THE LADY OF A SULTAN

THE LADIES OF THE ARISTOCRACY
BOOK 2

LINDA RAE SANDE

Twisted Teacup
PUBLISHING

ALSO BY LINDA RAE SANDE

The Secrets of a Viscount

The Widowers of the Aristocracy
The Dream of a Duchess
The Vision of a Viscountess
The Conundrum of a Clerk
The Charity of a Viscount

The Cousins of the Aristocracy
The Promise of a Gentleman
The Pride of a Gentleman

The Holidays of the Aristocracy
The Christmas of a Countess
The Knot of a Knight
The Holiday of a Marquess
The Snow Angel of a Duke

The Heirs of the Aristocracy
The Angel of an Astronomer
The Puzzle of a Bastard
The Choice of a Cavalier
The Bargain of a Baroness
The Jewel of an Earl's Heir
The Vixen of a Viscount
The Honor of an Heir
The Rose of a Sultan's Son

Note: Translations of select titles are available in German, Italian, Spanish and Portuguese.

CHAPTER 1
CONTEMPLATING A PAST

March 1841, on the western shore of the Aegean Sea

Even as a blazing sun washed out the brilliant colors surrounding him, Sultan Ziyaeddin I was seeing red. He was sure he had managed to sneak out of his holiday palace without being seen, but the hairs on the back of his neck rose to warn him of another's presence.

Who had dared follow him on this day, the first day of spring? The one day he deliberately kept his schedule clear so he might enjoy a rare treat. To simply stare out at the turquoise waters of the Aegean Sea whilst standing in his favorite place, a covered balcony that jutted from the golden-stoned walls of his *saray*. Leaning against the edge made it feel as if he was suspended in mid-air.

It had been her favorite place as well. At least, when she hadn't been curled up at his side in his bed late at night, satiated from their lovemaking and murmuring words of love and affection.

Twenty years. Had it really been twenty years since Afet's death?

Ziyaeddin swallowed hard in an attempt to clear his throat. Now was not the time to mourn.

Someone most definitely stood behind him, apparently waiting for an audience. He audibly sighed. "What is it now?" he asked in his native Turkish.

"My apologies, My Sultan," came the timid reply. "You asked that I provide an update on the plans for the new saray in Constantinople."

His shoulders immediately tensing, Ziyaeddin turned to find one of his emirs standing with his head bowed. Dressed in white baggy trousers, or *şalvar*, a pleated white silk shirt, and a white brocade kaftan, the man carried a leather pouch in one hand. The other held a sheet of parchment. He sported a simple white *kufi* on his head, the ends of its scarf wrapped loosely around his throat.

"And to give you my sincerest condolences on the anniversary of Sultana Afet's death," the emir added in a quieter voice.

Ziyaeddin regarded the young man with a look of annoyance, tamping down his initial revulsion at seeing Ertuğrul Efendi, his fifth son. "Thank you," he replied as he watched the emir quickly kneel and kiss the hem of his purple embroidered kaftan.

Could the emir choose a worse time to interrupt his reverie?

"This is the first day of spring. You may give me your update on the morrow," the sultan said.

Ertuğrul looked up from where he knelt. "As you

wish, My Sultan." He rose to his feet but continued to bow as he backed away from the ruler.

"Did you forget to bring a fez?"

Pausing in his retreat, Ertuğrul gulped. "You have not worn one since our arrival, so I thought it best to follow suit, My Sultan."

Ziyaeddin winced. Not only had he left Constantinople without more than the clothes on his back—he no longer employed a dresser who might have seen to packing his more European style top coats—he hadn't brought any of the scarlet red felt hats with him, either. The wardrobe in his private chamber was filled with the older style of clothes and headwear, though, and so he had simply adopted them for his stay at the palace near the shore of the Aegean Sea.

"Very well," he replied, realizing Ertuğrul was attempting to do him a favor. He already appeared out of place when in the company of his oldest sons and the other members of his cabinet due to his age. His manner of dress needn't add to the issue. "We shall find you a wife this year," Ziyaeddin added before the emir had taken a fourth step backwards.

His startled gaze lifting to meet the sultan's, Ertuğrul blinked. "Very well, My Sultan." Without waiting for a verbal dismissal, the emir crept away.

Sighing loudly—Ziyaeddin wanted to be sure Ertuğrul knew he was unhappy—he returned to the edge of the balcony and closed his eyes.

"Promise me you won't make him marry some spoiled rotten vizier's daughter, Baba."

The words, spoken in English, had Ziyaeddin whirling

around to discover one of his daughters standing at the other end of the balcony.

From where had she come?

"I haven't yet decided who he will marry," he replied, wincing at how the foreign words sounded in his ears. "And why are we speaking in English?"

Sultana Sevinc, his second daughter, approached and bowed to kiss his ring and then touch her forehead against the top of his hand. When she straightened, she said, "For practice making perfect, My Sultan."

Ziyaeddin took her face between his hands and kissed her forehead. "I am not sending you to Cambridge University," he stated, managing a smirk despite his poor mood. "They do not accept women."

Sevinc's face showed disappointment, but only for a moment. "Oxford, then?" she countered, one of her dark brows arching in a tease. "Or the university in Paris?"

He scoffed, dipped his head, and shook it in pretend frustration. "We are never going to find you a husband willing to abide you, are we?" he asked rhetorically. He almost wished he didn't have to arrange a marriage for her given how much he enjoyed her company. She argued her point of view far better than any of his viziers did.

Sevinc angled her head to one side as she crossed her arms. The move only enhanced the young woman's height and pleasant figure, both inherited from her mother, a Greek beauty gifted to Ziyaeddin upon his eighteenth birthday. "Not in the entirety of the Ottoman Empire," she agreed with a grin.

Rather than a simple head scarf, she wore a more traditional *baslik*, this one a felted hat wrapped in a scarf and festooned with beads and an occasional gemstone. Gold earrings dripped from her plump earlobes. Dressed as she was in a yellow *şalvar* and a golden yellow *entari* over a darker long gold waistcoat, Sevinc looked the part of a Turkish princess from the previous century.

Given her level of education, she did not wear it well.

"I am reading about titled men in England," she said. "I could be a duchess, or a marchioness, or a countess, or a—"

"You are *not* marrying an Englishman," Ziyaeddin stated, his manner suggesting they'd had this conversation in the past. "Now, is there a reason you've come out here without a...?" he glanced around, in search of the eunuch that should have been her chaperone.

"Samsa is just there," she replied, lifting her chin in the direction of the rather large bald bodyguard who, breathless, stood near the entrance to the balcony. From the sheen of sweat on his black skin, it was obvious the eunuch had been in search of her. "I thought to spend a few minutes with you whilst you mourn your second wife," she added in a quiet voice. "The first day of spring is always so hard for you."

Ziyaeddin dipped his head. "I am glad for your thoughts," he said. "And for remembering." Of all of his children, only Ertuğrul and Sevinc seemed to acknowledge the anniversary of Afet's death. He supposed it was because they were her children, even if Sevinc didn't know it.

"Mother is worried about you. She says you have not taken her to your—"

"Sevinc," he scolded, holding up a palm to reinforce

5

his warning. "Who I take to my bed is not for you to know." He had to think a moment as to which concubine Sevinc knew as her mother. One who had nursed her while another saw to her twin brother, Ertuğrul. A gentle scolding was in order.

Ignoring the warning, Sevinc said, "You haven't been with *anyone* in over a fortnight. Are not you... lonely?"

Although his silver eyes blazed for a moment—did the women in his harem speak of such things in front of his daughters?—Ziyaeddin merely stared at Sevinc until she dipped her head. "How often I bed my *kadins* is none of your concern, *kız evlât*." He was about to add that her use of the word 'fortnight' was entirely incorrect. It had been more than two months since he had invited one of his concubines to his bed.

"I am sorry, Baba. I only wish for your happiness," she murmured. "Perhaps you could take another wife," she suggested, visibly wincing when it was apparent her father's patience with her was at an end.

Although Ziyaeddin was about to scold her again, he felt his throat tighten. "I will never love another as I loved Afet," he vowed, now glad they were speaking a language few in the palace could understand.

Sevinc leaned closer and lowered her voice. "Never say never, Baba."

Knitting his dark brows together, Ziyaeddin gave her a look of suspicion. "Who told you that?"

Her confidence flagging, Sevinc glanced in the direction of the eunuch before saying, "I learned it from one of my brothers, who I think learned it from his tutor."

Ziyaeddin rubbed his face with one hand, smoothing

his long, salt-and-pepper beard into a cone shape. He had a passing thought to trim it shorter. Perhaps the gray wouldn't be so evident. "There are times I think I shouldn't have had you educated," he whispered hoarsely.

Having heard this particular claim many times before, Sevinc shrugged. "But who would you converse with when you need to practice your English?" she countered.

"One of your brothers," he answered without pause.

She giggled, glad he was no longer angry.

His dark-rimmed eyes suddenly rounded. "Why is it you think I need to practice my English?"

Sevinc lifted her shoulders in a shrug. "You never know when you will need it," she replied.

Scoffing, Ziyaeddin straightened, his fists going to his hips. "Never say never," he mocked.

Rolling her eyes, Sevinc grinned, gave her father a deep bow, and waited for him to kiss her forehead. "Courage, Baba."

Ziyaeddin watched her hurry off, the eunuch barely able to keep up as she disappeared down one of the corridors that led into the bowels of the palace. When he turned his attention back to the Aegean waters, he witnessed a sunset made up of a multitude of reds and purples. "I miss you, Afet," he whispered, unaware he had spoken the words in English.

CHAPTER 2
CONTEMPLATING A FUTURE

eanwhile, in Sussex, England, near the village of Kirdford

As the late afternoon rain soaked the grounds around Wisborough Oaks, Charlotte, Dowager Duchess of Chichester, leaned against the window sill in the parlor and examined the pattern of the wallpaper. She grinned when she remembered that *she* had been the one responsible for choosing the floral pattern.

A quarter of a century ago?

Her mouth rounded as she realized it had indeed been that long. Would she choose the same pattern if given the choice today? *Probably not,* she considered as she smoothed a hand over the wall, remembering when this wing of the Georgian house had been under construction. Although a huge fire had claimed the original, Garrett McElliott, her husband's best friend and the foreman of Wisborough Oaks, had overseen its reconstruction.

Not yet married to Joshua Wainwright at the time, Charlotte had seen to the choices for the decorating.

She sighed as she stared out the parlor window and pondered what she would do next.

If she was to actually do what she had decided to do only the week prior, when her friends were present and repercussions were of no consequence, then she should have Parma, her lady's maid, begin packing her trunks immediately. She should secure a ticket on a ship bound for the Mediterranean and travel to Portsmouth to meet the ship.

Making plans to tour Europe whilst surrounded by her very best friends made it seem so easy. Now that they had departed to rejoin their husbands in Mayfair, Charlotte was having second thoughts.

Given the death of Joshua, their eldest son John had taken his place as the new Duke of Chichester. His wife, Arabella, was expecting their first child before Christmas. Like everyone else in the household, Charlotte claimed it would be a boy but secretly hoped it would be a girl.

Youngest son James was somewhere in Italy or perhaps Greece, enjoying his Grand Tour. From his most recent letter, he was contemplating a delay in his itinerary.

Although there was more to Sicily and Rome than expected, there is much to explore here in Greece. David is of the same opinion, more because he has met a young lady for whom he feels affection. Please do not tell Aunt Elizabeth, or I feel she will expect him to return with a wife and child in tow, whereas I do not believe his affections are more than a passing fancy.

Charlotte grinned at the mention of Elizabeth. The

9

Viscountess Bostwick, Elizabeth Carlington Bennett-Jones was not really her sons' aunt, but she had been Charlotte's best friend since their youth. She had also been in residence at Wisborough Oaks only the week before, as had Hannah Slater Foster, Countess of Gisborn.

Hosting her two best friends for a fortnight—without their husbands—had been exactly the hen party Charlotte needed as she ended her year-long mourning period. The three of them had folded and packed her widow's weeds, black stockings, and black veiled hats into old trunks and watched as footmen had taken them up to the attic.

The two women had also helped her remove the last of her late husband's personal effects from the master bedchamber, placing some into a carton for John and the rest into a canvas bag for the servants to claim.

Her own possessions had already been moved into an apartment at the other end of Wisborough Oaks so that on the morrow, John and Arabella could move into the master and mistress suites.

"Your Grace?"

Charlotte gave a start and turned to discover Gates, the butler, standing on the threshold.

"What is it, Gates?"

"Mr. McElliott has requested a moment of your time, Your Grace."

Although she wasn't particularly surprised the foreman of Wisborough Oaks would pay a call at the main house, Charlotte was concerned that he did so in the morning. Usually he saw to informing her and John of any issues with the dukedom later in the day.

Glancing over at the tea service that had been delivered only moments ago, Charlotte decided there were enough biscuits on the silver salver to accommodate the foreman. "Do send him in," she said as she moved to stand before the settee.

Still as tall and straight as the day she had met him, Garrett McElliott entered the parlor and performed a deep bow.

"Oh, Garrett, you needn't," Charlotte said as she curtsied and rushed to take his hands in hers. Not an easy task given their large size and the length of his fingers. Although he had been born in Scotland, Garrett had been raised in London, so there wasn't a hint of a brogue in his voice. "How is Jane?" she asked, referring to the foreman's wife. The two had been married as long as Charlotte had been married to Joshua.

The thought of Joshua would usually bring tears to her eyes and a lump to her throat, but Charlotte was determined to put on a brave face.

"Well, she's not with child, if that's what you were thinking," he replied with a smirk.

Charlotte's eyes rounded. "I was not," she replied defensively. "Come. Have a cup of tea with me," she urged as she moved back to the settee.

Garrett did her bidding, settling into an adjacent chair facing the fireplace. Given the rain and the chill in the air, a fire had been set. A few logs burned, their bark occasionally crackling. "Still using wood in here, I see," he commented.

"Coal makes such a mess on the ceilings," Charlotte commented as she poured tea for them both. From the five-and-twenty years she had known Garrett, she knew how he took his tea and prepared it accordingly.

Placing several biscuits on his saucer, Charlotte was about to hand it to him when he said, "Are you determined to spoil my appetite for dinner?"

Undaunted, Charlotte gave him the cup and saucer. "It isn't even noon yet," she replied. "Besides, I rather doubt a few biscuits will ruin your dinner." She picked up her own cup and angled her head to one side. "Since I would expect you're bringing the most critical ducal property concerns to John these days, I have to wonder why you've paid a call on me?" she commented.

He took a sip of tea. "It's about the dowager cottage, Your Grace."

Charlotte blinked. "We have one?"

A look of guilt crossed Garrett's face. "Apparently you've forgotten that Jane and I are living in it," he replied.

Charlotte scoffed. "As you should be," she countered. "You've done all the work on it," she added, remembering how Garrett had seen to an addition of several rooms for his brood of four children.

"Still, aren't *you* in need of it now? It's been a year—"

"I am not," Charlotte firmly stated. "I've moved into the old apartments at the other end of the house. They're rather comfortable, and the vantage from my window is better than in the mistress suite." When he didn't look convinced, she added, "I spoke with Arabella. I've made it abundantly clear that she is now the mistress of this household. She's fine with me staying here in the house, and actually, I won't be underfoot much longer."

Garrett nearly spilled his cup of tea. "What's this?"

Deciding that putting voice to her plans for a trip to Europe would ensure she would actually take the trip, Charlotte leaned forward and said, "I'll be off on a tour of Europe very soon."

"Europe?" he repeated in alarm. "Alone?"

About to respond, Charlotte hesitated. "Well, I'll take Parma, of course. Start in the Mediterranean. Mayhap Greece or the Kingdom of the Two Sicilies. It's not fair that Lord James has all the fun," she added.

"For how long?"

Charlotte realized she hadn't yet decided on a complete itinerary nor a timeline. She had no idea how long she would spend in each country. She supposed it would depend on if she required a guide. How easy or hard would it be to employ drivers? How long should she plan to stay in each city? "Two years, perhaps?" she finally responded.

Furrowing his brows, Garrett settled back in his chair. "That long?"

Charlotte hesitated. "It's no longer than the boys are taking for their Grand Tour," she replied defensively. When she noted his look of worry, she asked, "What is it?"

He allowed a shrug. "I cannot help but think some down-on-his-luck Italian count is going to make you his countess," he murmured. "And expect you to pay all his bills."

She tittered. "I promise I shall be very circumspect when I'm around Italian aristocrats," she said. When he still displayed his concern, she added, "I shall be very careful. Besides, what's the worst that could happen?"

Scoffing, Garrett waved a hand. "Oh, I don't know. Your ship could go down in the Mediterranean. Or pirates might attack your ship—that still happens around Spain, you must know."

"So I've heard," Charlotte murmured, amused by his scenarios. "I do still read *The Times*."

"What if you're robbed of all your money?"

She shrugged. "I'll find a rich Italian count?" she teased. Sobering, she added, "Elizabeth gave me a few pointers. She has family in Italy I can call on if necessary."

Garrett sighed. "Don't take more than two trunks."

Charlotte straightened in her chair. "Why only two?"

He winced. "Any more than that, and you'll be announcing the fact that you're an aristocrat. That you're someone with means and money. Best not to draw attention to yourself."

She nodded her understanding. "What else?"

Inhaling, Garrett seemed to consider her query for a moment too long before he said, "Don't gamble."

Displaying a look of disbelief, she said, "I wouldn't."

"Don't even play cards," he warned.

She scoffed. "Who would I play with?" she countered, not sure why he would mention card games.

Shrugging, Garrett seemed at a loss to explain himself. "A simple game will seem innocent enough until suddenly playing for money will come up, and the next thing you know, there will be some serious blunt involved."

"Spoken as if you've been had," Charlotte murmured.

Garrett winced. "I admit I speak from experience, although it was Joshua..." A grimace crossed his face. "The late duke who was swindled," he finished. "Long before you two were married," he quickly added.

Charlotte was about to ask for more details, but she thought it best she not know more about Joshua's time as a second son of a duke. Not expecting to inherit the Chichester dukedom, Joshua Wainwright had spent his early twenties with Garrett gambling and carousing in London.

The fire had changed all that.

His entire family had died in that fire, and Joshua had nearly joined them given the severity of his own burns when he attempted to save his sister, Jennifer.

Even after two decades, those scars had barely faded, their ropy texture and taut appearance requiring him to wear a mask whenever he was in the company of others lest he frighten someone. The physician had even said they might have been the cause of his death, given how his tight, scarred skin made it difficult for him to stand up straight. As he aged, he grew more crooked, making it harder for him to walk. When *His Grace with half a face* was forced to walk with a cane, he was saddled with a new moniker.

His Grace, the half-faceless cripple.

With his breathing becoming more difficult—Charlotte was sure his lungs had been damaged by the smoke from the fire—Joshua took his last breath on a Sunday evening after dinner and a walk in the back gardens.

"He loved you very much," Garrett murmured.

Charlotte gave a start, wondering how he could know she was thinking of Joshua. "I loved him very much," she replied. "So much so, I rather doubt I will ever again have that sort of true love in my life."

Dipping his head, Garrett sighed. "Never say never, Your Grace," he whispered. "You never know who you'll meet in Europe."

CHAPTER 3
ENGLISHMEN ON HOLIDAY

*M*eanwhile, in Athens

Watching a young lady bearing a jug of water on one of her hips, Lord James Wainwright sighed appreciatively. "Why can't English girls look like that?" the second son of the late Duke of Chichester asked.

David Bennett-Jones, heir to the Bostwick viscountcy, scoffed. "I wouldn't want them to," he murmured. When James aimed a look of surprise in his direction, he added, "I like how English girls look. Skin, the color of moonlight—"

"Pasty white," James interrupted.

"—petite and delicate—"

"Skinny."

"—blue-eyed and blonde-haired—"

"Boring."

David rolled his eyes as the girl made her way into a small house made of white marble blocks. He was fairly sure the marble had been pilfered from an ancient temple or government building. He and James had seen evidence of repurposed materials everywhere they had visited on their Grand Tour.

"Me thinks it's time we made our way to one of the islands," he said, a map of the Greek mainland spread out before him. The parchment had been unfolded and refolded so many times, the printing was no longer legible in the creases. "What about Rhodes? It's the largest of the Dodecanese islands. I hear there is an impressive acropolis there. A Venetian castle, too."

"The Palace of the Grand Masters," James murmured.

"The Knights of St. John occupied the island. That's why there's a castle," David explained. "Apparently there are several of these Venetian castles scattered about this region," he added as he circled a finger around the islands in the Aegean. They had acquired the illustrated map at a shop upon their arrival in Athens. "I don't know if the Greeks have possession of Rhodes, though."

"There are supposed to be Greek ruins all along this coast," David said, motioning along the eastern Aegean and Mediterranean seas. "From a whole string of city-states that used to exist."

James glanced up at his friend. "That's the Ottoman Empire," he said. "Not exactly sure we'd be welcome there."

David furrowed his brows. "Why ever not? We have money—"

"We're *English*," James stated. "We sided with the Greeks in their war against the Turks, remember?"

"We sided *with* the Turks and the French just last

year," David countered. "Against that viceroy that was attempting to take Syria and the Holy Lands."

Pretending the wars were of little consequence, James shrugged. "Well, if anyone asks, we can always say we're from somewhere else."

The two had already explored the Greek ruins on the island of Sicily and spent time in Rome and Naples. From there, they had taken a ship across the Ionian Sea to Greece, hired a guide to take them to Delphi, and a driver for the trek to Athens. Along the way, they had come across other Europeans on their Grand Tours, young men who made recommendations or gave them warnings of what to avoid.

"Rhodes, it is," David announced. "Looks like there are several islands along the way we can tour for a day or two," he added, his finger tracing the path to Rhodes. He opened a small notebook, the edges of its pages feathered from use. "According to my notes, we need to find a ship out of a port city called Piraeus. Apparently it's not far from here."

James studied his best friend for a moment. "Are you sure you wish to leave Athens? A few weeks ago, you were in love—"

"Lust," David interrupted. "It was only lust. And I've studied all the mosaics I could find." He glanced up toward the Acropolis. "I was really hoping the Parthenon would be in better condition."

"Damn Venetians," James murmured, remembering the story they had learned from a local about how the Athenian temple had been used to store gunpowder by the Turks and then been blown up when the Venetians, in an attempt to take back Athens from the Ottoman Empire during the Morean War, scored a direct hit. The walls of the temple's cella had blown out, columns toppled, a frieze was ruined, and a cascade of architraves, metopes, and triglyphs tumbled to the ground.

"Damn wars," David corrected him. He glanced around, noting how aged some of the women appeared. Given the harsh glare of the sun and the lack of any sort of hat to protect their skin, he supposed it was common to see fairly young women appear older than they were. "When this young Englishman is ready, I shall be happy to find an English miss to make my bride," he commented. "And by then, I probably won't be so young anymore."

His brows furrowing, James remembered what his father had said about being a young Englishman. About how easy it was to fall in love with the first pretty young woman he danced with at a ball.

She turned out to be your mother, his father had said, his eyes twinkling in delight.

Mother wasn't your first dance, James had argued. His father had agreed, but added that it was his first memorable dance, made more so because Charlotte was betrothed to his rake of a brother and he remembered feeling jealous because he wanted her as his wife, not as a sister.

James blinked when David's hand waved in front of his face.

"Where were you?" David asked quietly.

Blinking again, James merely shook his head. "You didn't ruin her, I hope."

It was David's turn to blink before he realized who they were talking about. "I didn't. She led me to those ruins I took you to. We talked, but... I knew even before I escorted her home that nothing could ever come of it," he explained.

"You talked about her for a fortnight," James accused.

David's face took on a decidedly reddish cast. "If things were different, I might still be talking about her," he countered. "But I know how hard a time a Greek girl would have in Mayfair. Can you imagine?"

James tried to imagine Ophelia, the girl for whom David had pined only the week before, at a ball. Although she was a classic beauty, what with her raven black hair and olive-skinned complexion, her stilted English and ignorance of the British aristocracy would make her the laughing stock of all the other pasty white, skinny, boring young ladies.

Which had him wondering what David saw in her if he truly preferred young ladies with skin the color of moonlight, blonde hair, and blue eyes.

"My grandfather married an Italian woman," David stated, as if he could read James' mind. "Whilst he was on his Grand Tour. He thought he preferred typical English ladies, too, but Grandma Adeline changed him for life. I think he's still as horny for her as he was when he was my age."

James burst out laughing, well aware of David Carlington's behavior when it came to his marchioness. "The Marquess of Morganfield is a legend," he agreed, sobering after a moment.

"My father told me that Lord Everly met his wife in Greece," David mused, his thoughts still on Ophelia.

"He met her at a *ton* ball," James countered. "She was the Duke of Westhaven's daughter."

"But he didn't fall in love with her until he found her on Mykonos," David argued.

"Delos," James corrected him. "He thought she was Aphrodite come to life. Or else a mermaid. He's told the story both ways whilst at White's."

"Lady Everly did not have an easy time of it," David said in a quiet voice. "My mother attended finishing school with her in London," he added, referring to Elizabeth Carlington Bennett-Jones, Viscountess Bostwick. "Girls can be so cruel."

James dipped his head. "Is that why you're not pursuing Miss Ophelia?"

David nodded. "Part of the reason."

"And the rest?"

Allowing a wan grin, David gave a shrug and said, "We haven't yet been to Venice."

He ducked away when James' fist nearly impacted his shoulder, his attention suddenly diverted by a fashionable open carriage for hire. "There's our ride to Piraeus," he said with a grin. He waved until the driver acknowledged him.

James followed his gaze, a look of astonishment rounding his eyes. "You might be saved from Cupid's arrow this time, Bennet-Jones, but we've a good deal of the Aegean left before we cross back over the Ionian Sea," he teased.

David chuckled as the carriage pulled up next to

them. "Just you wait, Lord James. Cupid's got an arrow for you, too."

The two had barely made it into the carriage, the driver loading their trunks onto the back, when a breathless young boy ran up to them and held out a folded note. "Lord James," he said in heavily-accented English. "This came for you."

James reached out and took the missive, tossing a coin to the boy. *"Efcharistó,"* he said absently as he studied the wax seal on the back.

"What is it?" David asked as he settled onto the seat next to James.

"Note from home," James replied as he popped the wax seal and opened the letter. He took a moment to read the feminine script, his brows furrowing in disbelief.

"Is something wrong? Did something happen?" David asked in worry.

"Mother is taking a holiday," James replied, handing the letter to David. "She's coming to Greece on a Greek merchant vessel. Syros and then to Athens."

David glanced at the note, scoffing when he read the last line.

I don't expect to cross paths with the two of you, as I'm sure you've already completed your Greek tour. Do enjoy Venice for me.

"We aren't going to attempt to find her, I hope?" David asked as he handed the letter back to James.

"Of course not. It would be like finding a needle in a

haystack," James replied. "Although I suppose we could be on the lookout for her ship. "

David gave him a quelling glance. "She didn't mention the name of it," he countered.

James shrugged as the carriage rumbled off toward Piraeus. "How many Greek merchant ships come from England?"

Forced to agree there wouldn't be many, David settled onto his seat and studied the architecture of the buildings they passed along the way.

CHAPTER 4
A DEPARTURE

*M*eanwhile, in Portsmouth

As a porter saw to the trunks and Parma followed her with a valise in hand, Charlotte regarded the merchant marine ship with worry. "Mr. McElliott, are you quite sure this is the right ship?" she asked as she studied the foreign lettering on its starboard side.

ἥλιος του Ἀπόλλων

Although there were two masts with square rigging on both, there were no sails evident.

The tall man gave a nod. "Indeed. A Greek brig called *Sun of Apollo*. Fairly new, too," he explained.

Charlotte's gaze lingered on the ship's moniker before moving to a gray-bearded gentleman who had made his way down the ramp from the ship. He casually leaned against a post and lit a cheroot.

"Now, I've made sure you and your lady's maid have your own cabin, and you'll be eating with Captain Popodopolos for the morning and evening meals,"

Garrett explained. Noticing Charlotte's attention wasn't on him, he briefly glanced back before adding, "He captained a Greek vessel in their war for independence, and since we fought alongside them, he rather likes Brits. And he speaks English."

"That war wasn't so very long ago," Charlotte commented. At Garrett's look of surprise, she added, "I read *The Times* every day."

"Oh," he replied. "Well, he says it should take about three weeks to reach Syros—that's one of the Greek islands—"

"Where the ship was built," Charlotte stated.

Garrett gave a start. "How is it you know that?"

"I asked someone last night. At the hotel," she replied, her attention once again on the gentleman who was smoking. She recognized him as the man she had spoken with at the Star. "Whilst I was having tea in the dining room."

His gaze briefly darting to the lady's maid, Garrett furrowed his brows. "You weren't alone, I hope?"

"Parma was with me," Charlotte said. "I merely asked him if he knew anything about the ships that sail to Greece, and he told me all about the ships they build in the town called Hermoupolis," she explained, fighting the urge to yawn.

If the *Sun of Apollo* hadn't been scheduled to depart so early in the morning, the trio might have made the forty mile trip to Portsmouth that morning. Instead, they had traveled in the Chichester coach the day before and spent the night at the Star Hotel.

"Hmph," Garrett responded before he held out two

pasteboard tickets. "From Syros, you'll board a ship to Athens. The captain said he would see to your transfer personally."

"How much did you give him?" Charlotte asked.

Garrett blinked. "What?"

The duchess angled her head to one side. "You bribed him, did you not?"

Inhaling to respond, Garrett glanced over to where the ship's captain was still smoking as he waited for the last of some crates to be loaded. "I might have slipped him some extra blunt," he admitted. "Your Grace, I chose this vessel and this captain because I believe it is safer and certainly a faster option than a smaller sailing ship."

Charlotte gave him a wan grin. "I'm not scolding you, Mr. McElliott," she said. "But you had better tell John so that he can reimburse you for your trouble."

Garrett nodded. "If you insist." He glanced around. "You'd best get on board, but first I'll introduce you. He assures me his crew won't bother you, and should you need anything—hot water for bathing or tea—his cook will see to it."

It was Charlotte's turn to blink. "His cook?"

Garrett rolled his eyes. "The cook heats the water," he explained.

"Ah," she responded, giving Parma a quick glance. She expected the lady's maid to display a look of worry, but the East Indian woman seemed anxious to get on board. "Lead the way," she said with a nod to the captain.

As if on cue, Captain Popodopolos tossed the remains of his cheroot into the water and straightened his coat.

"Ah, we meet again, Your Grace," the captain said as

LINDA RAE SANDE

he lowered his head. He lifted her gloved hand and kissed the back of it.

"You might have mentioned you were the captain of the vessel I'm to travel on," Charlotte replied, giving him a slight curtsy. "My lady's maid, Parma," she added, urging Parma to step forward. She rarely included the servant in introductions, but given the tight quarters they would would be inhabiting, she thought it best he know her name.

"Apologies, Your Grace. My intention was not to withhold my identity from you, but rather from others who might wish me or my ship harm," he explained.

Charlotte's eyes rounded. "Why ever would anyone wish to do you harm?" she asked in surprise.

"Why, indeed?" he countered. He reached out and shook Garrett's hand before waving the women up the ramp.

Charlotte rushed to Garrett, embracing him as she said, "Do say a farewell to Jane for me," she whispered.

"I will, Your Grace. Safe travels," he replied as she released her hold on him.

Giving him a watery grin, Charlotte joined Parma on the ramp and the two boarded the ship.

CHAPTER 5

A VISION FOR THE FUTURE BLURS

Meanwhile, in Ziyaeddin's Aegean palace

As arguments for and against Ziyaeddin's latest proposal raged on amongst his viziers, several his own sons, the sultan finally raised a fist.

Silence fell over the men who sat around the low table in his throne room as ten pairs of eyes turned to stare at him.

"This university *will* be built," he stated. "A first of many before I die," he added, his voice betraying his impatience. "As will the new palace in Constantinople."

The viziers all bowed their heads and murmured their grudging agreement.

"We are here to decide if the first university will be in Konya or in Constantinople," he stated, absently smoothing his long beard into a cone.

Emir Ertuğrul Efendi straightened. When Ziyaeddin acknowledged him, he said, "We can do both at the same time, My Sultan."

Ziyaeddin blinked while others around the table

gasped at the suggestion. When Ertuğrul offered him a parchment, he took it and examined the drawings the architect had done. "What is this?"

"My proposal for a university based on the plans used by the one in Paris," Ertuğrul replied. "Altered, of course, to employ the materials available to us here."

The sultan furrowed a salt-and-pepper brow. "At what cost?"

Ertuğrul pulled another parchment from his pile. "We have it in the budget to build both. The man who would oversee the construction says the initial buildings can be completed in a year's time. The remaining in another year or two, depending on what disciplines you wish to feature."

Studying the detailed budget Ertuğrul had provided him, Ziyaeddin felt a combination of pride and annoyance that it was his fifth son who seemed to have the answer to every question. The solution to every problem. He'd been raised with the expectation that he would be that son, though. Raised with higher expectations than those of the six sons who came before.

Only four of those still survived, the other two having succumbed to pneumonia before they reached their second years. After Ertuğrul, infant mortality among Ziyaeddin's other children hadn't been as bad, but of the twenty-six babes born to his *kadins*, only nineteen were still alive.

Two *kadins* had died in the childbed. One wife, as well.

The familiar pang of loss had Ziyaeddin's heart constricting as a wince crossed his face. Would he ever get past the hurt he felt whenever he thought of Afet?

Given that the son she had birthed still lived—despite the difficult labor and him being the second of twins—and knowing he seemed to overcome every obstacle put in his path, Ziyaeddin supposed Ertuğrul was destined to succeed. At some point—when it came time to choose an heir for the sultanate—Ziyaeddin would have to choose either the eldest son who was in charge of the treasury or the one who had caused his mother's death.

Since dealing with matters of state had become drudgery, especially given his viziers' lack of vision for the future, Ziyaeddin was nearly ready to make his announcement. But not yet. He could rule for another year or two. He had to. Unless someone assassinated him, only his natural death would result in a new sultan.

"My Sultan?" Ertuğrul whispered.

Pulled from his reverie, Ziyaeddin gave a start. "Disciplines?" he murmured, remembering Ertuğrul's query. "I should like one to have subjects of Oxford and the other to be like Cambridge," he stated.

The viziers all exchanged curious glances. Of those at the table, only three had attended university in England —all of them his own sons. Two had attended the one in Paris. The rest hadn't been educated beyond the tutors their fathers had hired on their behalf. As a result, they couldn't understand their sultan's insistence that the empire have its own universities. Couldn't understand the need to have an educated populace. Couldn't understand the need to modernize buildings. To build a modern palace on the Bosphorus Straights.

Ignorance was costing the empire far too much.

"It shall be as you say, My Sultan," Ertuğrul replied, gathering the architectural drawings into a neat pile.

Ziyaeddin glanced over at the colored glass window. Given the golden wash of color that illuminated the carpet with streaks of yellow and red, he knew it was a sunny day. He longed to be outside, even if it meant merely lounging on his balcony. Longed to breathe in the Aegean Sea air, its salty tang mixed with a hint of the citrus trees that lined the enclosed garden below.

The sound of a clearing throat had Ziyaeddin once again giving a start. "We are done," he announced, ignoring the startled look of his second oldest son. Bamsi no doubt wished to discuss Russia and their recent acquisition of the empire's lands to the north. As the minister of defense in charge of the army, he was always in search of a battle. Ziyaeddin had grown weary of war, though, and defending the empire's sprawling borders had become too costly.

Despite his knees protesting his quick rise from the low table, Ziyaeddin managed to keep an impassive expression on his face until all the viziers had left the throne room.

All except for Ertuğrul.

"Are you displeased with the plans?" he asked.

Ziyaeddin shook his head. "I am most pleased with them," he replied. "I am merely tired and wish to see the sun before it sets."

Ertuğrul's eyes rounded slightly. "Yes, My Sultan." He backed away, bowing as he did so, and took his leave of the throne room.

With everyone else gone, Ziyaeddin hurried to the

secret door that led to his private quarters and its open balcony. A moment later, he lifted his face and closed his eyes as the warmth of the sunshine washed over him. Breathing deeply, he turned and faced west, intending to watch the fishing boats come in with the daily catches.

Instead, a two-masted ship on the far horizon caught his attention, and he frowned.

Either it was the ship from the Kingdom of the Netherlands bearing a shipment of cocoa powder and stroopwafels or trouble was coming.

CHAPTER 6
CAPTURED BY PIRATES!

*E*arlier *that morning, in the Aegean Sea*
Inhaling the scent of sea on yet another clear morning, Charlotte leaned against the ship's railing and surveyed the horizon in search of land. She calculated how many days she had done so, understanding now how travelers could lose track of time whilst on holiday.

The days on board the merchant ship had passed as quickly as the cutter sliced through the water. One storm had rocked the ship, but only at night. Although Parma had experienced seasickness as a result, Charlotte had slept through the entire ordeal.

There were times she was sure she could make out land above the swells of the aquamarine waters of the Mediterranean, but after a few minutes, she thought her eyes had deceived her.

Spotting another ship's sails several days before, Charlotte had watched them for a few minutes. When they didn't disappear, she hurried up to one of the Greek sailors and pointed.

He glanced out, his expression conveying brief concern before he merely shrugged and continued his work on the deck. When the distant ship moved on, its sails disappearing beneath the horizon, Charlotte relaxed.

She continued her vigil of watching for other ships, especially when a few days before, they had experienced a threat from a ship flying a green pennon bearing a skull.

"Who are they?" Charlotte had asked as Captain Popodopolos aimed a spyglass at the smaller ship.

"What's left of Barbary pirates would be my guess," he murmured. "Arabs from Africa. There aren't many of them out here. Rogue crews, mostly, but still dangerous."

A game of cat and mouse had begun when they passed a series of islands near Sicily. As a result, the captain had diverted their course, sure he could outmaneuver the smaller vessel that seemed to reappear as if out of nowhere only two days later. The chase was on, the cutter adding another sail and changing course to come more closely to an island in the Aegean Sea.

A shout from the starboard side of the ship had Charlotte tensing this morning. Before she could make her way across the deck, Captain Popodopolos hooked her arm with his. "Get to your cabin now. Lock the door. Keep quiet," he ordered.

Knowing better than to argue, Charlotte nearly collided with Parma as she descended the gangway. She repeated the captain's instructions, rushing into their small cabin and slamming the door shut.

"Pack everything of value into the false bottom of the larger trunk," she instructed. The jewelry that wasn't paste was already there, but there were other gowns with money sewn into the hems that should be hidden as well.

When the ship seemed to surge ahead—another sail had apparently been hoisted—Parma hurried to do Charlotte's bidding as the duchess gathered items from around the cabin and tossed them into the other trunk. About to place a small jewel box onto the growing pile, she paused to open it.

They might have been paste, but her favorite earrings were there. She plucked them from their compartment and stuffed them into her pocket. Before she could close the box, Parma cried out at the sound of boot heels above. The crew were obviously running about the deck, the captain shouting orders.

Parma had the false bottom out of the trunk but was struggling with the piles of clothing she had removed. Charlotte hurried to help even as she knew there were far more men on deck than those who made up the crew of the *Sun of Apollo*. "Hurry," she whispered needlessly. "Keep quiet."

When they had finished repacking the trunk, Charlotte secured the clasp and turned around to discover the jewelry box was still on the table. About to retrieve it, she couldn't when something pounded against the door. The frame splintered and the door burst open, carrying with it a long-haired sailor who was as surprised to discover them as they were to see him. Charlotte knocked the box from the table, surreptitiously kicking it beneath the furniture as she stepped back and gasped.

A string of incomprehensible words spilled from the foul smelling man's mouth as another man appeared behind him, this one apparently of higher rank. He wore a brown *kafiya*, and his bronzed complexion was obviously due more to the sun than to genetics.

Parma whimpered, her arms wrapping around her shoulders as she sat atop one of the trunks. Meanwhile, Charlotte straightened and moved her hands to her hips, giving the intruders her haughtiest glare. "How *dare* you come into my cabin without knocking," she stated.

The two exchanged quick glances of bewilderment before they both burst out laughing.

"I am Aukmed," the second brute stated. "And I dare."

CHAPTER 7
SOLD TO A SULTAN

later that day
A hard bump and a round of shouts roused
Charlotte from her state of half-sleep. Sitting next to her,
Parma whimpered as her eyes lifted to the ceiling of their
cabin.

She had no idea what had happened to Captain
Popodopolos and his crew when the pirates had overtaken the *Sun of Apollo*, but she and Parma had been left
in their cabin, the jamb so broken, the door could no
longer be secured. The contents of both trunks had been
tossed as one of the swarthy men had pawed through
their contents.

Charlotte remembered wincing as she watched, quite
sure he was leaving marks on her clothes with his soiled
hands. He had paused and directed an angry question in
their direction, but not understanding his language,
Charlotte could only reply with a shrug and a quick
glance at Parma. Had her hands not been tied in front of
her, she would have waved her arms about in an effort to

confuse him.

"Gold," he stated.

Charlotte blinked. "No gold," she replied.

The pirate pointed to her fingers. "Gems."

"No gems." When he gave her a look of disbelief, she added, "I was told not to travel with any valuables, so I left them in England."

Aukmed entered, his gaze settling on her a moment before he said something to the first man. When he shook his head and began searching the other trunk, Aukmed turned his attention on Charlotte, his eyes narrowing. "English?" he asked.

"I am," she replied, nodding.

"Her?" he asked, pointing to Parma.

"My lady's maid."

He scratched his forehead. "Where is the gold?"

Inhaling deeply, Charlotte said, "There is no gold, sir. At least, none that I know of. I was told not to travel with valuables." She held up her tied hands and spread her fingers. "No jewels, either."

Scrubbing his stubbled face with his hand, he rolled his eyes. "Have to sell you then."

Charlotte blinked. "Sell me?"

He crossed his arms and started to lean against the door jamb, but when the wood gave way, he nearly stumbled backwards. A string of curses in what Charlotte realized was Arabic filled the cabin for a moment.

"Are you a Barbary pirate?" Charlotte asked, pretending awe. It wasn't hard. At the mention she would be have to be sold, an intense fear had gripped her stomach, one she hadn't felt since the morning she had learned Joshua had nearly burned to death.

The pirate narrowed his eyes. "If I am?"

Charlotte's eyes rounded with feigned delight. "I was warned about Barbary pirates," she claimed. "Oh, how exciting! How do I address you?"

Staring at her in disbelief, the pirate scoffed. "I am called Aukmed."

"Do you often capture ships?"

"Often enough," he replied. Then he straightened. "What have you heard?"

Realizing she would have to come up with a story, Charlotte shrugged. "All my friends in England. When they heard I was going to Greece on holiday, every one of them said my ship would be invaded by pirates. And here I thought they were exaggerating," she claimed. "What will you do with the ship?"

He lifted his chin, apparently confused by her response. "Haven't decided. Might sell it. Might scuttle it."

"Oh, sir, but that would be a shame," Charlotte said. "It's quite new. It was built on the island of Syros only last year."

He stared at her in disbelief. "Was it now?" Aukmed asked, once again scrubbing his dark-bearded face with a hand. "And how might you know this?"

Charlotte lifted a shoulder. "I asked the captain, of course. I didn't wish to get on board until I knew it was seaworthy. I've never been on a merchant vessel before." Truth be told, before this attempt at a holiday, she hadn't been on any sea-faring ship in her entire life.

Frowning, the pirate narrowed his eyes. "You are educated?"

Straightening, Charlotte said, "I am a graduate of Warwick's Grammar and Finishing School in London. I can read, write, speak French, dance, paint, draw, play the piano forté, plan a ball and..." She glanced up at the ceiling again. "Do arithmetic."

The swarthy man narrowed his eyes. "So you're worth a good deal of gold to someone," he murmured.

"Uh... possibly," Charlotte hedged, resisting the urge to swallow. She didn't want him paying witness to her panic.

He chuckled. "Well, I guess we're about to find out," he said in his heavily-accented English. He pointed down at the trunks. "Are those all your clothes?" He made a cursory glance of the entire cabin, as if he expected to find more traveling trunks or valises despite the tight quarters.

She nodded. "I would have brought more, but I was told not to."

Growling, he murmured something in his native language, gave some instructions to the first man, and took his leave. Charlotte heard him climb the gangway ladder, his voice adding to a chorus of shouts that had started when the ship seemed to collide with something. The first pirate tossed the clothes from the floor back into the trunk and slammed the lid shut. Then he hefted it onto a shoulder and left. A moment later, another pirate entered and took the second trunk from the floor before he, too, disappeared through the broken doorway.

"Oh, my lady, what's to become of us?" Parma whispered.

Charlotte huffed a sigh. "I've no idea, but if we are to be sold..." She clamped her mouth shut at the reappearance of Aukmed. She realized he was the one in charge. The others seemed to follow his orders.

"Time to go," he said, waving a hand.

Parma waited to stand up until Charlotte had done so. The two made their way out of the cabin, the pirate following behind. At the base of the gangway stairs, Charlotte stopped. In order to climb them, she had to gather her skirts into her hands, but with her hands tied together at the wrists, she had a hard time gripping the rail given all the fabric of her bell skirt. With a huff, she dropped her skirts, held out her wrists and said, "Untie me, sir."

Giving her a quelling glance, Aukmed merely bent down and lifted her over one shoulder. Charlotte let out an "oomph" when she ended up hanging over his shoulder, some of her hair coming loose from its pins.

"Let me down," she demanded as the pirate climbed the thin stairs.

"Quit wiggling, or I'll drop you," he warned.

Charlotte immediately stilled, and although her face was already red from her being held upside down, she felt it heat even more when they emerged onto the deck to a round of hoots and hollers.

"*Hadi!*" he shouted.

The other pirates immediately quieted, turning back to whatever they'd been doing to secure the ship to a dock. From her position, Charlotte could see Parma had made it up the gangway without assistance, and she was following close behind. The sound of wood falling onto wood turned out to be the ramp lowering to the dock, and the next thing Charlotte knew, she was standing rather unsteadily next to a cart, a lock of hair hanging in front of her eyes. Parma rushed up to her. "Are you all—?'"

"I'm fine," Charlotte replied, not wanting Parma to use her honorific. If the pirates didn't know she was a duchess, things might go better for them.

Her gaze went to the ship. Captain Popodopolos and his crew weren't visible from her vantage, and she winced at the thought that they might have been killed by the pirates and tossed overboard.

The men charged with the trunks were next over the ramp, and the two wooden boxes landed with a thud in the back of the cart.

That's when she noticed the driver.

He couldn't have been more than twelve, his head adorned with a dark red fez. The rest of him was covered with light-colored clothes that appeared to be appropriate for sleeping.

Aukmed pointed up a curved dirt road that led to a huge stone building. "Start walking," he said, pointing in the direction of what could have been a castle if it had any crenelations. He turned and seemed to shout more instructions to his crew before he hopped onto the cart next to the boy. The two that had carried their trunks sat on the back of the cart, their legs dangling over the edge.

"Where are we?" Charlotte asked, her gaze sweeping over the turquoise water and then the land as she began to make her way up the road. She winced at the thought of her slippers being ruined. The least they could have done was allow her to put on a pair of half-boots for the journey.

"You'll find out soon enough," Aukmed replied, the cart moving ahead of her and Parma.

Charlotte glanced behind her, thinking perhaps she and Parma could get away by running toward the dock and making an appeal to another crew. But the Greek ship was the only vessel anchored to the dock. Other smaller fishing boats were pulled up to the rocky coast, but they had been abandoned, their owners having taken their catches with them earlier that day.

To the north, Charlotte could barely make out the whitewashed square buildings of a village where the land jutted into the water. To the south, the rocky beach continued without interruption. There were no buildings, no other villages or towns nearby.

After they had been climbing for about five minutes, Charlotte turned to stare down at the dock, realizing it only existed to serve the huge building before them. Appearing nearly gold in the late afternoon sun, it featured unusual but decorative architecture. A number of openings were visible along the tall walls—balconies, she supposed—and a horizontal band halfway up the wall suggested an exterior corridor wrapped around the building.

She struggled to catch her breath and attempted to push the lock of hair to one side so it wouldn't impede her vision. At the sound of a shout, she turned around to discover one of the pirates on the back of the cart was about to come for her, so she quickened her steps to catch up to Parma.

"I fear for you," Parma said, her own gaze locked on the sandstone building.

Charlotte put on a brave face. "But not for yourself?"

"I have always been a servant," Parma said.

Giving a start, Charlotte realized what her lady's maid meant. If they were to be sold, Charlotte would probably end up working in service. Doing what, she had no idea.

In this place, whatever it was.

She had a passing thought of what might happen should anyone pay witness to the scar on her back. The horse whip her father had employed in a fit of anger would make it appear as if she had been a slave to someone. Only a few of her dinner gowns were cut low enough in the back to expose the wound, the track of stitches Dr. Regan had used to close it barely faded after twenty-five years. Otherwise, it was always hidden under her clothes.

As bad as Joshua's burn scars had been, she had always believed her whip scar far worse. She had earned it, she supposed, for having gone against her father's wishes. For not having married the man he had chosen for her. Her friend Hannah was married to that man, the epitome of a fairy princess a far better fit for the Earl of Gisborn than Charlotte ever would have been.

Charlotte had always been destined to marry Joshua Wainwright. Despite his horrendous scars, she had been happy to be his wife. His duchess.

She fought back the urge to weep. To shed more tears at having lost the love of her life.

With the sun beginning to set in the west, the golden sandstone structure fairly glowed. Glints of color reflected off the windows, which she could now see were stained glass. From the way the windows were stacked at regular intervals, she surmised the building was three stories tall.

If anyone occupied one of the balconies, they were hidden from her vantage.

At least until a figure appeared in the middle of one of them.

Charlotte gave a start. A man stood staring down at them from a balcony on the third story.

Wondering who watched her with such an intense gaze—she couldn't make out the details of his facial features, but she knew he was staring back at her—Charlotte slowed to a halt. She would have continued the staring match, but one of the pirates gave a shout that sounded like a curse. The cart was about to go around the corner of the building.

"Coming!" she called out, hurrying to catch up. When she rounded the corner, she gasped, as did Parma.

From this vantage, it was evident they were about to enter a palace. A magnificent foreign palace.

Lush gardens lined the paved path leading to a pair of doors made of metal latticework. Colorful tiles outlined the archway and the windows that flanked the doors. Two guards armed with swords stood with their weapons drawn, their stances indicating these visitors were not welcome.

A verbal exchange commenced as the donkey that had been pulling the cart began to bray in complaint. Some sort of agreement was met, and Charlotte's arm was grabbed by one of the men while Parma was taken by the other.

"Ouch!" Charlotte complained, attempting to free herself from the annoying pirate. When he lifted a hand as if he intended to hit her, she dipped her head and did her best to keep up with his larger steps.

They climbed a set of marble stairs and passed through the massive doors. In the atrium, which seemed to be as high as the building, sconces were lit along the tile-decorated walls, and a continuous row of colorful large cushions lined the facing walls.

Another guard met them and led them down a wide corridor. If not for the lit sconces, Charlotte was sure it would have been too dark to see. They walked for what seemed the length of two streets in London before they paused in front of another pair of doors guarded by men wearing fez hats and strange clothes. Their swords were still sheathed in curved scabbards.

The babble of foreign tongues had Charlotte frowning. She couldn't begin to make out what was being said, but she soon noticed Parma was staring at her with wide eyes.

"What?" she mouthed, sure her escort wanted her to remain quiet.

"We're in the Ottoman Empire," Parma whispered.

Charlotte swallowed as she attempted to remember the map of the Mediterranean Sea the captain had shown her. The Ottoman Empire bordered the sea in several places, but she had no idea where the ship had docked with respect to the mainland of Greece.

Her reverie was interrupted when the doors were opened by the guards and she and Parma were shoved into one of the most opulent rooms Charlotte had ever seen.

She blinked. She attempted to study the gilt and mosaic ceiling above and the Turkish carpeting below, the colored glass windows on one side and the frescoed wall opposite. Attempted, because she was shoved forward and then forced to kneel, her petticoats barely providing a soft landing for her knees. The loose lock of hair once again fell over one eye, leaving her unable to see anything to her right.

Anger flashed through her, and she was about to scold the pirate who had pushed her down when her gaze was caught by another.

The man who had been staring at her from the balcony.

Charlotte blinked again. She dared a glance to the left, thinking she would see a doorway to a balcony, but there was no opening in the wall.

She knew from Parma's slight whimper that her maid was to her right, and she said a quiet "shush" in an attempt to calm her. All the while, she kept her fiery gaze on the silver-eyed man.

He was dressed in finery far more expensive than anything Prinny had worn in court. His hands bore several rings made of gold and silver, each one sporting large gemstones. A turban made of fabric suitable for a ballgown was wrapped around his head. Despite his long beard, it was easy to see that his otherwise perfectly sculpted face was marred on one cheek. Given Charlotte's experience with her late husband, she was careful not to stare.

Seated in a throne made of shimmering gold mounted atop a dais that spanned the width of the room, it was apparent he was a ruler, at least in this room. When he suddenly stood, he began shouting in a voice filled with anger and rebuke.

About to state her case, Charlotte realized she probably wouldn't be understood. He was speaking in a language that was sometimes guttural and sometimes singsong. Aukmed obviously understood, for he answered, his tone more reasonable.

The two continued to trade responses—Charlotte had expected a negotiation but didn't have the sense they were coming to any sort of agreement—until suddenly the man in charge shouted and raised a fist.

The entire room fell silent. She held her breath in anticipation of what was about to happen next. Continued to hold it when the man stepped down from his dais and stopped directly in front of her.

Charlotte lowered her eyes, unable to keep up the staring match.

He said something in his language and she glanced back up, giving her head a shake. "Apologies, sir, but I do not understand," she said in a clipped tone. It was at that moment she could make out the details of the scars on one of his cheeks, just above the line of his long beard. They appeared to have been made by a blade, the three slashes deep. None of the cuts reached his dark-lined eyes, however.

Aukmed apparently stepped forward with the intent

of hitting or kicking her, for the next thing Charlotte knew, the man in charge had a sword drawn and was holding it to the pirate's neck.

Awestruck, Charlotte remembered to close her mouth, but her eyes remained wide as Aukmed slowly retreated. A scuffle behind her followed by a muffled curse had her wondering what was happening, but she dared not move. After a moment, she knew the three Barbary pirates were no longer in the throne room.

The sultan moved to stand before her and she watched in horror as he lowered the sword between the front of her body and her tied hands. A flick of his wrist, and a second later, the rope fell away from her wrists.

"I am Sultan Ziyaeddin the First," the man stated. "You are now in my possession."

Charlotte inhaled sharply.

Possession?

Although she was relieved to be free of the pirates, she now wondered if she was any better off than she was before.

Despite all her years as a member of the British aristocracy, she had no idea how to address a sultan. "Your Highness," she finally replied, lowering her head in a bow. Had she been standing, she would have curtsied.

Her response obviously pleased the sultan, for a grin lightened his face and made him appear at least a decade younger.

"Highness," he repeated softly before he chuckled. He used the sword to slice through Parma's bindings, and she dipped her head in thanks.

"Is there a more appropriate honorific, Sultan Ziyaeddin?" Charlotte asked meekly, thinking 'Your Eminence' wasn't royal enough. It was then she remembered hearing his name. Seeing it in print. She couldn't give it more consideration at that moment, though, for he was regarding her with the most curious expression.

Ziyaeddin shook his head before he lifted a hand and waved a finger. "Highness is good," he responded, his smirk reappearing. In his own language, he called out instructions. Within a few moments, two women appeared next to Charlotte and Parma to help them to stand and take them from the throne room, both bowing several times as they backed out of the chamber.

Charlotte's gaze caught the sultan's just once before the doors closed. She had hoped to determine his intent, but the humor he had shown only the moment before had been replaced with an impassive expression.

The memory of his gaze stayed with her for the entire time she and Parma were escorted down another long corridor and into a stone-walled chamber dimly lit with several oil lamps. A small dressing table and taller cushion were pushed up against one wall, and two long cushions looked as if they were intended to be used as beds. Brightly woven blankets were stacked at the end of one of them, and Parma inhaled softly as she unfurled one of them. That was when Charlotte noticed the patterned Turkish carpet that covered the floor.

"This is as fine as any Aubusson carpeting," she murmured as she knelt to run her palm over the wool fibers.

The sight of a platter of fruits set atop the dressing table was a reminder they hadn't eaten since that morning. Helping herself to a cluster of grapes, Charlotte thought they tasted better than any she had eaten in England. She held out a bunch to Parma, and grinned when she noted how her eyes rounded in appreciation.

About to select an apple, Charlotte gave a start at seeing her trunks and the valise shoved up against one wall. Apparently the luggage had been delivered to the chamber whilst they were in the sultan's presence. She winced at seeing their condition, though. A quick glance inside showed their clothes appeared the same as when the pirate had tossed them about. She found a night rail and pulled it out, grimacing when she noticed the fabric was stained with fingerprints left by the pirate. Parma was quick to pull out another for her, and the two prepared for bed.

Feeling ever so exhausted, she gave Parma an encouraging word as she helped herself to one of the blankets and settled onto a long cushion. The light from the oil lamps barely reached the ceiling, but what she could make out appeared to be images of either Greek or Roman deities. She soon realized they were not paintings but rather mosaics made up of tiny tiles.

Despite her tiredness, she remained wide awake as the images above were replaced by those of their host as they filled her mind's eye.

Sultan Ziyaeddin I.

She *had* heard of him. As the ruler of the Ottoman Empire, his name had been spoken with both respect and with hate in London. He had been both an enemy and an ally.

What would she be to him?

An image of his face haunted her mind's eye. He hadn't tried to hide his scars when she was close enough to see his face. Perhaps he thought they made him appear more formidable. More frightening. Or perhaps he had no idea of their affect on those new to him.

Or maybe he didn't care.

Joshua's burn scars had been so bad, he felt forced to hide them behind a mask. He'd had no desire to frighten anyone. For a time, he had preferred not to accept any callers, not wishing to take a chance his appearance might offend someone.

Charlotte wondered at the odd sensation she'd felt when the sultan had turned his attention on her. Even with the scars, he was handsome in a rough sort of way. No amount of brocade and gold threads could soften his obvious masculinity. Usually a man of such harsh features wouldn't appeal to her.

So what was it about Sultan Ziyaeddin that had her staying awake on this night?

CHAPTER 8

AN INTRODUCTION TO PALACE LIFE

he following morning
"What do you suppose will happen to us, my lady?" Parma asked from where she had settled onto a stack of cushions near a colored glass window. If she pressed her cheek into the glass and stared hard enough, she could see through it, although the scene beyond appeared distorted.

Charlotte was staring into a different glass, an ornately framed mirror hung above the dressing table. All things considered, she thought her appearance no different from when she had departed Wisborough Oaks.

That morning's bath had certainly helped, even if it had required she undress in front of two burly bare-chested men whose upper arms were larger than her thighs. Both were bald, dark skinned, and unlike the guards she had seen stationed around certain doors, they didn't sport beards and mustaches. Their fierce expressions were quite at odds with their livery, for they wore loose white şalvar and pointy-toed slippers.

When Charlotte scoffed at the suggestion she step into the small bathing pool with the two men present, the Greek servant who had escorted them to the bathing chamber revealed why she had been chosen for the duty.

She could speak English.

"They are eunuchs, here to see that no one interrupts your bath," the slender woman whispered in heavily accented English. "Other than the sultan, no men are allowed to see the women in here."

The servant had then bowed and removed her and Parma's dressing gowns. She kept them folded over one arm as she stood and waited with a stack of linens so finely woven, Charlotte thought the fabric suitable for a dinner gown.

"Do you have a name?" Charlotte asked in a quiet voice.

The servant gave her a quelling glance, as if she was offended by the query. "Elena. We all have names here."

"I am called... Charlotte, and this is my lady's maid, Parma," Charlotte said, hesitant to mention her title.

Elena merely shrugged, as if she had no reason to know their names.

After they had both been forced to bathe under the harsh gaze of the two eunuchs, Elena took them back to their chamber. When asked what would happen to them, she merely shrugged. "I do not know."

Parma had been able to style Charlotte's hair from the few pins that had remained after their ordeal with the pirates. "I'll look for some more in the trunks," she promised when she stepped back to assess the simple coiffure.

Now that she was suitably dressed in a lavender day gown and had applied her usual perfume and cosmetics—lip color and faint rouge—Charlotte felt more herself. She considered their shared fate. "Well, if the sultan wanted us dead, he would have seen to it yesterday with that sword of his," she reasoned. As for what he intended to do with them, she really had no idea.

"That servant was a slave," Parma stated, referring to Elena.

Charlotte blinked as she turned to face Parma. "How do you know that?"

Her lady's maid displayed a pained expression as she handed her mistress a fan featuring hand-painted flowers. "Those men with the sultan yesterday... they were Turkish. He is Turkish. Except for his wives, all the women in this palace are no doubt slaves, and his wives may as well be, too," she claimed. "He probably has a harem of at least a hundred women."

Swallowing, Charlotte suddenly understood why Parma seemed so worried about their fate. She was from India. There were sultans there, too. In her youth, she had no doubt heard stories of women being captured and sold into slavery. Women who disappeared by the walls of a palace, never to be seen again.

Charlotte wished she had been able to understand the verbal exchange that had occurred between the sultan and the pirates the evening prior. Perhaps she and Parma had been sold as slaves to the sultan. If so, what sort of service would they be required to perform?

Surely the sultan wouldn't want her in his bed. She was a widow. Although she probably wasn't too old to bear a child, she certainly didn't possess the exotic appearance of the few women they had seen since their arrival, their lower faces covered with veils so only their dark outlined eyes and brows were visible. The other was Elena, the Greek servant who had witnessed their bath.

When the same servant arrived a moment later, Charlotte attempted to learn more from her. "Can you tell me where we are? What's to happen to us?"

The servant shook her head. "I can only say that I am to escort you to my sultan. Do you have something to hide your face?" She made a motion to indicate the space between the top of her nose down to her chin.

Charlotte scoffed. "I've a fan, of course," she replied as she lifted it to shield the lower half of her face from view.

Parma was quick to retrieve another fan from the valise. She turned her attention to Elena. "Should I use one as well?"

"You are to remain here," Elena stated.

Charlotte exchanged a worried glance with Parma before she nodded and followed the servant through a series of wide corridors to the same chamber where the pirates had unceremoniously dumped her and Parma at the ruler's feet only the evening prior. She was glad for the fan as it gave her something to hang onto—even if it wouldn't work as a weapon.

One guard knocked on the door, disappearing for a moment before he motioned for the other two guards to open both carved doors. Due to the pandemonium of the day before, Charlotte hadn't given a thought to their manner of dress. To the odd cylindrical hats made of scarlet felt. To the black leather boots that bore a resemblance to those worn by the gentlemen who rode horses in Hyde Park. To the curved scabbards that hung at their sides, decorative sword hilts clearly on display.

Her gaze darting to Elena, Charlotte wondered why the woman had quickly stepped away from her. Now she was waving frantically, motioning for Charlotte to enter the sultan's throne room.

Charlotte turned her attention to the man who sat at the other end of the stone-walled chamber. She would have liked a moment to marvel at the gold-tinged walls, the mosaic-tiled ceiling, and the rich fabrics that covered a series of cushions which lined the Turkish carpet leading to the sultan's throne, but the appearance of the man himself captivated her.

Ensconced on the simple gilded throne and wearing a blue brocade coat embellished with gold embroidery, the sultan was leaning on one elbow. His attention was on a parchment another similarly dressed man had apparently just delivered. That man bowed deeply before backing away from the sultan. After a few steps, he turned and rushed out the door, his kaftan flying open to reveal a long red embroidered tunic and darker red şalvar.

Charlotte was tempted to watch the man's exit after he passed her, but her gaze remained fixed on the sultan.

His beard was definitely shorter than it had been the night before. His black-outlined eyes appeared as if they were made of silver and were set in a face that could have been chiseled from stone.

All she had remembered had been his fierce expression

as the pirates presented her and Parma. The sharp tone of his voice when he replied to their words. The scars on his cheek. His long beard, streaked with gray. His announcement of his title and name. His perusal of her and Parma as they were led away by the two female servants.

Although she probably should have feared him the day before, she hadn't. He was no different than a king. She had attended Prinny's court enough times in her capacity as Duchess of Chichester to understand the rules of addressing such a head of state. As a duchess, she also knew not to cower. To stand as straight as possible, holding up her chin as if a book rested upon her head and needed to remain there as she moved.

Nevertheless, she had been relieved when she realized she was to remain in whatever this stone-walled structure was, surrounded by opulent drapes, plump cushions, ceilings covered in mosaics, and floors covered with patterned carpets. She would have felt fear if she'd had to go with the pirates, for their intentions obviously involved using her to earn some blunt.

When the sultan raised his gaze from the document he held, his eyes locked with hers, and it was everything Charlotte could do to withhold an audible gasp. To display a pleasant expression. To pretend she didn't notice the severity of the scars on his right cheek.

His shorter beard made the three scars much more apparent.

By no means were they as severe as the scars her late husband had sported since the fire that took his parents' lives. His older brother and younger sister, too. Nearly half of Joshua's face had suffered burns, as had some of his left torso.

Charlotte had seen him when the burns were fresh. Smelled the charred flesh. Fought the resulting nausea and vowed she would do whatever was necessary to see to it he had the very best doctor. That he would live to claim the Chichester dukedom as his own.

Even though Dr. Regan hadn't expected Joshua to live, she had seen to it that the he did.

A deep voice spoke words she couldn't understand, and Charlotte was pulled from her reverie. The sultan, his dark brows furrowed, used a hand to beckon her, the parchment he held apparently forgotten.

Barely aware her feet were moving, Charlotte was reminded of her first presentation at King George III's court. She had been seventeen at the time, wearing a ridiculous Georgian-era gown with wide panniers and so many furbelows, she might have been mistaken for a rather large cake. Her current gown's bell skirt and snug bodice wasn't much different, she supposed, although it was devoid of the excessive decorations. Coupled with the golden light from a nearby window, the lavender fabric practically glowed.

At the end of the cushions that lined the carpet runner beneath her feet, she stopped and dipped a low curtsy. Her head bowed before she straightened to see the sultan regarding her with the oddest expression.

A stream of what sounded like a scold came from somewhere behind her, but Charlotte kept her gaze on the sultan. His attention went to the source of the harsh sounding words, his eyes blazing with anger as he lifted one arm and made a dismissive motion.

Although she desperately wanted to see whoever it was who had spoken, Charlotte resisted the urge to turn around.

A response came in the form of a murmur—an apology, perhaps?—and she heard the doors behind her close.

The sultan turned his attention to her, and Charlotte had to resist the urge to stare. Had to keep her pleasant expression from conveying her momentary horror.

The scar she had noticed from a distance was definitely caused by a blade, the three cuts deep and arranged so they formed a 'Z.'

Z for Ziyaeddin? she wondered as she waited for him to finish his perusal of her.

He spoke directly to her, which had Charlotte blinking. Prior to the day before, she had never heard the language he spoke. "Apologies, Your Highness, but I do not understand," she said, bowing her head again.

The sultan regarded her a moment. "You are English?"

Charlotte's eyes rounded. "I am, Your Highness."

He took the step down from in front of his throne and stood only a few feet in front of her. The way his head lifted and turned slightly suggested he had caught a whiff of her floral perfume. "Your name?"

Deciding it would be best to tell him—surely a ruler would have more regard for a foreign aristocrat than a commoner—she replied, "Charlotte, Duchess of Chichester."

His slight recoil meant he knew enough English to understand her words.

"A king's daughter?" he guessed, his brows furrowed as if in thought. "No, for then you would be a princess," he murmured.

"An earl's daughter," she said. "The Earl of Ellsworth was my father," she replied. "My late husband was the Duke of Chichester."

He clasped his hands behind his back as he processed the information. After a moment, he huffed. "I am Ziyaeddin Sultan the First." The last word was said with a smirk, as if he found 'the First' amusing.

Charlotte angled her head, not about to remind him that he had introduced himself the night before. "Is it true you are the ruler of the Ottoman Empire?" she asked in awe, remembering Captain Popodopolos' mention of the man over dinner the first night of the voyage. His name had been spoken at the last ball Joshua and she had attended in London as well.

"I am," he replied, a brow arching in surprise.

His name had also been spoken again later by their youngest son, James. Something about an heir... "Do you have a son attending university in Cambridge?" she asked.

Both of Ziyaeddin's brows arched, and his expression conveyed surprise. "Two of them. My seventh and my ninth. You... you have heard of them?" His eyes rounded. "Has one of my sons done something so egregious they have earned demerits?"

Even as Charlotte was forced to suppress a grin—did all parents think their sons were causing trouble whilst at university?—she feared he would be disappointed if he learned his name had been said in passing, and not always in a favorable way. "I have heard of you, of course, Your Highness."

Ziyaeddin frowned. "Followed by a curse, no doubt," he murmured. "The English were our enemies in the war with Greece."

"But allies only a year ago," she countered. "Your name was spoken with respect, sir," she quickly added. "As for your sons, I have heard no rumors of demerits. I'm quite sure if they had earned any, my younger son would have mentioned it prior to completing his studies. He attended Cambridge as well. Before he set off on his Grand Tour."

Straightening, Ziyaeddin regarded her as a slow grin lifted his lips. "You will walk with me," he stated.

"I would be honored, Your Highness," she replied, once again dipping a curtsy. She expected him to offer an arm as she turned to join him on his way to the door. When he didn't, she made sure to keep more distance between them, not sure of the protocols in his court.

His hands still clasped behind his back, Ziyaeddin led them down the same corridor from which Charlotte had come, but they passed by the door to the room in which she and Parma had spent the night. When they turned into another corridor, he slowed his steps and glanced back, as if he feared they were being followed.

"What is it, Your Highness?" Charlotte asked in a quiet voice.

"Emir Efendi seeks an answer I am not yet ready to give," he replied. He paused in mid-step and regarded her with a look of surprise. "How did you know...?" He allowed the query to hang in the air as he rolled his eyes.

"You seemed distracted, is all. Which cannot be helped given your position, of course," she replied, hoping she had guessed correctly. "Your empire is rather large—"

"Not as large as it was when I inherited—"

"And covers a good deal of ground. It must be very difficult to oversee all the details."

He blinked as he regarded her with suspicion before he resumed walking. "There is much to do when one is a ruler," he finally agreed. His measured pace wasn't hurried nor was it a stroll as they made their way down a long carpeted corridor lit with decorative sconces. "Especially when there are those who think they can do it better when in fact they only want the power and will do it wrong."

The corridor ended and daylight streamed onto a balcony surrounded by a stone balustrade. He took a deep breath, his eyes closed as he lifted his face to the sun.

Charlotte watched in fascination, sure he was praying. When the palms of his hands lifted to his face, she quickly diverted her attention to the land beyond the palace walls. Although the air suggested a body of water was near, she saw only forested hills in the distance and low, white-washed buildings scattered near the base of the palace walls. From their height in the balcony, she knew she was three stories above ground.

"How did you come to be in possession of the pirates?" he asked.

Surprised by the change in topic, Charlotte furrowed her brows. "They boarded the ship I was traveling on early yesterday morning," she replied. "Captured the crew and imprisoned my lady's maid and me in our cabin." she explained.

"What ship?"

Inhaling softly, Charlotte realized the sultan would learn the truth from someone else if she didn't offer it. "It was a merchant ship, sir. *Sun of Apollo*," she replied. From the name, she knew he would guess it was Greek.

"The captain's name?"

Charlotte swallowed. "Popodopolos," she hedged. "My passage was arranged by the Chichester dukedom's man of business."

"For what purpose?" he asked, his fierce expression having returned to make him appear angry.

Sighing, Charlotte realized she may as well tell him the entire truth. "A European holiday," she replied, trying hard not to wince. Why had she allowed her best friends to talk her into the trip? Why hadn't she abided Garrett's plea that she remain at home? "My mourning period ended last month—"

"Mourning?"

"Yes. The Duke of Chichester died a bit over a year ago."

The sultan narrowed his eyes. "So... you are not married?"

She shook her head. "I am a widow, Your Highness."

His expression softened as he stared out toward the forested lands. "Another has not yet claimed you?"

Charlotte gave a start at hearing the odd phrase. "I've

not yet returned to Society," she responded. "Nor would I have accepted any suitors if there had been anyone. It would not have been proper before last month."

His head jerked back as if he'd been punched in the face. "I thought all English took lovers," he murmured. "Mistresses," he added, as his brows furrowed in concentration. "Lovers."

Charlotte cleared her throat. "Not all, sir."

"But your husband had a mistress."

Blinking, Charlotte wondered why he would say such a thing. "He did not, sir."

Once again, the sultan looked shocked before he chuckled. "Perhaps he did so secretly."

Annoyed by his suggestion, Charlotte countered, "I'm quite sure I would have known."

His eyes once again narrowed. "How?"

Her chin lifted in defiance. "We shared a bed, Your Highness. Every night," she claimed. Although it wasn't completely true—there had been times when Joshua was sick with a head cold and she retired to the mistress suite —she had secured a promise of fidelity from Joshua even without asking. After all, he was convinced no other woman would abide his awful appearance due to his burn scars.

"You were his only wife?" Ziyaeddin asked in awe. The man's entire bearing changed, as if he was attempting to learn something he couldn't comprehend.

"Of course," she replied. Then understanding dawned when she remembered Parma's earlier comment. "Oh. In England, men are allowed only one wife. Women are allowed only one husband."

Ziyaeddin stared at her until Charlotte briefly glanced away, uncomfortable under his harsh glare. "How is an Englishman to have a suitable number of sons with only one wife?" he asked, his expression betraying his confusion.

Charlotte stared at him a moment before she said, "They merely require one heir. And a spare, in case something should happen to the eldest son." She glanced to the side before she leaned in and asked, "Pray tell, how many sons do you believe are a suitable number?"

Ziyaeddin shrugged. "I have eleven who still live from the sixteen who were born."

"Sixteen *sons*?" Charlotte repeated in shock. "How...?" She clamped her mouth shut, remembering there was a harem somewhere in the palace. A collection of women available at his beck and call. For a moment, she imagined him with more than one in his bed, and the oddest sensation flitted through her.

What if he intended for her to be one of them?

She quickly fanned her face, sure she displayed a blush.

From the brief opportunity she was able to study his profile as they walked, Charlotte noted how long his dark lashes were. She had wondered what created the black lines surrounding his eyes when she realized it was entirely due to his black eyelashes.

For a moment, she imagined what he looked like with his eyes closed, those lashes resting atop his high cheekbones. Given his kohl-black beard included a few streaks of silver gray, she imagined the hair beneath his turban was much the same. She wondered if it was long or short. If it was long, did it fall past his shoulders? Or was he bald?

Was his chest covered in dark hair as well?

An image of him without the turban and completely naked flitted past her mind's eye, and she inhaled softly. Even as she mentally scolded herself for such wanton thoughts, her own body's reaction couldn't be ignored. Not when her nipples tightened and the space at the top of her thighs dampened.

What was wrong with her? She shouldn't be having such thoughts, especially not in the presence of a barbarian.

Nevertheless, she rather liked it when his sideways glance drifted down the front of her gown and back up to her hair. Despite his ramrod straight bearing and confident manner, she was quite sure he didn't know what to do about her.

Which was just as well. She didn't know what she was going to do about him.

CHAPTER 9
A LESSON IN NAMES

*Z*iyaeddin surreptitiously studied the beautiful Englishwoman who stood next to him, not sure why he was so amused by her discomfort at learning he had so many sons. Although she knew more about the Ottoman Empire than he would have expected a foreign woman to know, perhaps she was unaware of his right to possess a harem. To have multiple wives and concubines. His power as a sultan was somewhat dependent on it.

"I have twenty concubines, although only ten have blessed me with children," he stated proudly, his amusement apparent when his guest displayed a look of shock. He didn't add that three had died in the childbed or shortly thereafter.

"Only ten?" Charlotte murmured sarcastically, her brows shooting up in in wonder. The fan quickened its movement although her wrist barely seemed to move.

"They are excellent mothers," Ziyaeddin said, his hands clasping behind his back as they resumed their walk along a covered exterior corridor. The air had warmed considerably in the few minutes they had been outside of the palace, and yet the duchess didn't appear bothered by the heat. Perhaps her fan was more effective than he thought. It was certainly good at sending wafts of her floral-scented perfume in his direction.

He nearly stopped in his tracks when he realized she walked alongside him, even when others passed going in the opposite direction. Not a step behind him as his surviving wife or concubines would do. Perhaps her station in England afforded her such a privilege. He found he didn't mind, though. It made it easier for their conversation to be kept quiet. More intimate.

He experienced a moment of surprise. This fair creature had been dragged kicking and complaining into his palace and then dumped onto the floor before him as if she was no better than a slave. Despite her poor treatment by the pirates who intended to sell her and her lady's maid to him, she had kept her pride. Kept her wits about her even if she had appeared rather bedraggled upon her arrival.

Ziyaeddin was remembering how her golden red hair had come undone from its pins, a lock falling over one of her eyes as she pinned him with a cornflower blue stare that might have turned lowlier men to stone.

A stare he remembered from long ago. One he had not seen in twenty years.

It was everything he could do not to smirk at the memory. To keep his cock in check. For at that moment, it reacted in a way it had not done so in a very long time.

Perhaps it had been too long since he'd taken a concubine to his bed. As for his first wife, she was at one of their palaces in Constantinople with two of his younger sons—the sixth and eighth—a situation he was finding untenable. A courier had delivered a message only the day before, one sent by a eunuch claiming she had taken a lover since her return to the capital city.

Although the news had angered him at first—had she thought she could do such a thing and not be discovered? —he decided he no longer had feelings for the woman. Perhaps he never had. Their marriage had been arranged by his father with her father, a member of the ministry of state.

His brief reverie was interrupted when Charlotte asked, "And you? Are you an excellent father?"

Apparently the duchess was unaware she could be offending him with such a question.

Deciding not to take offense—he was enjoying the momentary diversion the Englishwoman provided during a morning filled with bothersome problems and the annoying emir with his letter of demands from some minor administrator—Ziyaeddin considered the query a moment and finally said, "I believe so. I did spend... or *do* spend time with them. I have seen to their education. I have clothed them." Pausing a moment—he was waiting for Charlotte's reaction—he added, "But I have not always allowed them a life of what you would call luxury."

Charlotte furrowed a brow. "So... you require them to work for their livings?"

He nodded, glad she understood. Something about the way she held her head and kept her gaze on him had the oddest sensation gripping his chest. Her interest seemed genuine, her concern apparent. "My first son, whom I have chosen as a finalist to inherit my sultanate, sees to the treasury," he explained. "The second and third are in charge of the armies. The fourth oversees what little navy we have left..." He paused, his features pinching at the memory of how Mohammed Ali had used the few ships they had left to attempt a takeover of Syria and the Holy Lands only the year before.

"Were you able to recapture your ships from that errant viceroy?" Charlotte asked.

Ziyaeddin stared at her in shock, wondering if she could read his mind. "How is it you know of him?" His entire empire had been put at risk as a result of Ali's thirst for power.

Charlotte lifted a shoulder. "I read *The Times*, sir," she replied. "The London newspaper." She dipped her head and added, "I apologize for asking. I can see that the reminder of it troubles you."

His eyes darting to the side, Ziyaeddin found he wasn't as troubled by what had happened the year before as much as he was by the aftermath. He knew other countries were watching his empire decrease in size and influence. That a woman would know of it should have bothered him more than it did.

Had she cast some sort of spell on him? One that made him ambivalent? Or had his plans for the future—universities, a different banking scheme, and a new, more modern palace—made the events of the past less important?

"Please, do go on, Your Highness," Charlotte urged.

Ziyaeddin inhaled even as his eyes narrowed. "If you

had not been delivered by pirates, I might believe you are a spy," he murmured. He absently reached for his beard, intending to clutch it and smooth it into a cone, but he had trimmed it so short that morning, his hand ended up empty and fisted against his chest. At least he no longer appeared as old has he had felt the day before, the trimming having removed most of the gray.

Charlotte's mouth dropped open in shock. "I'm hardly a spy, Your Highness. I am a mother of two sons, however, so learning how you keep yours out of trouble is of interest to me."

A hearty chuckle erupted from the sultan. "It is my fourth son who is in charge of the navy, which is now a small fleet of ships. My fifth sees to the... to the buildings."

"Government buildings?"

"Indeed. Another will see to food and its distribution when he is of an age to take on the responsibility. Another will see to collecting the taxes from the merchants who travel in caravans to trade at our bazaars." He waved a hand as he led her around a turn and into another corridor. "Of course, not all of my sons are of an age to begin their service to the empire, so they continue their education with their tutors here in this palace or in one of the others."

The two sons in Constantinople once again came to mind along with a concern his wife might be attempting some sort of coup. He hadn't yet decided what he would do when he had confirmation of her infidelity. Divorce was always a possibility, and if he did invoke the words necessary to end their marriage, it would come with a requirement that she marry her lover.

"My sons are both grown," Charlotte stated. "The oldest is now the duke. He is married to a woman he dearly loves," she explained.

"And the other? The one who attended Cambridge?"

Charlotte sighed. "On his Grand Tour. He is probably somewhere in... in Greece, I think," she said. "From the time he was a little boy, he has had an interest in anything Ancient Greek. Temples, statuary, the marbles from the Acropolis in Athens."

"I have seen those marbles," Ziyaeddin stated.

Charlotte angled her head to one side. "You have been to the British Museum?"

He grinned. "I traveled with my seventh and ninth sons when I took them to Cambridge," he explained. "I couldn't let them have all the fun."

Enjoying how she seemed so surprised by his words, Ziyaeddin wasn't prepared for how disappointed she sounded with her next question.

"How is it I did not learn of your visit to our country?" she asked, her features suggesting she felt left out.

"I did not announce it," he replied with a shrug. Despite the urge to continue gazing at the duchess, Ziyaeddin made sure to keep his head pointed in the direction they walked. He was aware of her repeated glances, sure she was studying his profile.

Charlotte waved her fan in an effort to cool her heated face. "So with all those boys... you must have had a daughter or two?" she commented. For a moment of near breathlessness, she thought Parma had deliberately tightened her corset too much that morning. When the corridor ended onto a large open balcony, she inhaled a lungful of Aegean Sea air in an attempt to stave off a faint.

"Ten daughters have been born to me," Ziyaeddin said proudly, his attention turning to her as they made their way to a balustrade. "Eight have survived." He would have allowed his gaze to linger longer—he was intrigued as much by the Englishwoman's curiosity as he was by her appearance, especially under the bright sun—but he sensed she was about to react with disbelief, and he resisted the urge.

Charlotte stopped in her tracks. "You had six-and-twenty children?" she asked in shock. "And nineteen are still alive?"

His gaze darted to the right before he nodded, impressed she could do the arithmetic in her head. "They are. They range in age from..." He paused as he raised one hand, the long, slender fingers seeming to tap the air in front of them. "Six to twenty-six." He stared at Charlotte a moment in an attempt to discover if she was impressed or appalled before he added, "My father had thirty-seven, but he had far more concubines and three wives."

Sure her face displayed a bright red blush—her fan was doing nothing to keep her cool—Charlotte dipped her head before she turned her attention to the distant horizon, her thoughts on how often he must have bedded all those women to have fathered so many children. At how skilled he had to have been to ensure their mothers were pleasured in the process in order to better their chances of a conceiving a babe.

At how skilled he probably still was.

She reached out to place a gloved hand on the balustrade that lined the balcony in an effort to steady herself. "How can you even remember all their names?" she asked, not bothering to add an honorific to the query.

Startled, Ziyaeddin displayed a frown before he shrugged. "I named them all, so of course I remember them," he claimed. When Charlotte lifted a brow, he dipped his head. "Are you challenging me, Duchess?"

Her expression of worry suggested she feared she had offended him, but he was enjoying their repartee too much to take offense. He was glad when he saw her grin.

"I suppose I am. Tell me your daughters' names."

He displayed a huge smile, his perfect teeth blinding white in the midday sun. "Challenge accepted," he stated. "My eldest is Aergul Sultana. Her name means 'a bouquet of blooming roses'."

Charlotte inhaled softly, obviously not expecting he would share the reason for the moniker. "Does she live up to the name?"

Ziyaeddin considered the query a moment. "Indeed. She has two children of her own now."

"She is married?"

"Oh, yes," he replied, about to scold her for suggesting one of his daughters would be bedded by a man prior to her wedding. "To a member of my... ministry," he added, pausing to recall the proper English word to describe his advisors and those who were in charge of various government departments. "Or is it a cabinet?" he murmured to himself. He gave his head a shake. "He is the son of an emir. Then there is Sevinc—"

"Which means?"

"Ah, 'delight'," he said. "And no, she has not always been a joy," he quickly added. "She is twenty years old, and she is what I believe you would call a... a rebel."

Charlotte inhaled softly. "You are disappointed in her?" she asked, noting how his brows furrowed, almost as if he regretted his words.

He shook his head. "Actually, I am very proud of her, but I also worry about her. Her brothers blame me for educating her too much, but I have hired the same governesses for all my daughters. All my concubines, too," he explained. "Of all the girls, Sevinc is the only one who has decided that our way of life must change. She has come to this conclusion of her own accord, so I know she must possess a wisdom unlike her sisters."

Charlotte decided she already liked his second eldest daughter. "How so?"

He inhaled to answer. "She doesn't believe men should have more one than one wife, although our religion allows us to have four." He paused when he saw how Charlotte's eyes rounded and then had to suppress the urge to chuckle. "She thinks there should be no concubines in a harem. Only a wife and all my sisters, aunts and female servants."

"I think I like her already," Charlotte murmured.

Ziyaeddin allowed the chuckle he had been holding in. "Tradition is hard to overcome," he said. "This has been our way of life since the empire was founded. But I am working to change things."

Charlotte furrowed a brow. "Do you plan to end slavery in your sultanate?"

He held up a bejeweled finger. "Actually, I already have, which is why I did not buy you from the pirates."

Charlotte gasped. "You... you didn't?" She glanced out, her gaze once again going to the horizon where the aqua blue sky met the turquoise waters of the Aegean Sea. "But... it sounded as if you were... as if you were *negotiating* with them," she murmured, remembering the odd exchange between Aukmed and the sultan as Parma cowered in fear for her life.

Although Charlotte had been frightened of the pirates and what they might do to her and Parma once they were off the Greek ship, she remembered feeling some relief when they were brought to the palace. Surely the ruler of such an opulent domain wouldn't be cruel.

"There was no negotiation," Ziyaeddin stated. "I told them, 'you will leave the ladies and their traveling cases or you will be executed for slavery'. Then I had them taken to the dungeons." He ignored her gasp of surprise and rounded eyes. "I sent a courier to their ship with the message that their men would not be returning and that they are no longer allowed to do business in my country."

Awestruck, Charlotte stared at the sultan in a whole new light. "Thank you, Your Highness," she said.

Although she was curious to learn what the pirates had demanded in the way of payment, Charlotte decided not to ask. She had no idea the value of Turkish money, if that's what had been requested. Given Aukmed and the other two pirates had been remanded to the dungeon, she thought perhaps they must have been too greedy with their price.

She hadn't dared ask when they might be released.

If Ziyaeddin intended to release them at all.

Ziyaeddin's chest puffed out as a grin lifted his lips. "It was my pleasure, I assure you," he replied.

"And the crew from the *Sun of Apollo*? The Greek ship?" Charlotte ventured, hoping to learn their fate.

Ziyaeddin suddenly furrowed his brows in a manner that had Charlotte wishing she hadn't asked about them. Even though it had been several years since the Turks had been defeated in the Greek's war for independence, she was sure the loss still stung. "They are bound for Rhodes, but their ship is no doubt forfeit to the pirates," he explained. "I had no say over the matter."

When his fearsome expression didn't change after another moment, Charlotte asked, "What is it, Your Highness?"

Ziyaeddin regarded her with the same fierce look for another moment longer before he asked, "Was one of them... *important* to you? One of the men on that ship?"

Charlotte blinked in surprise as she gave her head a quick shake. "Oh, no. Of course not," she replied, wondering at his reaction. "The captain was a kind man, though, in agreeing to take on me and my lady's maid as passengers. Those sorts of ships rarely do."

He scoffed. "They do for a price," he replied, his gaze sweeping the horizon, as if their talk of the Greek ship might have it appearing on the water. "I have discovered money can buy anything."

Not sure how much Garrett had paid for their passage

—Charlotte hadn't asked, and he hadn't offered to share the information—she said, "I wasn't informed of the cost of our tickets. The passage was arranged by my late husband's man of business."

This bit of information seemed to settle the sultan, but only for a moment. "Is he an honorable man? This... man of business?" He hadn't heard the phrase used before and wondered at its meaning.

Charlotte gave a start but said, "Very. He has seen to it the Chichester dukedom was well maintained while my husband was alive, and it continues to thrive under my son."

"Did he take you to his bed?"

He knew the moment he asked the question that she would react in a violent manner. Her eyes blazed much like they had the night before. So when she raised an arm in an attempt to slap him, he was ready and able to block the blow by quickly raising his hand. He caught her hand in his, brushing his thumb over her knuckles as her floral scent swirled about his nostrils. A familiar sensation had him blinking in an attempt to capture a memory from long ago.

"Apologies, Duchess. I do not know why..." He allowed the sentence to trail off, realizing he didn't know how to translate his thoughts into English. Now he wished he had spent more time practicing with Sevinc.

Since her attempted assault might have resulted in her own visit to the dungeons, Charlotte carefully withdrew her hand from his, took a step back and dipped her head. "I apologize as well, Your Highness," she said.

"Tell me more about this man of business," Ziyaeddin ordered.

Charlotte hesitated for a moment before she said, "I have known Mr. McElliott for as long as I was married to my duke," her voice quiet. "And I am very good friends with his wife and am practically an aunt to all their children," she added. "Not that it is any of your business, but I assure you, Your Highness, I have never been with any other man but my husband. In that way."

Ziyaeddin stared at her for a long time before he dipped his head. "So you have no protector now?"

Charlotte inhaled to answer and then seemed to rethink her response before she finally said, "My oldest son acts in that capacity."

"And your late husband? Was he good to you?"

Ziyaeddin knew she was about to scold him for asking such a personal question. He was sure she was poised to do so before she raised her chin and stated, "He was. We were in love with one another from the first moment we danced together at a ball in London." He watched as she swallowed hard in an attempt to keep tears at bay, and he suddenly understood.

"My concubine, Afet, was the love of my life. She bore me a son and a daughter," Ziyaeddin said quietly. "Twenty years ago."

Charlotte watched as his features softened and his eyes lost their focus. "Afet?" she repeated. "What does that name mean?"

Brought out of his brief reverie, the sultan sighed. "A woman of bewitching beauty," he replied. "Lovable. She was both."

"Was?" Charlotte repeated, her brows furrowing. "Did you... did you marry her?"

He dipped his head, pausing a moment before he replied. "I did. Four days after she was gifted to me by her father."

Once again, the memory of Afet's fierce expression came to mind. The defiance she had shown had been a welcome challenge. He had been so taken with her, he had decided he would do whatever was necessary for her to agree to marry him—willingly—and declare her love for him.

It had taken her three days.

He had been in love with her from the start.

"Gifted to you?" Charlotte repeated in a near whisper.

Pulled from his reverie, Ziyaeddin nodded. "He was a Greek. He wished a favor from my father, and she was the... cost," he said, wincing when he realized the word was a poor choice.

"What happened to her?" Once again, Charlotte's query was asked in a whisper.

"She died the day after she gave birth to the babe who is now my fifth son, Ertuğrul. I have always been thankful that I took her to wife before that fateful day. So that we might one day be reunited in death."

Charlotte inhaled softly. "I'm so sorry for your loss," she whispered.

He regarded her a moment, one of his brows furrowing as if he were determining her sincerity. "Thank you," he finally replied.

"And the baby boy?" she prompted, apparently unable to pronounce his name.

"Ertuğrul is one of my emirs now," Ziyaeddin stated, his manner suggesting he wasn't pleased with his son.

Charlotte recalled how Ziyaeddin had described his sons' duties and remembered the fifth son oversaw the government buildings.

That would be Ertuğrul.

Whatever had he done to anger his father?

Aware a pall had settled over their conversation, Charlotte straightened. "Those other daughters? What are their names?"

Ziyaeddin scoffed, but his eyes lit up in delight. "Ah, the test resumes," he murmured. He held up a hand and splayed his fingers. "Ekin, which means harvest. Then there is Defne, Miray, Nehir, Hiranur, and Aysun," he recited as his fingers bent one after the other.

Charlotte's mouth dropped open in awe before she clamped it shut.

"They are all beautiful girls, and the remaining seven will be married to men in important positions," Ziyaeddin explained proudly. His brows furrowed after a moment. "My grown sons have a harder time in what you call the marriage..." He paused, as if he was struggling to remember the correct word. "Agora?"

"Mart?" Charlotte guessed.

He lifted a forefinger. "Marriage Mart," he agreed with a nod. "Other than the oldest, they are blinded by beauty first and haven't yet learned there is more to a woman than meets the eye."

"You do not arrange their marriages?"

"I will for some of them," he replied. "Not for my

eldest three, though. They are already married or betrothed to suitable girls."

A servant silently appeared from within the nearby corridor, his head bent. When he didn't notice the man's arrival, Charlotte nodded in his direction.

Ziyaeddin turned and spoke in Turkish. The two exchanged a few words before the sultan waved a dismissive hand. The servant hurried off.

When he turned his gaze back on Charlotte, Ziyaeddin sighed. "My presence is required elsewhere."

"Of course, Your Highness," Charlotte replied, dipping a curtsy. She expected him to hurry off. Instead, he remained in front of her, regarding her with the oddest expression.

"I cannot leave you here, Your Grace," he stated. "You must go back to your chamber."

"Oh," she replied, not bothering to hide her disappointment. "Well, I think I can find my way back," she claimed, even though it was apparent she wasn't entirely sure she could. The corridors in the palace were practically a maze.

"I cannot allow you to roam about the palace by yourself," he countered. "A woman alone... it would not be seemly," he added. He wasn't surprised to see a flash of annoyance cross her expression, and he nearly chuckled.

When it was apparent she understood his meaning and had reconsidered arguing, she asked, "Will you escort me, Your Highness?"

He nodded, his mind still on the message his servant had delivered. At least he'd had the opportunity to learn more about his guests. More about the duchess.

Their conversation had been a necessary diversion in an otherwise decision-filled day. There had been too many of them of late, despite his insistence he had come to the Aegean palace in order to holiday. To spend his days visiting the nearby Greek ruins. Riding on his yacht on the turquoise waters. Hunting for grouse. Walking in the palace gardens. Reacquainting himself with one of his favorites from the harem.

Not once had he done any of those activities.

They were halfway down the first corridor when his guest decided to bring up the matter of her and her servant's fate.

"Pray tell, Your Highness, when might I be allowed to resume my travel to Europe?"

Ziyaeddin paused before the door to her chamber, his expression once again fierce. "It is best you enjoy my hospitality for a time, Duchess. I have no intention of sending you off on a ship with pirates so close." With that, he motioned to the guard to open the door and then hurried off in the direction of the throne room.

*C*harlotte stared after the retreating sultan, her mouth dropping open as a combination of anger and awe had her fists going to her hips.

"Infuriating man," she murmured in a huff before she stomped into the chamber.

The guard closed the door behind her, aiming a frown at her back as he did so.

CHAPTER 10
PREPARING FOR A TOUR

The next morning
When the sun's rays pierced the colored glass in Charlotte's room, she awoke with a start. She glanced around, heartened to see Parma already up and about carrying a pitcher of water and bath linens.

"Good morning, Your Grace," Parma said as she approached. "I was becoming worried."

Charlotte furrowed a brow as she sought some measure of time. There were no clocks in the room, and the thick stained glass of the window cast the room in a multicolored wash.

Alarm had her rising from the strange mattress. There wasn't a bed frame of any sort—the long cushion was simply another pillow on the floor—so she had to struggle to stand. "Why? What's happened?"

Parma poured water into a huge ceramic bowl, which only enhanced the intricately decorated pattern featuring dolphins and waves. "You slept later than usual, my lady. The sun has been up for hours." She waved at a tray brimming with fruits and two ceramic cups. "I hope you don't mind, but I helped myself to some of the food that the Greek servant brought. She introduced me to one of the palace laundresses, and she is seeing to washing the soiled clothes we wore on the ship."

Glancing at the tray, Charlotte gasped. A colorful array of cut and whole fruits filled the flat wooden circle. "Goodness, how many of us do they think are in this room?" she asked rhetorically. She turned her attention back on her lady's maid. "I don't mind at all."

She took the bath linen Parma offered and washed her face and hands. "Has anyone knocked or come to the door since breakfast was delivered?" she asked as Parma moved to undo her braided hair.

"No, Your Grace. But I found a note slipped beneath it." She stood and moved to the dressing table. "There was no name written on the outside."

Charlotte joined Parma at the table, taking a seat so the lady's maid could do her hair. "Did you read it?"

Parma shook her head as she held it out. "I did not, nor do I think I could," she replied.

Charlotte aimed a curious glance at her lady's maid before she took the parchment. As Parma brushed her hair and pinned it up, Charlotte struggled to make out the words.

Whatever device that had been used to transfer the ink onto the parchment was flat rather than pointed, which left the vertical strokes of each letter wide and their horizontal lines very thin. After a few attempts, she grinned. Although the sultan spoke English rather well—

she would have to ask how he had learned it—he was not an accomplished writer of the language.

Dear Duchess Sharlot,

It seems affairs of the State outway affairs of the hart. I beg you accept my apologees for I will not be able to escort you on this fine day about the Palace.

In my place I will send you my most trusted. Ask her anything you wish. She will anser your querees, probablee too honestlee.

Sultan Ziyaeddin

Beneath the writing was a blotch of wax with the sultan's seal pressed into it.

"*She*?" Charlotte murmured, chuckling as she tried to imagine who her escort might be. Was he referring to Elena? And just what did he mean when he referred to "affairs of the hart"?

"Your Grace?"

Charlotte looked up to discover Parma had finished styling her hair. "It seems I'm to be escorted about the palace by a woman," she commented before she furrowed a brow. "Unless the sultan has his pronouns mixed up."

She suppressed the urge to chuckle. At least Ziyaeddin had thought about her. With as many people as there were in the palace, she thought it would be easy for him to forget she was even there.

That last thought had her giving a start. His parting comment implied she wouldn't be allowed to leave the palace anytime soon, but surely he didn't intend for her to stay indefinitely. He had made it quite clear that slavery was no longer allowed in his empire.

Surely he would let her go. Help her to arrange transport on a ship to one of the larger Greek islands or to Athens.

Wouldn't he?

"What would you like to wear?" Parma asked as she made her way to the trunks.

"I suppose it depends on what hasn't been soiled by those detestable pirates," Charlotte said, fearing the worst. Parma had stitched some of their money into the hems of gowns while the false bottom of the largest trunk held most of her blunt as well as the jewelry that wasn't made with paste gemstones. "Or been taken," she added, thinking they might have discovered the jewels before they brought the trunk to the palace.

"Everything is here, as far as I can tell," Parma replied. Having already opened both trunks the day before to find a gown for Charlotte to wear for her presentation to the sultan, Parma began pulling out the gowns she had already refolded.

Rising from the dressing table chair, Charlotte joined her in front of the trunks. "Are you sure?" she asked in surprise. "They didn't pilfer anything?"

Although it had been apparent to the maid that someone had rifled through the trunks—the clothes had been carelessly tossed about—they were all there, as were the fripperies, petticoats, chemises, and stockings. "I refolded all the gowns after I checked the bottom. Apparently the pirates didn't know to pull up the panel. The money and jewels are all still there," Parma explained. "Your small jewel box is missing, though," she added as she pointed to the other trunk, an expression of disappointment crossing her face. "I don't think it was in either of the trunks when the pirates took over the ship."

Relief swept over Charlotte. After the events of their arrival, she had been so relieved when their ordeal had ended at the feet of the sultan, she hadn't given much thought to their belongings. "I had pulled out the jewel box to select what I was going to wear for the day," she murmured. "It was all paste, though." She indicated a summer gown of coral muslin trimmed in white. "I'll wear that," she said, remembering how hot it had been the day before.

For a time after the sultan had left her, Charlotte had wondered if she had felt overly warm due to the weather or if her discomfort had been caused by the man. She hadn't expected Ziyaeddin to be so imposing. To possess such charisma. To send her insides into a turmoil of flutterbies and fill her mind with erotic thoughts of what he was capable of doing late at night.

Her gaze shot to the mattress on which she had slept. The soft cotton bed sheets had caressed her heated skin and provided a bit of warmth as the room cooled during the night. Her dreams had been filled with images of Ziyaeddin. Of his dark outlined eyes and the ragged scars that marred his right cheek. Of his hands, with their long slender fingers and the large gemstone-encrusted rings that had decorated several of his knuckles. Of his expression when he announced she should accept his hospitality and remain in the palace.

Even as a frisson shot through Charlotte when she

imagined what he might do to her, she felt sick at remembering he still had a wife. A harem of women, half of whom had blessed him with children.

Would he expect her to join him in his bed?

As excited as the thought of him touching her made her feel, she recoiled at the reminder that he was married. She would be committing adultery.

"My lady?" Parma asked, one of her hands passing in front of Charlotte's face.

Charlotte gave a start, noticing Parma had shaken out the day gown and set it aside with several petticoats. "What is it?"

Parma motioned toward the door. "Should I answer the door? Someone has knocked."

Her attention going to the carved wooden door, Charlotte inhaled softly. "I will see to it," she replied, determined to put thoughts of the sultan in the back of her mind. "After I put on some jewelry."

She fished a pair of earrings and a bracelet from the bottom of the false-bottomed trunk and allowed Parma to help her to secure them in place.

Deciding she was as ready as she would ever be, she tucked her fan into a pocket, went to the door, and gingerly tested the handle.

She inhaled softly when it opened, stunned to come face to face with a palace guard.

CHAPTER 11
A TOUR OF THE PALACE

*A*lthough the guard regarded her with interest, Charlotte knew he wasn't the one who was to take her on a tour of the palace. She poked her head out of the door and looked both ways to discover a young woman reading a book on the balcony at the end of the corridor. Her head was covered in a bright bejeweled scarf and headdress that matched her outfit. A slight breeze caused the scarf to flutter so that it looked as if the girl had wings.

At first, Charlotte thought the clothes were an embroidered blouse and skirt with a fitted jacket, but when the woman glanced up and made her way toward Charlotte, it became apparent the skirt was actually a pair of what appeared to be loose pantaloons. The slippers she wore were ornately embroidered, their toes slightly curled up.

The young woman executed a perfect curtsy.

Charlotte followed suit. "I am Charlotte, Duchess of

Chichester," she said, realizing that as the oldest, she would be expected to speak first.

"It is an honor to meet you, Your Grace. I am Sultana Sevinc. My father asked me to escort you about the palace."

Sevinc's barely accented English had Charlotte's eyes rounding. "It's very good to meet the daughter who most vexes her father," she replied with a grin.

Sevinc's happy expression faltered as a blush colored her fair features. She seemed at a loss for words.

"Oh, do not be concerned," Charlotte said. "You might vex him, but I think he values you more because of it," she added. "May I ask what you're reading?" she queried, indicating the tome tucked beneath the young woman's arm.

Visibly relieved, Sevinc held out her book. "*Pride and Prejudice,*" she replied. "Please don't tell my father. I brought it back with me from England last year, and it has become my favorite."

Charlotte scoffed. "Why would he object? It's a perfectly acceptable novel for a young woman to read, I should think."

Shaking her head, Sevinc said, "He prefers I study more serious books."

Sobering, Charlotte angled her head to one side. "How serious?"

Sevinc's gaze lifted to the ornate ceiling of the balcony. "'Modern Building Techniques Utilizing Cut Stone' or 'The History of the Byzantium Empire'," she recited, tucking the book under her arm.

"You're not joking," Charlotte stated, reassessing in

her mind what the sultan had said the day before. All his concubines were educated as were his sons and daughters.

"Joking?" Sevinc repeated, her dark brows furrowed.

Charlotte shook her head. "Teasing... um... telling a funny," she stammered as her own gaze lifted to the ceiling. She nearly gasped at the detail in the colorful multicolored mosaic patterns that spanned the entire length of the balcony's ceiling. The individual tiles that made up the hunting scene looked as if they were no larger than the tip of her finger.

Sevinc dipped her head. "There is no... joking... when it comes to the sultan," she murmured. "And he becomes more and more serious the older he grows."

The two began to stroll down the open corridor, the pale gold stone palace wall to their left and a vast body of water evident in the distance beyond the carved balustrade to their right. Although she wanted to stop and take in the opulence of her surroundings—she had barely noticed them whilst in the company of the sultan the day before—Charlotte kept pace with Sevinc. "Do you know why?" she asked.

Sevinc turned her gaze on Charlotte long enough for the duchess to see that her eyes were brown. Framed with dark brows and thick eyelashes, they were almond-shaped. Her high cheekbones were much like her father's, but her broad mouth was probably from her mother. Her arresting beauty would have all the young bucks in London clambering for a chance to dance with her if she ever attended a *ton* ball.

"My father seems to have grown weary of life," she

replied, although there was uncertainty in her voice. "He has prevented palace intrigues and ensured his sons equal shares in the sultanate—"

"Intrigues?" Charlotte interrupted.

Pausing a moment, Sevinc leaned a bit closer and said, "Over the years, the various palaces in Constantinople have been home to traitors and patriots, devoted servants and spies, friends and foe—many of them relations. Petty jealousies led to assassination attempts, which is why the boys used to be kept in separate palaces as they grew up. It lessened the chance of one of them gaining too much power."

"Oh, dear," Charlotte murmured. "Sounds like the large family of an aristocrat in London." When she noted Sevinc's look of surprise, her own eyes rounded and she added, "I am joking. Our laws of inheritance only allow for the eldest to inherit a title and the lands associated with it. The other sons must remain in good stead with him to continue receiving allowances or find another way to make their livings."

Sevinc gave a prim grin and resumed the stroll. "My father has probably not rid the palace completely of the worst, but it is better than it was for his great-grand-fathers."

When they turned the corner, Charlotte discovered the open corridor continued along the entire length of the palace wall. "This palace is terribly large," she murmured.

"This one is actually small compared to some of the palaces in Constantinople," Sevinc remarked. "And this one is quite old," she added. "It was built before... I believe what you call the medieval age? During our first sultan's reign," she explained. "It was never meant to be a palace from which a sultan ruled but rather one he could go to when he wished to go on..." She paused, as if she struggled for the right word.

"Holiday?" Charlotte guessed, her gaze sweeping over the landscape of mostly water. The view alone was worthy of an escape from everyday life.

"Holiday, yes," Sevinc affirmed with a grin.

"The vantage is gorgeous. The sunsets must be amazing."

"Oh, indeed, they are."

Charlotte grinned, realizing Sevinc had acquired some of her command of the English language from having read books, most notably those by Jane Austen. "And the water. Is it an ocean or...?"

"The Aegean Sea," Sevinc replied, her expression suggesting Charlotte should have known.

Charlotte gasped as her gaze swept over the water. "Pray tell, where exactly are we?"

Sevinc blinked as she regarded the duchess. "On the western shore of our main lands. These are not the most western lands of the empire, though, given Cyrenaica and some other provinces are located across from the Kingdom of the Two Sicilies." Her gaze darted to the stone floor beneath them. "If I might be so bold, it would be wise of you not to bring up our borders with my father."

Inhaling softly, Charlotte angled her head to one side. "Other than Greece—?"

"We are a shrinking empire, and my father has lost his will to fight."

Charlotte resisted the urge to gasp, but curiosity had her asking, "Shrinking... how?"

Sevinc glanced around, as if she feared someone might be eavesdropping on them. "Russia has taken Abkhazia, Poti, Akhaltsikhe, and Bessarabia. Serbia and now Greece are no longer ours. I fear others will be lost before one of my brothers takes his place as sultan."

"Perhaps less land means fewer problems for your father to solve," Charlotte suggested. "Less war means more funds for other, more necessary services," she added, sounding ever so reasonable. "More money to pay for the upkeep of existing buildings."

Sevinc furrowed her dark brows, her expression suggesting she'd had an epiphany. "Perhaps that is why he is so impatient with Ertuğrul," she murmured.

At the mention of the sultan's son, Charlotte angled her head to one side. "The sultan mentioned he had been given one of the administrative tasks."

"Many, in fact. He is in charge of all the government buildings," Sevinc replied. "Father never seems satisfied even though Ertuğrul does his very best. Despite his youth, he is very good at what he does. He was a student of architecture."

When she paused and dipped her head, Charlotte asked, "What is it?"

"His mother, Afet—Ertuğrul's mother—was my father's favorite wife. Baba hasn't taken another wife since she died."

Remembering the sorrow the sultan had displayed the

day before when he spoke of Afet, Charlotte now realized it was no secret to those in his harem. Curiosity had her intrigued. "What of the other wife? I understand he had two wives."

Sevinc scoffed much like Charlotte did when she was annoyed. "Oh, he does not like his first wife," she claimed. She leaned in closer. "No one does."

Charlotte's brows furrowed in concern. "Do you suppose he is hard on Ertuğrul because he intends to make him his heir?"

Sevinc once again dipped her head. "I have never asked him that, but that could be the reason why he is so impatient with him. Why he expects so much more from him than he does from the older boys."

Charlotte considered this bit of information along with what she knew from the short time she had spent with the sultan the day before. "I should think the son of his favorite wife would have a special place in the sultan's regard."

Her eyes widening, Sevinc quickly shook her head. "I rather doubt it, Your Grace. Although..." Here she stopped and seemed to study something in her mind's eye.

"What are you thinking?" Charlotte prompted, pleased to see the young woman drawing her own conclusions. Her ability to think through possibilities would serve her well as the wife of someone in her father's government.

"Baba is concerned about education. He wants to build universities and a new palace... and begin a banking system," Sevinc explained.

Charlotte paused mid-step. "The sultan sounds as if he is an enlightened man."

The prim grin returned as Sevinc nodded. "He would be honored to hear such words from the members of his ministry," she said.

"But not from a woman?" Charlotte guessed. From the man's behavior upon their arrival, she was fairly sure he was far too proud to consider anything a woman might suggest.

"Oh, from you as well," Sevinc quickly put in. "That you would think so will have him quite pleased with himself." She dipped her head. "I think you have vexed him in a most unexpected way."

Charlotte wasn't sure she wanted the sultan to think any higher of himself than he already did. Although she realized it could have been a language issue, she had the impression Ziyaeddin already held himself in too high a regard. "As a duchess, I excel at vexing men," Charlotte said as she smiled. "I am joking," she quickly added.

"I have never seen him react to a woman as he did to you," Sevinc whispered, her manner suddenly more serious. "Yesterday morning, he was prepared to have you sent to Rhodes on a ship, but he stayed the order after meeting you."

"Rhodes?" Charlotte repeated in surprise.

"It is a large island near here. From there, you could have boarded a larger ship bound for Athens."

Charlotte's eyes rounded. "So... why didn't he? I should think he would wish to be rid of me," she said, keeping her voice low. "And I can certainly pay for my passage and that of my lady's maid."

Sevinc inhaled and let her breath out in a whoosh. "May I ask a personal question of Your Grace?"

Charlotte nodded. "Of course. Please, speak freely."

Dipping her head once more, Sevinc allowed a mischievous grin. "I believe my father is..." She paused, as if she was struggling with finding the correct English word. "Falling in love with you."

Her eyes rounding in shock, Charlotte was prevented from responding when the subject of their conversation called out from behind her.

"Ah, there you are," Ziyaeddin said as he approached, his arms wide. "I was afraid you had taken Duchess Charlotte to meet all of your sisters," he added as he stepped before his daughter, cradled her face in his hands, and kissed her forehead.

Sevinc rolled her eyes, a gesture Charlotte was sure the young woman had learned during her time in England. "You asked that I impress her," Sevinc replied with a smirk, her hands holding her book behind her back.

Ziyaeddin gave a hearty laugh before turning to Charlotte. He bowed and took her hand, bestowing a kiss on the back of it. "You are a vision on this day, Your Grace."

Apparently Sevinc didn't expect the courtesy, for her eyes rounded and she struggled to suppress a grin.

Charlotte curtsied and carefully withdrew her hand. "As are you, Your Highness. Your tailor has made you a most exquisite suit. You would be the envy of every man at a *ton* ball in London."

Ziyaeddin briefly glanced down at his long brocade kaftan. The thick purple fabric was adorned with swirls of embroidery done in gold threads. Beneath it, he wore a purple satin shirt with a collar that wrapped at his neck and purple şalvar that ended at the tops of gold metallic slippers. "Ah, I thank you for the compliment, but this is not how I usually dress."

"Oh?" Charlotte briefly wondered if he meant that he was wearing something more ornate than usual. She couldn't imagine him appearing more royal than he did at that moment.

"In Constantinople, I have adopted a far more European style of dress," he explained. "Unfortunately, very few of those clothes were brought here to this palace, so I am wearing turbans and kaftans when I should be wearing fez and coats."

"You would be quite celebrated in London, I should think," Charlotte said. She could just imagine the matrons in Mayfair fluttering their fans about in an attempt to draw the sultan's attention. "A guest at all the balls."

"Ah, but would anyone dance with me?" he asked, his eyes twinkling in delight.

"I would, of course."

He gave a start, his expression momentarily starstruck.

"As would every young woman but those who would be jealous of your purple satin," Charlotte quickly added. In reality, she had no idea what the young women would think of the sultan. Half would probably cling to their mothers in fright while the rest would wonder how they might have their modistes copy the *entari* his daughter wore.

Ziyaeddin's eyes narrowed. "Are you mocking me, Duchess Charlotte?"

She shook her head, wondering how he could think such a thing. "I am not. You see, unmarried ladies of a certain age are not allowed to wear anything but white gowns to balls, Your Highness. Purple... purple is a *royal* color, reserved for those in high positions, and it is quite becoming on you," she explained.

He bowed his head, apparently placated by the compliment. "I can imagine it is on you as well," he replied.

Charlotte angled her head to one side. "I do have a purple dinner gown in one of my trunks. You would not have to imagine," she said, her eyes darting to Sevinc in anticipation of the daughter's reaction.

She was not disappointed. Sevinc was doing everything possible to keep a giggle in check.

"Then you shall wear your purple gown when we share our first dinner together," he stated.

Charlotte felt an odd thrill at hearing the comment, so she was surprised at seeing Sevinc's expression change to one of shock.

Had she done something wrong? Been too bold? Or had she entirely misunderstood the situation?

Surely she couldn't be the only foreign aristocrat to visit the sultan. Perhaps there were others in attendance. Someone with whom she could arrange travel to a nearby port. "I suppose you must host many visiting dignitaries for state dinners," Charlotte hedged. "Are there others in residence this week?"

A flash of anger—or perhaps she imagined it—crossed

Ziyaeddin's face before Charlotte noticed Sevinc giving a quick shake of her head. "No other dignitaries are in residence," he stated.

"Oh," Charlotte replied as she dipped her head, her hopes of an easy means to leave the palace dashed. She noticed an elaborately dressed man rushing in their direction and knew they were about to be interrupted. "I look forward to receiving the dinner invitation, Your Highness," she said before she executed another curtsy.

Ziyaeddin nodded his agreement before the intruder made his presence apparent. The emir spoke in Turkish, the words sounding harsh to Charlotte's ears, and the sultan frowned and responded in clipped tones. Bowing, the emir backed away and said something that sounded apologetic, as if he had been chastised for having interrupted.

"I must leave you," Ziyaeddin said on a sigh. He directed his attention to his daughter and added, "I know you prefer to be out of doors, but do be sure to show our guest around the *inside* of the palace."

Sevinc bowed her head and said, "Of course, Baba."

Ziyaeddin took Charlotte's hand in his, brushing his lips over her fingers. A tremor passed though her arm at the same moment, which had her giving a start. He noticed, one of his brows arching slightly. "When we are next in one another's company, we shall not be interrupted," he stated. He turned and hurried off to join the emir, who had paused in his retreat to wait for the sultan.

Charlotte turned to Sevinc, noting that the prim grin had returned. "Should I be worried?"

Sevinc shook her head. "Please, do not. Your presence is a welcome distraction for him."

Nodding her understanding, Charlotte indicated they should continue their tour, and Sevinc led them to a set of open doors.

Although she had toured palaces and stately country houses in England, Charlotte knew the moment she passed by the ornately carved wooden panels that she was about to experience a completely different sort of opulence.

The pale gold stone walls that made up the interior of this part of the palace seemed to shimmer, as if flakes of gold had been applied to them. Turkish carpet runners extended along the entire length of wide corridors and past a series of doors—all closed—and intersected other corridors. The high ceilings made her feel especially small as Sevinc paused to open a door.

"The first room we shall go to is the *hamman*," Sevinc said. "It is much like a swimming pool. We bathe there."

"I was there yesterday morning," Charlotte said, wincing at the memory of the eunuchs watching her and Parma as they bathed.

"Ah, probably shortly after the younger girls bathed," Sevinc said. "They come very early in the morning to prepare for school."

"School?" Charlotte repeated in surprise.

For a moment, Sevinc looked as if she thought she might have used the wrong word. "School, yes. All the members of a harem are educated much like in an English-style girl's school or... or at a convent."

"All day?" Charlotte asked, remembering her experience at finishing school.

Sevinc nodded. "Six or seven hours, and then there is homework for another hour."

Charlotte blinked. Even when she'd attended Warwick's Grammar and Finishing School in London, she hadn't been in class that long. "What sorts of subjects?"

Sevinc shrugged. "The Quran, dancing, playing instruments, conversation, writing, needle-working, learning court etiquette, painting, learning how to serve coffee and sweets—"

"It *is* like an English finishing school," Charlotte murmured.

"—how to fill the sultan's pipe, singing, composing poems, and how to pleasure a man."

"Oh, we never learned that," Charlotte said as she smirked.

"After two years, concubines are given a final exam by the sultan's mother."

Charlotte gave a start. "She is here?"

Sevinc inhaled softly. "She is not. She died last year. But there are no new concubines that need educating. Only my younger sisters and..." She paused as she struggled to remember the correct English words. "Nieces and cousins."

"Oh. I am sorry," Charlotte replied. She imagined Ziyaeddin's mother must have been a rather formidable woman.

"Since she died, Baba is no longer accepting girls to his harem. Other than any daughters his concubines might have, but there hasn't been one born in six years."

"Daughters are part of the harem?" Charlotte asked in confusion.

"All of the women of the palace are in the harem. Concubines, daughters, aunts, servants... and they are all educated," Sevinc explained.

"But it was your grandmother who gave the final exams?"

"Yes," Sevinc replied.

Charlotte considered the subjects, including the last one Sevinc had mentioned. "And if a girl fails the final exam? What happens to them?"

Sevinc led them through the door into an ante chamber. "She becomes a kitchen maid or a cleaning maid. If she passes, she becomes a *cariye*... a potential concubine. But some *cariye* never make it to a sultan's bed. They spend their days helping to clean the palace, by sweeping and washing."

"And if they do make it to his bed?" Charlotte asked, annoyed when a frisson shot down her spine. The mere thought of the sultan in a bed had her aroused in a most unexpected manner.

"They are called *gözde*," Sevinc explained.

"I rather doubt I would make it to *gözde*," Charlotte murmured, thinking of how naive she had been when she first climbed into Joshua's bed.

Sevinc hid a grin behind her hand. "If a concubine is chosen, they must crawl on their hands and knees to his bed."

Charlotte tittered, thinking the sultan's daughter was teasing. She quickly sobered. "You're serious."

Sevinc nodded. "They must show submission," she

stated. "Then they kiss the edge of his bed." She scoffed. "It does sound awful for a woman," she said on a sigh.

"But that is the way of it," Charlotte countered, thinking most women were just as powerless in England. Her position as a duchess had afforded her liberties other women didn't enjoy while it limited her circle of friends. Resulted in special consideration by shopkeepers and modistes.

Privilege.

The two turned a corner and headed down another corridor. "Tell me more about your father's concubines," Charlotte suggested, her curiosity piqued.

"Well, in any harem, the favorite concubines are called *ikbal*, and those who give birth are called *kadins*. For my father, they are nearly the same." She paused a moment. "Were."

"Were?" Charlotte repeated.

Glancing about as if she feared she would be over-heard, Sevinc whispered, "Apparently father has not invited anyone to his bed since we arrived here last month. It was much like that in Constantinople, at least for a time before we left."

Charlotte furrowed a brow. "Perhaps he has much on his mind." She cleared her throat. "Tell me, why ever would a girl wish to be in a harem?" she asked. The idea of attending school and becoming no better than a servant girl held little appeal. The chances of becoming a *ikbal* or *kadin* seemed slim.

"They are paid, of course," Sevinc replied.

Charlotte blinked. "Paid?"

"Oh, yes," Sevinc replied. "It is a position, you see.

Concubines are expected to give birth. Those who bear sons are paid the most."

Charlotte wondered if it would be crass to ask how much, so she didn't.

"I am not supposed to know this, but one of my brothers says his mother was paid two-thousand *akçe* a day," Sevinc claimed in a whisper. "She was also given a village."

Although she had no idea what that amounted to in English pounds, Charlotte thought it sounded like a fair wage. "It's a wonder he doesn't go broke," she said, remembering how many children Ziyaeddin had fathered.

"I think my father is quite wealthy," Sevinc commented. "The empire is, at least." She opened a door. "Now, here is the *hamman*," she said when she led them into a steamy chamber. In the center of the room was a huge pool. "When the youngest are having their lessons, the rest of the women come to the *hamman* and prepare for the day."

Despite having learned of Ziyaeddin's concubines and wives, Charlotte felt shock at seeing so many naked women, young and middle-aged, splashing or lounging about the Turkish bath. Only a few had been there the day before. She inhaled sharply when her gaze fell on the two large men that had been present during her bath. Their arms crossed over their chests and their legs spread wide, they watched the women with dispassionate expressions.

"What are those men doing in here?" Charlotte asked in a hoarse whisper. "They watched me bathe in here yesterday."

As if she'd been overheard, one of the men, bald and barrel-chested, straightened and turned to stare at her.

"They are the guards," Sevinc replied in a whisper. "Eunuchs who make sure no men enter the *hamman*. Men are not allowed to see another man's harem, you see. And sometimes the eunuchs must help keep order."

Charlotte furrowed a brow, wondering what the young lady meant as Sevinc led her to another door. Beyond the room with the bath was a dressing chamber with a phalanx of servant girls stacking bath linens and folding clothes. There were even toilets along one wall.

Through another arched door was a huge carpeted room dotted with colorful cushions. Several young girls were seated with slates on their laps, copying a word an older woman had written on her slate.

A slight breeze had Charlotte turning to discover one wall was missing from the room. In its place stood several columns. A covered balcony extended past the line of Corinthian columns, its stone ceiling covered in mosaics. Beyond were the tops of several trees and a staircase that led down to a walled garden.

"This is glorious," Charlotte breathed as she surveyed the landscape. When she turned, she gasped when a young woman dressed only in transparent veils hurried past. Charlotte was reminded of the thin muslin gowns that had been popular when she was young. No one in London would dare wear one in public unless it was over another gown. The manner in which this girl was dressed left nothing to the imagination, though.

"She is a slave," Sevinc said. "Or rather a servant now,

I suppose," she corrected, as if she just then remembered her father had outlawed slavery.

Charlotte blinked. "She's beautiful." She glanced around, not seeing anyone else dressed like her. Despite the warm day, the other women wore gowns made from rich velvets, some with fur trim. Only a few were dressed like Sevinc.

"She wears veils so nothing can be hidden in her clothes," Sevinc stated, her voice kept low. Despite the number of women in the room, it was on the quiet side, perhaps in deference to the class that was taking place.

For a moment, Charlotte merely stared at the sultan's daughter. "Obviously not," she replied. Then one of her eyebrows furrowed when she realized she had missed Sevinc's meaning. "I don't understand."

"In a palace, there is always a danger of treachery. No weapons can be hidden if the clothes are transparent, so the servants who have not yet earned trust must wear them even when it is very cold."

Charlotte inhaled softly. "Oh." She was about to add, "How awful," but thought better of it. She glanced around the room, realizing she recognized a backgammon board. "You play games?"

"Oh, yes," Sevinc replied. "We play cards and backgammon, read books. Some like smoking a hookah. I do not." She waved to an arched doorway and Charlotte followed her through, well aware her presence had been noticed by most in the common area.

"These are all the chambers of the harem. Where everyone sleeps," Sevinc whispered as she indicated the long corridor. Matching painted doors lined both sides, and from their frequency, Charlotte realized the rooms beyond could not be very large. "Some of the women are taking naps, but they will all awake by five o'clock to resume cleaning and to serve the sultan his dinner. They all have jobs they must do."

"Where are the children?" Charlotte asked, remembering Ziyaeddin had some who were not yet adults.

"Through there," Sevinc replied, pointing to another arched door. "Not all of them, though. Two boys are in Constantinople with their mother. Two of my brothers are at Cambridge University." She rolled her eyes, obviously annoyed by the reminder.

"Who takes care of those that are here?"

Sevinc shrugged. "We all do, but mostly their mothers and the maids."

"And if their mother has died in the childbed?"

Dipping her head, Sevinc said, "There is always one who is willing to nurse a babe."

Charlotte glanced around, wondering how so many women could live together under one roof. She tried to imagine what would happen should the daughters of the aristocracy be forced to live in a harem. There would no doubt be fighting and hair-pulling, slapping and shouting after so much time in close quarters. "However do these women stay friendly with one another?"

Sevinc suppressed a chuckle. "Oh, they do not," she replied. "There was a time it felt as if we lived in a nest of vipers. Most every concubine wishes to become the sultan's wife, mostly for the power it brings, but my father has made it clear he will not take another wife, so it is not so... competitive as it once was."

"Oh? Why would he say such a thing?" Charlotte asked, thinking of the widowers of the aristocracy back in England. Most of them were quick to remarry if for no other reason than they required a hostess and someone to run their households. A few even did so because they discovered they were lonely.

Sevinc lowered her voice. "Baba says he is too old to abide another wife," she said with a grin. "But I think the death of his mother meant he no longer had to do her bidding."

"She wanted him married?"

"To keep his concubines under control," Sevinc explained. "But that is why we have eunuchs and the administrators and the sultan's mother when she was alive. They help to keep order in the harem."

Charlotte's attention was on a lovely young woman who lounged on a cushion, her attention on a book. She occasionally glanced up and looked around, boredom evident in her expression. "And if one of these women should wish to leave?"

Sevinc shrugged. "They do so. They are not prisoners," she replied. "They can visit their relatives. Go shopping. Take a boat out on the water. And if after nine years a girl is never called to my father's bed, she can receive permission to go free. Her status as a free person is certified in writing."

Charlotte scoffed, surprised by this bit of information. "Has that ever happened?"

Sevinc nodded. "Indeed. It is why my father's harem is not as large as those who came before him. He finds the girls excellent husbands, and they are provided with dowries and houses and sometimes an allowance," she explained. "They are highly desired because they have been educated and have ties to the court."

Charlotte nodded her understanding. She supposed it was no different than an aristocrat having a string of mistresses, although with much longer contracts.

"What about you?" Charlotte asked. "Marriage, I mean?"

Sevinc angled her head to one side. "My father will arrange something, probably with one of his viziers," she explained, her body shuddering as if she found the idea repulsive.

"I'm sure he knows that whomever he chooses must appreciate your level of education," Charlotte said. "You've a good head on your shoulders, and I shouldn't want you to end up with an old fart for a..." She stopped, inhaling sharply at hearing her gaffe. "Apologies."

But Sevinc was having trouble suppressing her giggles, a combination of a chuckle and a snort sounding from behind hands held to her mouth. "Oh, Your Grace. You have described the situation perfectly," she said with a huge grin.

Charlotte dipped her head. "Nevertheless, I do hope you can marry for love. As I did."

Sevinc sobered and bowed her head. "I will take you back to your chamber now. You are probably looking forward to a nap."

Although she hadn't thought of what she would do next, Charlotte liked the idea of lounging about her chamber as she had seen some of the women in the harem do. "I could get awfully spoiled here," she said when they stopped in front of her chamber door. "Thank you for spending time with me today."

"The pleasure is mine, Your Grace," Sevinc said as she curtsied.

Charlotte returned the curtsy and entered her chamber, stopping short when she paid witness to what Parma held in her hands.

"We've had a delivery, Your Grace," Parma said.

CHAPTER 12
A CAPTAIN BRINGS NEWS

eanwhile, on the south side of Rhodes

"What do you suppose happened to the Colossus of Rhodes?" James asked as he stared out at the harbor of the largest Dodecanese island. Legend claimed the Colossus of Rhodes was one of the Seven Wonders of the Ancient World, but from what he could see, nothing was left of it.

"Destroyed by an earthquake in 226 BC," David replied, his attention on the ships that made their way through the narrow opening into the harbor. He glanced down at a drawing of what the statue had supposedly looked like and scoffed. "I highly doubt they had the means to build a statue large enough to span that opening."

"Seventy cubits tall... that's just over a hundred feet," James remarked. "Snapped off at the knees. The broken parts apparently were left where they fell for over eight-hundred years."

David tried to imagine where the statue could have

been located so that when it collapsed, the upper part could land on dry ground. Any logical locations were surrounded by water. He was about to point out a possible spot when a ship entering the harbor caught his attention. "Do you see what I'm seeing?" he asked, nudging James.

But James had already turned his attention on the Greek merchant ship. "They're fighting with swords," he said with some excitement. "Do you suppose they're..." He was about to say 'play acting' when a blade flashed and impaled a dark-skinned man.

"Staging a mutiny?" David guessed, the drawing of the statue forgotten.

James pulled a pair of opera glasses from his satchel and aimed them at the ship. "I don't think that's a mutiny," he whispered. "I think those are... those are *pirates.*"

David wrenched the opera glasses from James and aimed them at the ship. One thing was apparent—no one was seeing to lowering the sails, and given the strong wind, the ship would either collide with another ship or run aground. "We're not the only ones who have noticed," he murmured, well aware of nearby sailors shouting. Several were already on one of the docks, waving their arms. A horn could be heard from some-where near the harbor entrance, its mournful sound accompanied by the repeated peals of a bell.

The two watched as one of the combatants aboard the ship finished off his opponent and rushed to the wheel, giving it a quick turn. Given the speed of the vessel, the resulting change in direction took a moment to happen, but it also had several of those who were fighting struggling to keep their balance.

"Come on. Let's get over there," James urged at the same moment one of the sails dropped to the deck. The ship was still turning, the wind no longer filling the other two sails.

The bell continued to ring, and sailors from other docked ships rushed out onto the wooden planks to discover what was causing the commotion.

David followed James as they made their way to the dock in a half-run. "Do you really think this is a good idea?" he asked as seasoned sailors ran past them. "That ship is about to collide..." He paused as his eyes widened. The merchant ship narrowly missed a fishing boat, the captain of the smaller vessel managing to move out of the way in time, his shouts and curses clear despite the wind.

At the entrance to the dock, James pulled up short and attempted to interpret what a nearby sailor was saying to another. "They recognize the Greek ship," he said to David.

"*Sun of Apollo,*" David said, reading the name emblazoned on the side of the ship.

"Something about it coming from England," James added with some excitement. The two watched as a pirate was sent over the edge of the railing, his body flailing as it fell into the water. Although the vessel was still moving, it had slowed considerably and was no longer in danger of taking out the dock.

A rope sailed through the air, expertly caught by a dockworker who quickly tied it to a post. Shouts continued to fill the air as sailors ran past them and more ropes were tossed from the deck of the merchant ship.

"They could use your help," an older man said from next to them. "Strapping young lads like you standing around gawking like it's your first day on the water?"

James acknowledged the man with a quick bow. "You're English?"

"Aye," the gray-haired man said as he waved a hand toward an old gunner. "Walker's the name. That's my ship, and I'd like it to stay in one piece," he added. Given the trajectory of the Greek vessel, the back of the captain's gunner was in its path.

"What do we do?" David asked.

"Help with the ropes. Pull that ship into port," he replied, waving a gnarled finger toward the *Sun of Apollo*. "Capt'n Popodopolos has obviously had some excitement on his latest run."

David and James exchanged quick glances before they hurried to the end of the dock, where they joined forces with the other sailors who were tugging on the thick ropes in an attempt to bring the Greek ship around and into a slip.

"My gloves are going to be ruined," David groused as he gripped the rope and pulled.

James glanced around at the other sailors, noting how most of them weren't wearing anything to protect their hands against the coarse hemp. "Small price to pay for some fun," he replied, enjoying the chance at some exercise.

Although it seemed to take the rest of the morning to haul in the *Sun of Apollo* and secure it, the sun wasn't yet at its zenith when the two young men watched the ship's captain doff his hat and wave it in the air, as if in triumph.

Cheers erupted from those on the dock, and a quick glance at the shoreline around the harbor had James realizing the incident had drawn a crowd.

Captain Walker drew up alongside James and David as they gazed at the shoreline and then turned their attention back to the ship's deck. "Now there's some fine teamwork," he said. He gave a wave to someone on deck, and the two gave him a nod.

"Glad to be of help," James said. "You know the captain of this ship?"

"I do," Walker replied. "And that's one of the newest vessels out of Syros," he added, referring to the *Sun of Apollo*. When the captain of the Greek ship walked down the ramp, Walker was the first to greet him. "Pirates? Again?" he called out as he displayed a huge grin.

"This time, it was bad," Captain Popodopolos replied, obviously not appreciating the British captain's humor as he shook hands with him. "There were nine of them that came aboard our ship from theirs," he groused. "Although our cargo is mostly intact, three of them took our passengers. Disembarked at the port of that Ottoman palace on the eastern shore," he explained. "The ship remained anchored for more than a day waiting for their return, but they never got back on board." He waved toward the deck. "Which means we only had to dispatch six of the bastards."

Walker sobered at hearing the Greek captain's words. "Turkish pirates?" he guessed.

"No. From northern Africa, I would guess from their language," Popodopolos replied. "When the one in charge didn't return to the ship, the rest of the pirates must have panicked. They pulled out of port and headed for here, not realizing we would know how to break out of our own brig."

Still standing near Captain Walker, David and James overheard the Greek captain and exchanged quick glances. "You came from England, sir?" James asked as he reached into his top coat pocket and pulled out the letter he had received from his mother before they had left Athens.

Popodopolos furrowed a brow, apparently noticing the young men for the first time. He nodded. "We set out of Portsmouth twenty-three days ago," he replied. "You are English?"

James said, "We are. The passengers you spoke of... who were they?"

The other captain cleared his throat, about to claim it wasn't any of their concern, but Popodopolos held up a staying hand. "Her Grace, the Duchess of Chichester, and her lady's maid."

David gasped and said, "Damnation!" before James could respond.

"That's my mother," he said, obviously shocked at hearing her name. "I am Lord James Wainwright," he added as he held out his right hand.

"Popodopolos, captain of *Sun of Apollo*," the older man said as he shook James' hand.

David offered his hand and introduced himself. "Her

lady's maid—Parma? You say she was taken as well?" he asked.

Walker exchanged a worried glance with the other captain. "Indeed," Popodopolos replied. He rubbed his face with his palm and glanced back at his ship. The bodies of the dead pirates had all been tossed overboard, and the crew were seeing to off-loading a couple of crates.

"We have to go rescue her," James stated.

"We have a shipment to deliver to Syros," Popodopolos countered, but his expression suggested he agreed with James.

"I'll pay you, sir," James offered.

"I can take your cargo," Walker offered. "I've a delivery to make to Syros after my crew finishes unloading a few more crates here."

"Are you sure?" Popodopolos asked, his gaze darting from Walker to James.

"Glad to be of help," Walker assured him. "I have to go there next to have some work done on the hull."

"When can we leave?" James asked, anxious to go.

"We have to check out of the inn. Get our trunks," David reminded him as he tugged on his sleeve.

James took a deep breath. "You're right."

"We can be off later tonight," Popodopolos said, ignoring Walker's scoff. "Sunset. The sooner we depart, the sooner we'll be there."

"What do you suppose happened to them?" David asked. "The duchess and the other pirates?" he added.

Popodopolos gave a shake of his head. "They went to

the palace, no doubt about it. If the sultan was in residence—"

"Sultan?" David repeated. "Do you mean the sultan of the Ottoman Empire?"

His brows arching in appreciation of the young man's query, Popodopolos said, "That's exactly who I mean." He displayed a sour expression. "If the sultan was in residence, they would have sold your mother and her maid to him, probably for his harem."

When James made an unintelligible sound in the back of his throat, David pulled on his arm. "Think, James," he said in a hoarse whisper. "We know his sons," he added when James gave him a look of confusion. "From Cambridge. "

Captain Popodopolos furrowed a brow. "What's this now?"

James stood staring at David a moment before he turned to answer. "My friend is right. Sultan Ziyaeddin— if he is indeed the one the pirates expected to find at that palace you mentioned—he has two sons who attend Cambridge University." He scoffed and shook his head. "But I specifically remember them claiming that slavery was no longer allowed in the Ottoman Empire."

"An edict of their father," David added, arching a brow.

Walker gave a grunt and the Greek captain rolled his eyes. "First I've heard of it," Popodopolos said with a frown. "But if the pirates couldn't sell your mother to the sultan, then why didn't they return to the ship?"

James swallowed, worried his mother might have ended up in the hands of slave traders farther inland.

"We can stand here and speculate, or we can get moving," David said, angling his head to one side as if someone had put him in charge.

"Boy's right," Walker stated. "Let's get that cargo transferred so you can be on your way," he said, directing his words to the Greek captain.

Popodopolos nodded as the other captain headed to his ship. "Be back here before sunset," he said to James. "Or I leave without you."

"Aye, Captain," James replied.

Without a backward glance, he and David rushed from the dock and headed to their inn.

*S*treaks of purple and peach colored the western sky as the *Sun of Apollo* left Rhodes, headed southeast.

James and David were on deck, their trunks stowed in a cabin where the door had been broken from its hinges. Privacy was the least of their concerns, though.

More of interest to James was the small box he held in his hand. He had found it on the floor beneath the room's only table, immediately recognizing the hinged, fabric-covered box as one belonging to his mother.

Finding the jewelry box had been a surprise. Discovering it still contained her favorite jewels had James feeling some hope as well as trepidation.

Why hadn't the pirates taken the jewel box?

CHAPTER 13
A BATH INTERRUPTED

*E*arlier, *in the guest chambers at the palace*
        Charlotte stared at the length of red sheer silk her lady's maid held up. The edges were adorned with tiny beads and the ends were sewn with small tassels. "What's this?" she asked as she moved to take the sheer fabric from Parma.

Parma shrugged. "A veil. It was delivered a few minutes ago along with this note. And Elena said that a bathtub is to be brought 'round so you might bathe in privacy."

The oddest sensation shot through Charlotte as she took the note from Parma. The words 'Duches Sharlot' had been written in a thick calligraphy on one side, and the edges of the parchment were held together with a wax seal. Embedded in the wax was an image Charlotte couldn't discern. Nothing like a coat of arms, the *tughra*, an insignia of sorts, appeared made up of a series of interlaced swirls with a couple of straight bars.

Sliding her thumbnail beneath the tughra, Charlotte

was careful not to break the wax as it gave way. "I wish to keep this," she said as she gave the wax to Parma. "Tuck it in with the jewels, won't you?" She unfolded the square note and arched a brow.

Dear Duchess Sharlot,

I learned you did not care for the hamman. Or probablee you did not like the eunuchs. They are grouches. A bathtub you shall have.

I would like it very much if you would wear the scarf over your hair when you join me for dinner tonight.

Zi

Charlotte glanced up from the note, her face reddening.

Who had told the sultan that she didn't like the Turkish bath?

She supposed she would have been fine with it if the eunuchs hadn't been present. It was unnerving to have men watch whilst she bathed, even if they had no interest in her. Besides, very few people had seen the scar on her bare back, and she wished to keep it that way.

As for the silk fabric, Charlotte held up a corner of the veil. Made of the finest silk threads and loosely woven, the fabric would work for an overskirt or for the sleeves of a gown. But in her hair?

"I know what to do," Parma said as she unfurled the veil and allowed it to drift down onto a cushion. "I will pin it into your hair when I have finished styling it."

"I hope he doesn't expect it will be the *only* thing I wear to dinner," Charlotte murmured, moving to the trunks to look for the purple dinner gown she had mentioned to the sultan earlier that afternoon.

"I have already pulled the red satin dinner gown, Your Grace," Parma said, indicating a gown spread out over several small cushions.

Charlotte inhaled softly, wondering at the excitement she felt at having been invited to the sultan's dinner. Before she could respond, there was a knock at the door.

Parma hurried to open it, and a moment later a copper bathtub was brought into the chamber under the direction of the Greek servant. Four men carried the slipper-shaped tub while a string of other servants followed with jugs of steaming water.

Charlotte watched as the water carriers poured the hot water into the tub and filed out much like they had come in. The servants departed, all of them bowing as they backed out the door but none of them making eye contact.

Charlotte acknowledged each servant with a nod as she realized she must have done something to please the sultan.

The odd sensation once again passed through her body, and it intensified when Parma stripped off her day gown. Charlotte stepped into the metal tub and sank into the hot water on a long sigh. The lady's maid hurried off to find bath linens.

Charlotte regarded her reflection in the bath water and lifted her chin, first angling her head to one side and then to the other. She drew a fingertip along the bottom of her cheek.

When had her jawline softened? When had the lines begun to show on her neck?

"I have always thought it unfair that British fashions do not allow for a woman's shoulders to be completely bare."

"I suppose any man would," Charlotte replied absently, her finger trailing over the top mound of a breast. She gave a start, realizing the comment had been made by a man and that he was in her chamber. She glanced over her shoulder, stunned to see the sultan approaching. "What are you doing here?" she asked, pulling her knees to her chest in an attempt to hide her nudity. Despite the size of the copper tub, she knew her bare back was exposed from her shoulders to just below the whip scar that stretched across it.

Ziyaeddin chuckled as he approached, his steps slowing when his gaze caught the evidence of the scar on her back. For a moment, Charlotte was sure he was going to ask what had happened, but he moved to the side of the tub to regard her first with appreciation and then a frown. His fists went to his hips as he gave her a quelling glance, which had his kaftan opening to reveal the opulent clothes beneath. "I wished to see you."

"But not all of me, I'm quite sure," Charlotte countered, her arms wrapped around her legs. For a moment, she was glad she hadn't allowed Parma to wash her hair, or she would have looked like a drowned rat.

"Do not tell me what you think I wish to see," he scolded. "Or not," he added. "I come this afternoon because I wished to see you."

Charlotte's face bloomed with color. "Well, here I am,

Your Highness," she said, still holding her folded legs against her chest so her knees hid her breasts.

Sobering, Ziyaeddin regarded her with concern. "You needn't be modest with me," he said. "I have seen most of the women in my harem unclothed."

Charlotte scoffed. "They are all nubile young girls," she complained. "They're all perfectly formed, with pert breasts and round..." She clamped her mouth shut, realizing she hadn't seen *all* the members of his harem nude. In fact, she had probably seen only a few of them in the bathing pool.

Ziyaeddin frowned. "Oh, I have not seen *them* naked," he said. "The young ones are all *odalisques*. Virgins. Too young for me," he said as he waved a hand dismissively. "I have only bedded those who are at least of an age to marry," he claimed. "And they are of all shapes and sizes." His arms dropped to his sides as he stared down at her, as if he thought she would do his implied bidding and allow him to see all of her.

Charlotte continued to stare up at him, not giving up her hold on her legs. "I would kiss the hem of your robe, Your Highness, but my hands are otherwise occupied at the moment."

A smirk appeared on the sultan's lips, which had her relaxing somewhat.

"I have come to discover if you will be present at my dinner this evening," he stated. "Did you receive my invitation?"

Whatever annoyance she still felt at the sultan's unexpected visit dissipated. "I did receive your gift, Your Highness. It was very generous of you. Thank you."

His eyes darted to the side. "I am not a barbarian," he said.

"I... I didn't say you were."

Swallowing, he appeared flummoxed for a moment, as if he was questioning his English. "You will come to the dinner?"

Charlotte continued to stare up at him. Despite how he towered over the tub, she didn't feel the least bit vulnerable. Nor did she sense any danger in his presence.

How odd.

"Yes, I will be there. What time should I come? And where do I go?"

He sighed, as if he was giving up on the idea of seeing any part of her—other than her shoulders—naked. "Sunset. I will send the Greek servant for you."

"I will be ready, Your Highness," she replied.

He suddenly knelt and pried one of her hands from in front of her calves. Bringing it to his lips, he kissed the back of it, but his gaze never left hers.

Charlotte swallowed, unsure of what to say or do.

When Ziyaeddin straightened, easily rising to his feet, Charlotte winced. Her own knees would not have allowed such a graceful move. She watched him give her a nod before he strode toward the door, calling out a command to the guard to have it opened before he reached it.

A moment later, he was gone, and the door was once again closed.

Straightening in the tub, Charlotte took a deep breath and let it out. "Parma?" she called out, wondering what had become of her lady's maid.

"Here, my lady," Parma replied, breathless, as she hurried to the side of the tub with a stack of linens.

"Were you hiding from him?" Charlotte accused in dismay.

The lady's maid's eyes rounded. "Him?" she repeated. She glanced back at the door in confusion before her eyes rounded. "The sultan was in *here*?"

"He only just left," Charlotte replied. "Wanted to be sure I received his invitation."

Parma inhaled sharply. "He didn't try anything untoward, did he?" she asked, her eyes still wide with alarm.

Charlotte gave her a quelling glance. "I'm a widow. I have two grown sons. He has a harem," she replied as she rolled her eyes.

Except why had he invited her to dinner?

They had briefly discussed it earlier, but she hadn't had the impression he would follow through with an invitation so quickly.

And why had he sent the veil?

"I had to step out. To get the linens," Parma explained. "The other servants in the palace are all very helpful. I met two others from India this morning."

Charlotte turned her attention to the door. Had the sultan deliberately waited until her lady's maid had left their chamber to make his appearance?

Did he expect to find her in the bath?

A pleasant frisson shot through her abdomen even as she scoffed. *The infuriating man!* Charlotte loosened her hold on her legs and stretched them out as far as they would go in the copper tub. Perhaps she had been too modest with the ruler, but she wasn't about to let him have his way with her.

"Parma, do you think the red dinner gown reveals too much when it's worn with my usual corset?" she asked, thinking of her décolletage.

Her lady's maid paused as she held out a bath linen. "More would be revealed if you wore the smaller one," she countered, not actually expecting Charlotte to choose the uncomfortable corset.

"I shall definitely be wearing it this evening."

Her eyes rounding once again, Parma nodded before offering a bath linen to her mistress. "Are you sure that is a good idea, my lady?"

Charlotte hesitated, wondering at her maid's concern. "What are you thinking?"

Parma lifted a shoulder. "Every woman I have seen in this palace is covered from neck to foot with layers of clothing," she said. "I would not wish to live here in the summers."

"Pull out an appropriate shawl," the duchess ordered as she stood from the tub and wrapped the linen about her body. "I've been invited to dinner, and I intend to discover when we're to be sent off to resume our holiday." If the sultan wanted to see more of her, she would only give him what he wanted if he gave her a departure date.

At least, she would give him what he *thought* he wanted. Once he saw more of her and realized she was an old matron, he would surely dismiss her.

Wouldn't he?

CHAPTER 14
DINNER WITH A SULTAN

*L**ater that night*
Parma slid the last two pins into Charlotte's elaborate coiffure and stepped back to admire her handiwork. "I wish I had a few more pins, Your Grace," she murmured as she held out the edges of the veil and then let it drop so it trailed down Charlotte's back. The beaded hem fell well below the whip scar. "Then I could do more with this," she said as she held the long lock of hair Charlotte had asked be left to drape over the front of her bare shoulder.

"I like it just the way it is," Charlotte replied, turning her head to one side to admire the red coral earrings Parma had discovered beneath the false bottom of the trunk. The matching necklace from the parure hung around her neck, its red coral and diamond pendant resting above her décolletage. One of her wrists displayed the bracelet, and she had added a diamond ring to the wedding band Joshua had given her the day they had exchanged their vows.

She had dabbed perfume on her wrists and behind both ears, sure the sultan had found the scent pleasing.

Given the manner of dress of the other women in the palace, Charlotte decided to forgo the long gloves she normally would have worn. She felt naked with her arms uncovered, but the shawl would help in that regard.

Unless she removed it.

She wasn't yet sure if that would happen. Perhaps when all the guests were called into the dining room?

What was the accepted dinner dress when dining with a sultan and his entourage?

How many people would there be for the sultan's dinner? she wondered as she stepped into a pair of slippers.

The Greek servant appeared at the door of their chamber, her eyes rounding at the sight of Charlotte in her finery. "I am to fetch you for your dinner, Your Grace."

"I am ready," Charlotte said, puzzled by the woman's expression. She pulled on the shawl, and the servant seemed more at ease. "Elena, what is wrong?" she asked, sure something about her manner of dress was offensive.

"Nothing," the servant said, quickly turning to lead her out of the chamber.

Charlotte narrowed her eyes, but followed the woman down the corridor. They passed the door for the sultan's throne room and turned into another corridor, pausing briefly before a door with two guards stationed on either side. "Where are the other guests?" she asked, hoping she wouldn't be the last to enter a room full of viziers, emirs and their wives.

No wives, she thought suddenly. The sultan had said there would be no other women present.

"Other guests?" the servant repeated. "I know of no other guests."

Inhaling softly, Charlotte was about to respond when the guards opened both doors. Giving the servant a quick nod when the woman waved her in, Charlotte lifted her head and strode into the room. The doors closed behind her before she determined she was entirely alone.

A low table was set with a number of covered dishes, but only two cushions were next to it. The serviettes and placesettings were simple—beautifully patterned china plates set with silver spoons and utensils that looked like they might pass for butter knives.

Charlotte was admiring the artistry on one of the plates when she realized she wasn't alone. She whirled around to discover Ziyaeddin watching her from an arched doorway. She dipped a curtsy. "I seem to be the first one here, Your Highness," she remarked.

Ziyaeddin glanced around the small dining room, as if he feared someone else might be there. "I did not invite anyone else," he replied as he made his way to stand before her.

Charlotte blinked and swallowed her initial response. Although his kaftan was made of a dark blue velvet as rich as the one he had been wearing earlier that day, it wasn't nearly as ornate. The şalvar featured a wide silver filigreed belt buckle festooned with gemstones of various colors. The rest of the belt was made of silver mesh.

When he reached for her hand, the silk shawl fell from her shoulders, the ends draping over her elbows so they hung nearly to the floor. She had to suppress the urge to smirk when she noticed Ziyaeddin's eyes widen and his breath catch.

He took her hand in his and kissed the back of it, his gaze lingering on her ring. "Your gown is very becoming on you," he said when he had finally straightened. "But it is not purple."

Charlotte winced and dipped her head. "The purple clashed with your most generous gift," she replied, pulling on the edge of the veil that Parma had pinned atop her hair. She had to admit it was perfect with her dinner gown, and the fabric felt divine against her bare skin. It also covered the scar across her back.

"Red is very becoming on you," he commented.

"Thank you, Your Highness. Your jewels are quite impressive."

He stared at her a moment, as if he were parsing her words. When Charlotte realized how they could be misinterpreted, she lifted a hand to her lips as her face bloomed with color. "The gems in your..." She waved a finger at his belt. "I do not know what your... your ornament is called."

Ziyaeddin blinked before a chuckle suddenly erupted.

Charlotte kept her hand in front of her mouth as her grin widened.

"It is a belt buckle," he stated. "One given to me by my father."

"And the jewels?" she asked, impressed by the workmanship of the settings. She would have liked to study it in more detail, but given its location on his body, she didn't dare allow her gaze to linger.

His eyes lit with delight. "Sapphires and rubies, I

think," he replied. "The diamond in the middle is the hardest."

Charlotte's eyes rounded as a rush of heat pooled at the top of her thighs. Did the sultan realize what he had said? Was his understanding of the English language good enough to include such double entendres? From the look of amusement he displayed, perhaps it was. "You are incorrigible," she gently scolded.

Amused, Ziyaeddin reared back, apparently not understanding that particular word. "You are the loveliest woman to set foot in this palace in twenty years."

Inhaling softly, Charlotte stared at the sultan in a new light. Even if English wasn't his first language, he seemed to understand most of what she said. Flattered by his compliment, she dipped her head. "I'm quite sure your late wife was far more beautiful than me," she replied.

The reminder of Afet didn't seem to affect the sultan as it had the day before. "She was a great beauty," he agreed. "And from the moment I met her, I was determined to make her a willing wife."

Charlotte blinked. "Oh?"

"She was brought to me by her father. As a gift," he explained, one of his brows arching as if he was expecting a different reaction from her. "Much like you, she stared at me as if her eyes were daggers and she wished me dead."

He wasn't disappointed when she replayed his words in her head, and her eyes widened in shock.

"You wished to...?" She clamped her mouth shut.

His eyes narrowed, as if he dared her to finish the question. "Go on," he prompted.

"I can hardly believe you were of such a mind the moment you met *me*," Charlotte argued. "When the pirates dumped me at your feet. I must have looked terribly—"

"Exotic."

"—bedraggled, and awfully—

"Bewitching."

"—Unkempt and—"

"Incensed."

"—oh, I was that," she agreed, suddenly aware of how the space between them was only a few inches. "But not at *you*, of course."

"I am glad to know it," he murmured. He placed his hands on either side of her face and dropped a kiss at the top of her forehead. His lips lingered for a moment.

Charlotte stared up at him when he finally pulled away. She had no idea what was meant by the gesture. Was she expected to return the kiss on his forehead? If so, he'd have to bend down a good deal.

Or was he about to kiss her on the lips?

A flock of flutterbies took flight in her belly, tumbling about in a manner she hadn't experienced in a very long time. The unexpected sensation had her gripping the edge of his kaftan as she stood on tiptoe and leaned against the front of his body. The slippery silk of his shirt caressed her bare décolletage as she angled her head.

When he made no move to kiss her lips, Charlotte inhaled softly and lowered her heels to the floor. "Apologies, Your Highness. I thought..." She knew her cheeks and neck were bright pink with her blush. She almost scoffed at the thought that at her age, she was still capable of feeling embarrassment.

He studied her for a moment, his brows furrowed. "You thought... what?"

Charlotte dipped her head. "I thought you were going to kiss me."

He turned his head to one side. "I thought I did," he replied. His eyes suddenly rounded in understanding. "Ah, you were expecting our lips to touch."

Nodding, she said, "Is that not done in your culture?"

Chuckling, Ziyaeddin stepped back and regarded her with an expression of bemusement. "Not out in the open," he explained. "But what two people do in the privacy of their homes is not for me to say. I would not forbid such a kiss."

"But you do not do it?" she asked, stunned at her reaction to his closeness. She itched to touch him. Even fully clothed, the man was charismatic. Handsome in a dark sort of way. In London, he would be considered a rake. The worst sort of libertine. And yet she was sure there would be a number of women lined up for the opportunity to share his bed.

"I have little experience with that sort of kissing," Ziyaeddin said, a slight wince suggesting he was lying. He and Afet had kissed many times, always in private and usually in the throes of passion. He hadn't kissed another woman on the lips since her death.

"Liar," Charlotte accused, a smirk accompanying her accusation.

Ziyaeddin's eyes darkened, and for a moment, she feared she might have angered him. Instead, she realized too late he had interpreted it as a dare. His hands went to her shoulders, pulling them forward as his head dipped down.

Charlotte's lips met his in a crushing kiss that almost immediately softened. She cupped one hand to his cheek as the other moved to the back of his neck, and she hung on for dear life as he plundered her mouth with his tongue.

When he ended the kiss, a soft mewl of protest sounded from the back of her throat. "I apologize. It's been a very long time since I have been kissed like that," she whispered, releasing him from her hold.

He captured the hand that had been on the side of his scarred cheek, and he brought it to his lips. His brows once again furrowed as his eyes refocussed. "Why do you apologize?"

Charlotte gave a slight shrug. "I am out of practice, Your Highness." *Out of practice and out of my league when it comes to understanding what is happening.*

Ziyaeddin remembered what his daughter had said earlier that week. That they were speaking English for the practice. "It has been far longer for me," he murmured. "Perhaps we must practice to make perfect."

Charlotte's eyes rounded, now sure he was propositioning her. She was saved from having to respond when he seemed to change his mind.

"Now is not the time, though," he said as he stepped back, still holding onto her hand. "Our dinner awaits." He led her to one of the cushions, and Charlotte knelt as she pulled her skirts to one side. She watched as he moved to the other side of the table and did the same, although he ended up cross-legged. She averted her gaze as he silently prayed, her attention on the collection of dishes set before them.

"Please, help yourself," he said as he lifted a disc of flat bread and tore it in half. He offered one side to her before he pinched off a small amount and ate it.

"Thank you," she replied as she admired the variety of courses set before them. Charlotte recognized only a few of the foods, all served in silver bowls or on silver platters. From the sheer number of offerings, she realized all the dinner courses had been delivered at once. "What would be considered the first course?"

"Ah, the soup," he said as he removed the lid from a small tureen. Steam poured forth along with a delicious aroma. "We eat it with the *pide*. The bread."

Charlotte ladled some into one of the small china bowls and offered it to him before serving herself. "Do you often host guests here at the palace?" she asked before taking an experimental sip of the soup.

"Not at this palace," he replied as he plucked a lamb kebab from a platter. "But always at one of the palaces in Constantinople."

"*One* of the palaces?" Charlotte repeated. "How many are there?"

Ziyaeddin blinked as his brows furrowed. "Three are there now, but Ertuğrul is overseeing the construction of a new palace. One more... modern," he explained. "It will be named Dolmabahçe."

Charlotte attempted to sort the word and realized she couldn't guess its English equivalent. "Which means...?" she prompted.

"Filled-in garden," he replied, apparently expecting the query. "I am assured it will be quite luxurious when it is complete in two years."

When his expression appeared troubled, Charlotte asked, "You don't think it will be?"

He angled his head to one side. "Oh, it will be, but at a huge cost. Ertuğrul says it could take a quarter of our yearly tax revenues to complete."

Charlotte's eyes rounded. She had no idea what that amount might be, but it seemed extravagant. Probably as expensive as the one Prinny ordered be built in Brighton before he was crowned King of England. "Of the entire empire?" She inhaled. "It sounds as expensive as a war."

Ziyaeddin arched his brows. "You have the right of it," he replied. "But when it is complete, it will exist. There will be something to show for the funds spent." He paused a moment, his gaze going to his mind's eye. "A war... these days, there is nothing but destruction after a war. And sometimes, there is not even land to show for it." Although it should have bothered him that his most recent land losses had been to Russia, the areas had been small and more trouble than they had been worth to the empire.

"You mentioned Ertuğrul. Was it his idea to build the palace?" she asked.

Shaking his head, Ziyaeddin said, "It was mine. He is merely doing my bidding." This last was said as if he found Ertuğrul lacking in some regard.

When she paid witness to his wince, Charlotte lifted a brow but she thought better of asking more about his son. Any mention of the man only seemed to vex the sultan. She returned her attention to the platters of food. "What are these?" she asked as she indicated a salver filled with small oblong meats.

"*Köfte*," he replied, his good humor returning. When Charlotte continued to stare at him, he added, "Meatballs. They're small. Eat several of them," he encouraged. He watched as she tasted a spoonful of *kisir*, a spicy wheat salad, its color due to the red hot peppers that provided its flavor. "Too... spicy?" he asked when she seemed uncertain if she should take another bite.

"I fear for my tongue," Charlotte replied, trying hard to keep tears from forming.

He grinned as he offered a spoonful of yoghurt, and she leaned over to eat it. From his look of amusement, she knew he had been waiting for her to try something she wouldn't like. "Much better," she said when she realized the yoghurt took away the heat of the peppers.

"Do you like lemons?" he asked.

Charlotte nodded. "I like the flavor," she replied.

He indicated another bowl of kisir, this one more yellow in color. "This version has a lemon seasoning," he said as he spooned some onto her plate.

"Oh, this is much better," she said as she tried it. "What is your favorite food?"

Ziyaeddin surveyed the dishes. "The meat, usually," he replied, indicating the kebabs and the meatballs.

"I do hope we're not expected to eat all of this food," she murmured as she spooned several *manti* dumplings onto her plate. She recognized them from the first meal that had been delivered to her room.

"When we have had our fill, I will have the rest taken

away," he replied. "The servants will finish it." Sensing she was going to ask if that would be their only meal for the day, he said, "No one goes hungry in my household."

Charlotte nodded her understanding. "It is the same in mine," she replied. "Or my daughter-in-law's, I suppose." When she saw his brow lift as if in question, she added, "My oldest son is the duke now. His wife— she is the Chichester duchess—she has the responsibility of the household."

"You are in agreement with this arrangement?" he asked, as if he didn't believe she should be. "Are you not the one who should be in charge?"

Charlotte was struck by his comment. Apparently he understood a woman's responsibility for a huge household. "I am in agreement because it is how things are done in England," she replied with a shrug. "Arabella is eager to learn. Eager to have her own household."

For a moment, Charlotte felt as if a rug had been pulled out from beneath her. As if Joshua's death had caused more of a shift in her life than just losing a husband. Despite not having a purpose at Wisborough Oaks, Charlotte felt a sudden need to return there. Surely she was needed. Would be needed. "Arabella is going to have a baby before the year is out. When do you suppose my lady's maid and I will be allowed to leave the palace?"

Ziyaeddin gave a start, his brows furrowing. "Leave? You've only just arrived."

Charlotte nodded. "Well, I cannot stay here, Your Highness."

"Why ever not?" He straightened, his manner suddenly serious.

She scoffed, her spoonful of couscous forgotten. "I must return to England—"

"You said you were on holiday."

"Yes, but I hardly think I should continue my holiday given what's happened," she argued. "Besides, I think I should like to be there for the birth of my first grandchild."

It was his turn to scoff. "The first will be no different from the rest," he countered with a wave of one bejeweled hand.

Charlotte's mouth dropped open in dismay. "Your Highness—"

"I should know. I have..." He paused and seemed to mentally count before he said, "Four, I think."

Her hands going to her hips, Charlotte really wished she could rise from the table, but her legs were nearly numb from how she knelt. "I cannot stay here," she said again. "I have availed you of your hospitality for three days already."

His reaction suggested he was surprised. "Hospitality I would gladly grant for a very long time," he said. "You are my guest."

Charlotte arched a brow as a shiver shot through her torso. She was about to offer a payment for the inconvenience of having to host her—there was gold sewn into the hems of her garments—but she decided it best she simply accept his hospitality for the time being. "You are very generous, Your Highness. Thank you."

As if he had guessed she was about to offer payment, the sultan appeared as if he was having trouble reigning in his anger. "You owe me nothing, Duchess Charlotte, and be glad the pirates brought you here instead of some-where else."

Inhaling softly, Charlotte stared at Ziyaeddin. Although his words weren't meant as a threat, they were a reminder that she and Parma might have ended up as slaves.

So why did she sense she was now a prisoner rather than a guest?

CHAPTER 15
A DIFFERENT SORT OF
AGREEMENT

Charlotte regarded the sultan's rather calm demeanor for a moment before she asked, "Why do you suppose the pirates thought to sell us to you?"

Grimacing, Ziyaeddin looked as if he was losing his patience with her. "I do not know, but I do not buy slaves," he stated, his silver eyes blazing. "Slavery is not tolerated in my empire."

Pondering his response, Charlotte finally said, "They were obviously unaware of your dictate."

Ziyaeddin dipped his head and did not respond for several seconds, as if he were struggling not to lash out at her. "Is it not enough that I freed you from them?" he asked in a quiet voice.

Inhaling softly, Charlotte stared at the sultan. "It is, of course, Your Highness," she replied. "I do appreciate it. Very much," she added, not wishing to seem ungrateful. "May I inquire as to what will happen to them? The pirates in your dungeon?"

Ziyaeddin's impatience was now clearly written on his

face. Apparent in how his arms crossed over his chest and in how his back stiffened. "If they behave, I will release them next week with the warning that they are never to step foot on my land ever again."

"And the ship they took?" She knew she was pressing her luck when it came to prying answers from the sultan, but she was desperate to learn if Captain Popodopolos and his crew were still alive.

Ziyaeddin shrugged. "The other pirates left on board realized their error and have sailed off," he said. "The *Sun of Apollo* is no longer docked."

Charlotte nodded her understanding, hoping the Greek crew members hadn't suffered for the loss of the three pirates. "I thank you for what you have done," she said meekly. "Surely I cannot expect you to do more on my account."

His eyes rounding at her comment, Ziyaeddin helped himself to another serving of kebab. "You must understand that to be a guest of a sultan means you must accept my hospitality for as long as I wish to extend it."

Charlotte's mouth dropped open. "Do you... do you intend to keep me as a prisoner here?"

Ziyaeddin's eyes darkened at the same time they narrowed. "You are not a prisoner, Duchess Charlotte. You are my *guest*. I wish for you to stay, so you shall." He returned his attention to his meal, as if the matter were settled.

It wasn't for Charlotte.

"For how long, exactly?"

He took another bite but did not immediately answer. "We kissed one another," he said quietly.

Charlotte swallowed even as the familiar shiver of pleasure shot through her again. "We did."

"I thought it was what you wanted," he said, his attention on his meal.

Dipping her head, Charlotte realized she had to tell him the truth. Surely he would know if she lied. "I liked it very much," she admitted, heat once again burning her face and neck.

"Good. For I wish for you to share my bed this evening."

Charlotte's eyes rounded. "*Me?*" she squeaked. She might have imagined what it was like to be kissed by the sultan, but she surely hadn't imagined what might happen after the dinner was done. "You have a harem of beautiful women, and you wish to bed *me?*" she asked in disbelief.

His brows furrowed as if in concentration as he translated her words. "I do," he affirmed. "And yes."

She stared at him in awe, really wishing her body wasn't reacting as it was.

In betrayal.

The space at the top of her thighs was already throbbing in anticipation. Her nipples had long ago puckered, apparently in the belief they would be kissed and suckled, as if she was to be the dessert course. "Because we kissed?" she whispered.

He finished the kebab and inhaled slowly, as if in resignation. "Yes. And because..." For a moment, he seemed uncertain. "You may think you are undesirable because you are a widow, Duchess Charlotte, but I will show you that the dead do not expect us to live as if *we* are dead."

Charlotte inhaled as if she intended to protest, but the words caught in her throat. Joshua had spoken of what she should do after his death. *Find another worthy of you*, he had whispered when he knew he didn't have long to live. *And love him until the day you die.*

Well, she didn't yet know if the sultan was worthy of her, but she rather doubted she would ever grow to love the man. He was infuriating. Stubborn. Spoiled with the power of his position.

And entirely too damned handsome.

What was Joshua thinking now? she wondered as she swallowed, her gaze meeting the sultan's. "I have never been with another man but my husband," she blurted.

His dark brows furrowed as he angled his head to one side. "I understood English aristocrats took lovers after the heirs and spares were born," he stated. "And yet you did not do this?"

Charlotte shook her head. "I did not wish to," she replied. "I loved my husband."

Ziyaeddin drank deeply from a tankard, his expression suggesting he was deep in thought. "After the death of my favorite wife, I did not bed another of my concubines for a very long time. I..." His face screwed up in concentration. "I vexed my mother for a month."

"Your mother?" Charlotte responded, before she remembered Sevinc's comment on the matter. "What ever did she have to do with whom you took to your bed?" It was then she remembered his mother had been the one to give the concubines their final exams. The one to keep order in the harem.

Heat suffused Charlotte's face as she wished she could take back her question.

The query had Ziyaeddin's brows rising, almost as if he found it amusing. "Until her death last year, she was in charge of the harem," he explained. "She saw to the education of the concubines as well as my sisters and my daughters. She trained the concubines, you see. Kept track of who had given birth. She was the paymaster and was in charge of the... the payroll," he said, the last word giving him some trouble.

"Payroll?" Charlotte repeated. "For your servants?"

He shook his head. "For my concubines. They are paid according to their... to their rank. According to how many children they have given birth to."

Charlotte rolled her eyes. "As if they are prostitutes," she stated, remembering how Sevinc had described the concubines' compensation. Hearing the information from the sultan made it seem as if his harem was a business enterprise. As if he had to pay those who gave birth to his children.

Ziyaeddin blinked, obviously surprised by her reaction. "Is it not fair for them to be compensated? They spend their life in my palaces," he explained. "At my beck and call." He winced after saying the last, as if he thought his choice of words was wrong.

"Living a life of luxury, I should think," Charlotte countered, waving a hand to indicate the riches surrounding her.

"Or in a gilded cage," he replied.

Charlotte blinked. From what she had seen earlier that day, she hadn't thought any of the women to be unhappy. "Are you saying they don't wish to be here?"

Ziyaeddin shook his head, obviously frustrated with his inability to explain the situation in English. "No. But they are free to leave, should they wish to—and if I am in agreement," he added. "If I do not bed them, I am sure to find them a suitable husband so that they might have the opportunity to have children."

Despite what Sevinc had told her, Charlotte wondered if he was ever really in agreement with someone who wished to leave his palace. "Have any of them ever asked to leave?"

A smirk lifted the corners of his lips. "You did, only a moment ago."

Inhaling softly, Charlotte stared at him before she looked away, her cheeks red with embarrassment. "I wasn't aware I had become a member of your harem," she whispered.

"Of that I have not yet decided," he murmured, the smirk reappearing as if he were teasing her. He leaned over and captured one of her hands in his. "But I beg you allow me to prove myself to you." He waved his free hand. "So I may decide I do not desire you."

Charlotte blinked, momentarily offended. "I'm not sure you realize what you just said."

A huge grin lighted his face, and Charlotte was struck at how happy he seemed. How young he appeared. How his grip on her hand tightened just enough to hope he didn't let go.

"Oh, my English is not the best, but I know what I

said," he replied as he let go of her hand and suddenly straightened from the cushion. A moment later, and he had moved to her side of the table to help lift her to standing. The move seemed effortless, as did the way he led her through a pair of doors beneath an arch.

Charlotte inhaled softly at what was on the other side, well aware he had closed the doors behind them and bolted the door.

Had he done so to prevent them from being interrupted? Or to keep her from attempting to escape?

Off to the left was the balcony he'd been standing on the night when she'd been brought to the palace. From the color of the sky, it was apparent the sun had set. Directly in front of her was a huge sofa behind small tables scattered with papers and books. Several oil lamps cast the room in a golden glow. Off to the right, dressed in what appeared to be satin fabrics, was the largest bed Charlotte had ever seen in her entire life.

"Oh," she breathed when he pulled her close and kissed her forehead.

"Oh, indeed," he murmured as he urged her onto the balcony. With its vantage over the Aegean Sea and the vivid twilight to the west, it could have been a favorite spot for a painter.

"I don't think I've ever seen these colors before," she whispered, awestruck by the bands of purples and peaches that seemed to rest above the line of water on the western horizon.

"They would look stunning on you," he replied. "I shall have some silk delivered to your chamber on the morrow."

Charlotte gasped as she tore her attention from the fading sunset to stare at the sultan. "That's rather generous of you," she replied, relieved when a cooling breeze caressed her face and upper arms. She couldn't remember another time in her life when being out of doors seemed so perfect.

"I am a generous man," he said before he inhaled deeply. His gaze swept the horizon, as if he was in search of something.

"What is it?" she asked, well aware of how close he stood. She could feel the warmth of his body. Smell the spicy scent of a cologne she didn't recognize.

"I am expecting a ship from The Netherlands," he replied.

Charlotte tore her gaze from the stripe of purple sky and glanced over at him. "Bringing something special?"

He shook his head. "Supplies, mostly. Some stroopwafels and cocoa powder, I hope."

Gasping, she turned to face him. She could understand his desire for cocoa powder. The Dutch produced the very best. But she was unfamiliar with the other word he had said. "Stroopwafels?" she repeated. "I would have thought you would be expecting tulips."

"I like delicious foods, Charlotte," he murmured. "We shall have stroopwafels and chocolate for breakfast here and at the new palace." He regarded her with a quirked brow. "As for tulips, we already have them."

Charlotte angled her head. "Did you get them from the Kingdom of The Netherlands?"

He chuckled. "They got them from us," he replied.

"Oh," she replied, realizing she knew little of the

history of the empire. "But... does it get cold enough here to grow tulips?" she asked, knowing the flower required a winter to set the bulb for the next season.

He frowned. "If it does not, the gardeners will dig up the bulbs and surround them with ice," he said with a shrug.

Charlotte's mouth rounded into an 'o.' The sultan seemed to share the late English king's penchant for expensive things. "Are you a spoiled man, Your Highness?" she asked in a tease.

Ziyaeddin frowned as he parsed the words. His eyes suddenly widened with understanding. "If you are asking if I get what I want, then I suppose I must admit that I do," he replied. "Else what would be the point of wanting?"

Scoffing, Charlotte turned to regard him with wonder. "What if the *having* is not as great as the *wanting*?" she countered, crossing her arms as she tapped a slippered foot.

He furrowed a brow as he moved to stand even closer to her. "Are you speaking of my want for you?" he asked.

Her eyes darted to the side before she dared meet his gaze. "I suppose I am," she admitted, swallowing when she remembered he intended for her to spend the night with him.

"Then let us discover the answer together."

Charlotte inhaled sharply as he pulled her shawl so the ends came free of her elbows. He turned her around, his fingers working to undo the few fastenings at the back of her gown as they stutter-stepped back into his bedchamber. For a moment, she felt a fingertip trace the line of her whip scar, and she shivered as his touch tickled.

"You will tell me about this, but not now," he whispered.

Turning her head so it rested on her shoulder, Charlotte replied, "If... if I must," she stammered.

Although she expected that what was to happen next would be quick—he'd have his way with her and then dismiss her—she soon realized he had other plans. Plans to undress her. Slowly.

"You are tied up," he murmured as he spread open the back of her gown.

Nervous, Charlotte couldn't help but chuckle at the comment. "It's a corset, Your Highness."

He grunted. "What happens if I untie it? And these?"

Well aware of his fingers pressing on the undergarment as well as the ties for her petticoats, as if they would give way of their own accord, she said, "I shall... *explode* out of all of it." She wished she had been facing him, to see his expression as he sorted her reply.

"Explode?" he repeated. "I do not think you know the meaning of that word."

She angled her head to the side, her chin pressed to her shoulder so she could see him. "Oh, I know what it means, and so will you if you untie those bows and the corset."

One of his arms wrapped around her waist as he tugged on the ends of the bows. Charlotte inhaled sharply, surprised by his move and relieved when the ties loosened, making it easier for her to breathe.

"You did not explode," he accused, pulling her body against the front of his.

She glanced up at him, her head against his shoulder. "Well, not exactly, but I certainly have more room to breathe and..." She paused and followed his line of sight down the front of her loose bodice. "I no longer have a décolletage."

He frowned, apparently unfamiliar with the word. But his warm breath on her neck had her shivering. "I wish for you to undress me," he whispered, his eyes nearly closed as he inhaled deeply.

Charlotte blinked, wishing there had been wine at their dinner. Had she known what was to happen, she might have drunk an entire bottle. "Are you quite sure? Because..." She turned in his arms, which had her petticoats dropping to her knees. When she faced him, her front now pressed to his, she gulped.

His erection was evident through his şalvar.

"I have never been more sure, Duchess Charlotte." He pushed the sleeves of her gown down her arms and over her hips. The satin slipped from her body, and then her corset followed as he pushed it from her torso.

Left wearing only her chemise and standing in the middle of a pile of fabrics, Charlotte winced. "If you're sure," she murmured.

Chuckling, the sultan slid his hands beneath her arms and lifted her from the clothes, backed up a few steps, and set her back down. He didn't pull his hands away, though, instead allowing them to roam down the translucent cotton of her chemise and over her near-naked body.

She shivered when a frisson skittered under her skin.

Reaching up, she pushed the kaftan from his shoulders. The shirt beneath, a wrap style tied at the side of his waist, was easy to undo. The rest of his unusual clothes proved a challenge for her, though.

"How do I undo this belt?" she asked, breathless from his unhurried ministrations. She was doing her best not to stare at his chest, his skin and nipples nearly hidden with whorls of dark hair. One of her hands skimmed down the front of his torso to the bejeweled buckle.

He chuckled as he easily unhooked the silver ornament and tossed it onto the nearby sofa. "Patience," he whispered softly, one of his hands reaching behind her head to pull it forward. He once again pressed a kiss against her forehead. "We have all night."

Charlotte inhaled softly. "Oh, I don't think you'll be keeping me here that long," she replied, undoing the fastening at the top of his *şalvar*. About to push them down, she couldn't when his hands covered hers.

"Why do you say that?" he asked, his silver eyes blazing.

Blinking, Charlotte sighed and stepped back. She shook off his hold on one of her hands and swept it down the front of her body. "Your Highness, I am old. I've given birth to two boys. Whilst you still have the body of a Greek god, I have these awful white marks on me, and my breasts are all saggy and..."

She couldn't continue her rant. Not when his lips covered hers. Not when he pressed the evidence of his erection into her belly and groaned through the kiss.

When his lips let go of hers, he moved them to the top of one cheek and then next to her ear. "None of that matters," he whispered. "Although I shall reward you greatly for comparing me to a Greek god," he added, his eyes twinkling in delight.

Charlotte swallowed as he easily lifted her onto the bed. Trembled when his lips continued their trek down the length of her torso, leaving trails of cooling moisture in the night air. Shivered when his hands splayed over her heated skin and slid over her engorged breasts. Whimpered when his lips captured a nipple and briefly suckled it through the fabric of her chemise.

"How long has it been since a man has done this to you?" he growled.

Charlotte nearly scoffed at the query. Did he honestly expect she would be able to provide a coherent answer? He had her so addlepated, she barely knew where she was. "More than year," she finally replied. "Nearly two, probably," she added, her hands skimming down the sides of his torso until they could grip his buttocks.

Ziyaeddin's body jerked in her hold before he reached for each of her wrists in turn and moved them so they were on either side of her head. When she mewled her uncertainty, he lifted his head and shook it. "Do not touch me, Charlotte. Not yet," he whispered.

"What are you—?"

"Patience," he interrupted, his mouth once again covering one of her breasts.

She arched into him and then slid a foot along the side of his leg. He paused in his ministrations and lifted his head, one of his dark brows arching in warning.

"Not even with my toes?" she whispered in confusion. He was going to make love to her, of that she was now quite certain. None of her arguments had put him off, nor had the sight of her wearing only her chemise and jewelry. Her body was waging an internal war with what was left of her ability to reason, and she knew reason was about to lose.

Would it anger him if she told him to stop?

Her body would certainly do something in protest. Every nerve ending was on high alert. Excited. Hungry for his touch.

She swallowed and closed her eyes, the very end of her ability to think bringing to mind that she was doing this for England. For Queen and country. After all, wasn't this what aristocrats meant when they spoke of foreign relations?

For a moment, she relaxed, the tenseness in her body flowing away. In the next, she opened her eyes halfway and regarded the sultan in an entirely different way.

He was a man. Merely a man. Like any other man, he had needs. If he had decided she could meet those needs, then who was she to argue?

Her body certainly wasn't going to. Her nipples were ruched. The space at the top of her thighs throbbed. She yearned to touch him. To discover what gave him pleasure.

"If I cannot touch you, however am I to learn what you like?" she asked in a whisper, the words sounding as if someone else had spoken.

A grin finally lightened his expression. "I would like you wet with need of me. Open for me," he whispered.

Charlotte inhaled as she spread her legs wider. A quick glance down the front of his body, and she nearly gasped at the sight of his turgid manhood. The bulbous tip of it was nearly purple, its length and girth greater than her late husband's. Her eyes rounded in fright. "Your Highness," she rasped as she attempted to pull her knees together.

"You shall call me Ziyaeddin when we are in private," he whispered hoarsely.

"You're enormous," she countered.

He had wrapped his forearms beneath her knees and had the tip of his cock at her entry when he realized what she said. "You say that as if it is undesirable."

She opened her mouth to respond but a most pleasant tremor shot through her entire body. "Oh!" was all she could get out before he nudged his way into her.

"Open for me," he whispered, his lips lowering to her forehead.

Lifting her hips and gripping his thighs with her own, Charlotte did his bidding. He growled as he entered her, paused to emit a groan of what might have been pleasure, and then said something unintelligible when he was fully inside her.

Charlotte cried out when his hands covered hers, the move preventing her from hanging onto his shoulders. Preventing her from using them to caress the sides of his torso or grip his buttocks or cup his sac as he simply hovered over her.

"You *are* wet for me," he whispered, as if in awe.

Blinking, Charlotte struggled to breathe. "How could I not be?" She attempted to lift her chest from the bed, wanting his lips to continue what they'd been doing only the moment before. "The way you were staring at me during dinner? As if I were to be your dessert?"

Ziyaeddin furrowed his brows. "You are the one who is starved," he accused, before his head dipped down and he once again suckled a breast. "I have hungered for you for a very long time."

Swallowing, Charlotte had a thought that his sense of time was all wrong. "And yet you could have had a feast delivered to your bed with a mere snap of your fingers."

He shook his head. "Table scraps," he murmured.

She managed to free a hand from his grip and place it on the side of his head, her fingers spearing his hair. Without his turban, the silver streaks in his otherwise black hair glinted with the flame from the room's oil lamps. "Let me hold onto you, dammit," she ordered.

He let go of her other hand and placed his on either side of her shoulders. "Very well," he replied, his eyes glinting at hearing her curse.

Then he began to move.

He nearly pulled himself all the way out of her body, but Charlotte had slid her hands to his buttocks and was holding on as if her life depended on it. When he thrust into her, stars sailed before her eyes. He pulled out and thrust into her again, but this time she was ready. She knew how to do this. Knew how to counter his thrusts by lifting her hips. Ziyaeddin was far larger than Joshua had been in his best health, though. The sultan's shoulders were broader, his thighs thicker. She could feel the power of him even as she lifted her hips to meet his thrust.

Her move had obviously been unexpected, for he murmured something in his native tongue that might have been a curse or a prayer before he resumed his thrusting. Charlotte met each and every one with equal fervor, amazed that her body remembered what to do. How to do it. Even when she knew she couldn't hold back what was to come—she could already sense her insides contracting in anticipation—she continued to hold on.

Perhaps Ziyaeddin felt it too, for he quickened his movements and then rose above her, his head thrown back as his groan filled the room and her orgasm sent her into ecstasy.

For a moment, it was as if they were suspended in time, neither moving but both experiencing a mutual pleasure they dared not interrupt.

Charlotte wasn't prepared for what happened next. She had expected he would fall atop her or roll off to one side. Instead, he gripped her hips as he brought his knees beneath him and knelt on the bed, which left her fully exposed when his gaze swept over her.

Missing the closeness of his body, Charlotte pushed herself up until she could wrap her arms around his back and embrace him, her head tucked into the small of his shoulder. His arms supported her, one around her shoulders and another across the middle of her back.

This she had never done before, at least not after having made love. She realized the sultan had to possess enough strength to keep them both upright as she trembled in his hold, frissons darting throughout her body as her orgasm finally subsided.

When she used her inner muscles to grip his erection, she took delight in his hearing his sudden inhalation of breath, and then she gasped when she felt the sudden wash of warmth that told her he'd finally taken his own pleasure.

How had he staved it off for so long?

He tightened his hold on her as his body seized. His lips took purchase on one of her shoulders, his long groan muffled before he had to take a gulping breath.

When he pulled back to regard her, his brows were furrowed. He looked as if he intended to say something, but instead he merely struggled for air. Charlotte felt one of his arms give up his hold on her as he used it to leverage the two of them down to the bed.

Not about to let go of her hold on him, Charlotte ended up atop him, unable to suppress a grin of satisfaction as he closed his eyes and seemed to fall asleep.

She speared his hair with her fingers and smoothed it back from his forehead, noting how the creases had disappeared from above his brows. The dark lashes lining his eyes rested atop his high cheekbones, making him appear far younger than he was. She lowered her lips to each eyelid and gently kissed them both. Then she studied the shape of his nose and the outline of his lips before she drew a finger along his jawline.

In England, his features would be considered too harsh, too rough for polite Society. He could pass for a pugilist, though, or a dunner at a gaming hell. Normally, she wouldn't give such a man a second glance. But from the moment she had seen him watching her from his balcony, she had felt an attraction she couldn't explain. A pull so intense, she should have been frightened by it.

Instead, she now felt empowered. Or perhaps she was

merely drunk on the aftermath of their lovemaking. She was determined not to compare the experience with any of those she'd had with Joshua, but how could she not? She had no other point of reference. Had no other experience of feeling worshipped at the same time she was being ravaged.

Giving Ziyaeddin one final kiss on the corner of his mouth, Charlotte settled her head into the space between his neck and shoulder and closed her eyes.

"I will have you one more time this night," he warned in a voice that sounded far away.

She lifted her head to discover his eyes were still closed. "Only one?" she countered, managing to sound disappointed.

He chuckled quietly as he tightened his hold on her, and they both fell asleep.

CHAPTER 16
A RESCUE CREW SETS SAIL

*M*eanwhile, *off the island of Rhodes*
The sun had completely set when Lord James Wainwright, the brother of the Duke of Chichester, and David Bennett-Jones, heir to the Bostwick viscountcy, were approached by the ship's captain.

"Cook has dinner ready. Come join me in my cabin," Captain Popodopolos said by way of invitation.

The two young men pushed away from the railing of the *Sun of Apollo*, giving their affirmative answers in unison.

"Your mother was a guest at my table every night she was on board," the captain added as they made their way to a dining table set for four. The other to join them turned out to the be the ship's navigator. "This is Ensign Knox," he said, waving to the young man who looked as if he wasn't any older than James and David.

"Good to meet you," James said as he shook hands with the ensign. "When do you suppose we'll be there? Wherever *there* is?"

LINDA RAE SANDE

Ensign Knox poured wine for the four of them. "Tomorrow, if the winds favor us, and they should." His English had James realizing he was from somewhere in southern England and probably the only Englishman on the crew. Everyone else was Greek.

"That soon?" James asked.

"We'll have land in sight by dawn," Popodopolos stated as a young sailor delivered their meal. He acknowledged the boy with a nod before he lifted the dome from a salver containing a baked turbot. "The palace is to the south. It has its own dock, and then it's a bit of a hike to get up to it. We'll be seen, of course," he added with a wince. He indicated the young men should help themselves to the meaty fish first, and they did so.

"But they will recognize your ship," James reasoned, as he filled his plate with the various foods the sailor had delivered.

"That's what I'm afraid of," Popodopolos replied, helping himself to a serving of the fish.

"Have you had dealings with the palace in the past?" David asked, tucking into his meal. With all the excitement that morning, they hadn't stopped to eat in Rhodes.

"Unfortunately," Popodopolos replied. "Greek War for Independence. I captained a ship that sank several Empire ships," he said. "The sultan was aboard one of them."

"You sank his ship?" David asked in alarm.

"Not with him on it," the captain replied. "I... took him aboard mine, but not as a prisoner."

"What?" James scoffed. "You could have finished him off—"

166

"As much as I hated the Ottoman Empire, and I did, I knew they would still be a powerful nation after the war. Their lands practically surround Greece," he explained. "There was no need to kill him, especially considering who might have taken his place."

David and James exchanged quick glances, realizing the captain referred to the viceroy who had attempted a coup only the year before. "The enemy you know," James murmured as he arched a dark eyebrow.

"What did you do with him?"

Popodopolos leaned forward, his elbows pressed into the edge of the table. "I hosted him on my ship. Shared my dinner with him. Took him to the same palace we're on our way to now, and I left him there."

"You're joking," James breathed.

The captain shook his head. "He didn't take offense at what I did, but I think he might have preferred to die a martyr to the cause." About to say more, he seemed to think better of it and drank his wine.

"He has made important reforms since the war," David said before taking a sip of his wine. "He's abolished slavery—"

"And yet the pirates who took this ship intended to sell the duchess to him," Popodopolos interrupted.

"It's a relatively new reform," David murmured. "Perhaps they weren't aware." He glanced over at James. "But if they couldn't sell her to the sultan..."

"There might have been other less scrupulous traders who would take her in exchange for gold," Popodopolos finished for him. "We'll find out on the morrow. If we can get into the palace..."

"How do we do that?" David asked.

The captain shrugged. "Walk up to the front door, I suppose. Introduce yourself."

"They won't shoot first?" James asked, concern evident in his expression.

"I suppose we can go with white flags," Popodopolos said before he finished off his wine. "Maybe flash some gold."

"Speaking of gold," James said suddenly. "What do I owe you for our passage? We didn't settle on an amount."

The captain shook his head. "When I made arrangements to take on the duchess as a passenger, I promised Mr. McElliott I would see to it Her Grace was delivered to Syros and that she had passage on a ship bound for Athens," he said. "I still intend to keep that promise."

"That's very honorable of you, Captain," James replied.

"As long as it doesn't get me killed," Popodopolos murmured. "Or you." He returned his attention to his meal, and the others followed suit.

*D*espite the relatively calm seas, James found it hard to sleep that night. Worry coupled with excitement had him turning in his cot. He wondered how his mother had put up with the accommodations.

"I know you're restless, but can you please try to sleep?" David asked from the other cot. "You're making me nervous."

James huffed. "Sorry," he replied. "But what do you suppose they've done with her?"

"In the palace?"

"Yes. Popodopolos said earlier that the three pirates who took her and Parma ashore never returned to the ship."

There was a pause before David inhaled and blew out the breath. One of the benefits of being assigned to the cabin two women had occupied meant the air held a hint of floral perfume instead of the rank odor of unwashed bodies. "The Turks probably killed them," David reasoned. "Especially if they don't allow slave traders."

"You think my mother is a prisoner in the palace?" James asked.

David sighed again. "I don't think a sultan would imprison a woman quite like you're thinking," he replied carefully.

"So, not in a dungeon?"

Scoffing, David chuckled. "Not in a dungeon," he affirmed, but he didn't offer what he thought as the alternative.

A harem.

CHAPTER 17
A NIGHT INTERRUPTED

*B*ack in the sultan's chamber at the palace
The sensation of a fingertip drawn up one of her bare arms had Charlotte giving a start. She awoke to discover Ziyaeddin lounging against a stack of cushions, one leg bent and splayed wide. He had pulled her so her body rested against the side of his, her head in the small of his shoulder.

She glanced down the front of his body, grinning when she noticed his morning tumescence on full display. Sliding a hand down his hirsute chest, she used a fingertip to do the same to his engorged cock as what he was doing to her arm.

He jerked and quickly covered her hand with his, pressing it hard around his cock. "Do you like it in the morning?" he asked, his voice sounding gravelly from sleep. "Making love, as you call it?"

Charlotte lifted her head from his chest. "I do, although I should like to use a chamber pot first," she whispered.

He growled but let go his hold on her. "Through there," he whispered, motioning toward an arched doorway.

Although the sun wasn't up, dawn had broken, and the dim light from the open balcony coupled with a still-burning oil lamp lit the room enough for Charlotte to find her way. She paused to straighten her chemise. Catching sight of a silk banyan puddled at the end of the bed, she scooped it off the carpeted floor and wrapped it about her body, chuckling at how large it was on her small frame.

Her entire body buzzed with what the sultan had done to her in the middle of the night. She had awoken to discover him leaving the bed, his long strides taking him to the balcony. When he didn't immediately return, she slipped out of the bed and followed.

The sight of him standing naked, barely lit by the light of a quarter moon, had her inhaling softly. He heard and turned to beckon her to join him.

"What woke you?" she asked in a whisper.

"I thought I heard something," he murmured, his arms wrapping around her until he had her pressed to him. "The front guard is on duty, though," he added, lifting his chin in the direction of a sentry who was posted near the entrance to the palace.

When she jerked in his hold, he chuckled. "He cannot see you, nor would I allow him to," he whispered. While carrying her back to the bed, he added, "Only I shall have the honor."

Charlotte swallowed at hearing his comment. Although it would be easy to believe him, she wondered how long it would be before he didn't hold her in such high regard. How long it would be before he tired of her in his bed. Tired of her company.

Surely then he would let her go. Send her away. She would always have the memories of this night.

He had taken great delight in pleasuring her, in teasing her body to readiness for his manhood and then denying her in favor of another form of pleasure. By the time he had impaled her, she was nearly bone-less. He had spent himself within a minute, his thrusts quick and frantic. When he'd finished, he had placed a splayed hand over her belly and gently rubbed it.

"What did you do that for?" she had asked as she struggled to catch her breath.

He lowered his lips to the space above her mons and kissed it. His short beard set off a series of frissons which had her entire abdomen contracting in another orgasm. "A daughter, I hope," he whispered. "You do want one, do you not?"

Charlotte inhaled sharply. "I rather doubt I can at my age," she had murmured.

"You are not too old, Duchess Charlotte," he had said. "I would be honored to see to it."

Scoffing, Charlotte remembered staring at him in disbelief. "I cannot stay here," she said quietly. "I must return to England... at some point."

He had frowned in that manner that had made her realize she had angered him. "Apologies, Your Highness—"

At that point, his hand had covered her mouth, his

thumb brushing along her lower lip. "Now is not the time to argue with me," he had warned.

Charlotte blinked, stunned when he gathered her into his arms and held her close. "Not when we have shared my bed and kissed one another."

On the one hand, Charlotte knew it would be easy to simply mind the sultan. Mayhap bring up the topic of her leaving at another time during the light of day. But a sense of panic had settled in her chest. Ziyaeddin must have felt the change in her, because he allowed a long sigh. "Say what you must," he ordered.

"I cannot stay. At least, not for much longer," she murmured.

"How long were you to be away on holiday?"

She inhaled to answer and then sighed. "That's not fair," she whispered.

He gave her a quelling glance.

"Two years," she finally admitted.

He arched a brow. "Then you shall stay with me for a year," he replied. "Go with me when I return to Constantinople."

"Constantinople?" she repeated in alarm. "I can't go to Constantinople."

"Well, you cannot stay here when I am not in residence," he reasoned.

"You intend to keep me as your... your prisoner?" She meant for the words to sound light. Almost teasing. But Charlotte knew she had said the wrong word when she saw how his expression darkened, how his brows furrowed as if in anger. "Forgive me, Ziyaeddin. You said you did not buy me."

"I did not," he hissed. "But I have given you refuge. Hospitality—"

"Which I greatly appreciate."

"—your own chamber—"

"You are a very generous man."

"And yet you wish to leave?"

She inhaled to answer and then sighed. "Well, perhaps not right away, I suppose," she had murmured. "But... what must I do to gain my freedom?" she had asked, even as a war waged inside her. A sultan was offering her a place to stay—accommodations in an opulent palace with delicious food and gorgeous views and perhaps—dare she hope?—a baby.

"We will speak of this in the light of day," he had replied. "I will think more on it then... as should you."

Charlotte had watched as he settled back into the cushions, his even breathing suggesting he had fallen asleep. But when she had pressed the front of her body against the side of his, she had felt the tension in him. Despite kissing the top of his arm, he remained rigid.

"My father horse whipped me when I refused to marry the man he had chosen for me," she whispered, deciding that moment was as good as any to explain the scar on her back.

She knew he heard her for his hold on her suddenly tightened. For a moment, the chamber remained silent.

"So I am not the first man you have vexed," he whispered hoarsely.

Charlotte inhaled sharply, not sure if his words had been said with humor or not. Anger had her struggling to move away from him, but he was quicker. His arms reached around her and pulled her hard against him. Even as she writhed in an effort to free herself, he held her close. "Had I been there, he would have died by my sword, Charlotte," he stated. When the fight seemed to leave her all at once, he splayed one of his hands over her back as he held her and added, "Daughters are always to be treated better than our sons. *Always.*"

Tears pricked the corners of her eyes at hearing his words. "So you would not do such a thing to one of your daughters? Even if they vexed you?" she asked in a whisper, her thoughts immediately going to Sevinc.

"I would not," he replied, one of his thumbs brushing a tear from her cheek. "Nor would I strike a woman. Unless she held a weapon to my neck, in which case, I would seek to disarm her before doing her bodily harm."

Charlotte gave him a watery grin and then kissed him on the forehead. "Thank you," she whispered.

He sighed deeply and seemed to relax beneath her. "You will not vex me intentionally?"

Not sure how to respond—if she said she would, did that mean he would let her go?—Charlotte finally sighed. "I will not." A thought struck her at that moment, and she asked, "Is that what you think your first wife is doing?" The words were out of her mouth before she could stop them, and she held her breath in anticipation of him responding in anger.

But he didn't.

"Perhaps she is not doing it intentionally," he whispered, although from his furrowed brow, it was apparent he had his doubts. "She has been discreet. The only reason I know she has taken a lover is because the eunuch who sees to her security has sent word," he murmured.

"If she was trying to hurt you... to vex you, she would not try to hide the *affaire*," Charlotte reasoned. She knew about such relationships. The aristocracy was rife with infidelity.

"Still, I do not wish to remain married to her if she loves another," he countered.

Charlotte lifted her head from his chest. "You would divorce her? You... you can do that?"

"Of course," he replied. "But I would not unless she had his promise of marriage or protection."

It was at that moment Charlotte was reminded that what they had been doing was adultery. She swallowed, never having thought herself capable. "It may only be for this night, but... you're having an *affaire* with me," she murmured.

"This is not an *affaire*, Charlotte," he stated. "It is different in our culture. I am a sultan. I have a harem." He appeared to be keeping his dismay in check even as his expression displayed it. "We'll not speak of this again until daylight." With that, he had rolled over onto his side, leaving her staring at the wide expanse of his back.

So when Charlotte had awoken atop him with one of his arms wrapped around her, she had been surprised. A bit relieved, too, thinking he might have forgiven her stubbornness. Or perhaps he simply required a quick release and didn't care that it was she who lay in his arms.

As she replayed their conversation in her head, she entered the bathing chamber and stopped short. Besides the floor to ceiling mosaics in dark blue and gold, a built-in wash basin, and a toilet, there was a man crouched against one wall. She caught a whiff of him before he leaped at her, the smell of him all too familiar.

That of Aukmed.

Her attempt to call out was silenced by the hand that covered her mouth. A curved knife appeared in her line of sight, and she immediately stopped struggling.

"I am getting out of here, and you are coming with me," he hissed, his other arm wrapped around her middle.

Charlotte resisted the urge to struggle or attempt to bite his hand. Her heart hammered so hard in her chest, she was sure her pulse could be heard across the tiled room. As far as she could tell, there was only one way in and out of the chamber, which meant Ziyaeddin would see them as the pirate made his escape.

Unless he had fallen asleep.

She remembered the sultan saying the three pirates had been put in the dungeons. If so, how had they escaped? Where were the other two? Had Aukmed been in the sultan's chambers the entire night? Or come in to the room whilst she and the sultan had slept?

Ziyaeddin had bolted the door to the bedchamber. But there was the balcony, and it hadn't been closed off before they made their way to the bed.

The balcony. Ziyaeddin had said he thought he heard something when she had joined him in the middle of the night.

LINDA RAE SANDE

"Move," Aukmed whispered, aiming her in the direction of the arched doorway.

She hadn't even taken two steps when Ziyaeddin appeared in front of them, his silver eyes blazing as his naked body tensed. His fists clenched at his sides.

Her own body's response was visceral, her heart slowing and her breathing calming at the sight of him. Surely he would know what to do. Surely he would save her.

For a moment, she wondered if he would. Was he still annoyed with her? Perhaps he would be glad to be rid of her. He had offered her a place at his side. A chance for a child. In his defense, he had every right to be offended by her ungratefulness.

Determined not to show her fright, Charlotte merely stared at Ziyaeddin as he seemed to assess the situation.

"Stop right there," Aukmed warned, the knife held to her throat. He said something in Turkish, and the sultan seemed to think about it for a moment before he stepped back and to the side. He waved an arm as if he had decided to let the pirate pass.

Charlotte nearly whimpered as tears pricked the corners of her eyes. As she feared, he wasn't going to fight for her. But what could she expect? He was naked. He had no weapon.

Angling his body so he could keep an eye on the sultan at the same time he made for the balcony, Aukmed shoved Charlotte forward.

Not to the bolted door, but to the balcony.

How did he expect to escape by way of the balcony?

Charlotte thought of the height. They were three stories up from the ground. Had he climbed a rope?

"The way down will be quick," Aukmed hissed. "If you let go, you fall."

Whimpering, Charlotte's eyes rounded when she realized what he meant for her to do. There was a rope of sorts, apparently made of strips of linen with knots every few feet. Secured from somewhere up above—probably the roof—it disappeared over the edge of the balcony wall.

"I can't," Charlotte whispered. "I... I haven't the strength."

"You will. You'll go first."

"But you won't make it," she countered. "The guards—"

"Will not be there, or I shall kill you."

The words were said loud enough for Ziyaeddin to hear, and he cursed in Turkish.

"You could have just paid for her like you would any of your other whores," Aukmed said in disgust, tugging on the red veil with the hand that held the knife. "This will fetch a good price as well."

Almost to the balcony, Charlotte was the first to realize there was yet another man present. Crouched on the balcony wall, off to one side. Not yet in the line of sight of the pirate. "You bastard," she said, responding to Aukmed's comment even as she dug her heels into the carpet in an attempt to keep him from seeing what she was seeing.

Surely he was a guard.

Or perhaps he was one of the other pirates.

The thought had Charlotte gasping.

Given his attention was on the sultan, Aukmed didn't notice the crouching man. His words were directed to Ziyaeddin. "Don't you dare come any closer, or I'll throw her over the wall," he warned.

Charlotte thought it odd the man spoke in English, as if his words were meant for her ears. She didn't react to them, though, but rather to the way the crouching man was jerking his head to one side. He was holding a bow and had an arrow cocked to shoot.

Friend. Not foe.

She suddenly leaned to the side he indicated, and a second later, an arrow pierced the pirate's eye. His hold on her tightened for only a moment before he fell backwards. Escaping his grip, Charlotte whirled around and pressed her back against the wall as the man from the balcony entered and shot another arrow into the pirate.

No longer able to hold herself up, Charlotte gripped the edges of the veil and banyan around her and whimpered as she slid down the wall. She never made it to the floor, though, for Ziyaeddin was there, pulling her up and into his arms.

"Charlotte?" he whispered hoarsely.

"Are you hurt, My Sultan?" The words came from the man with the bow.

"Ertuğrul?" It was Charlotte who asked, her eyes widening when she recognized the man with the bow.

He bowed. "Your Grace."

"How did you...?"

"I discovered the guard below was missing whilst on my morning hunt," Ertuğrul explained. "I saw the rope as it fell from the roof." He directed the next words to his father. "Apologies, My Sultan. I hurried as fast as I could to the roof, but he had already made it down. I knew your door would be bolted, and there was no other way in."

Ziyaeddin nodded his understanding. "What of the other pirates?"

"Dead. They are up on the roof," Ertuğrul replied, his head jerking up.

Nodding his understanding, Ziyaeddin turned his attention to Charlotte. "Did he hurt you?" He moved his hands to her face, his brows furrowing as he studied her cheeks and neck.

"No. I am... fine," she murmured, a profound sense of relief having replaced the odd senses of dismay and disappointment and fear she had felt only moments ago. His arms once again wrapped around her back to keep her close. It was then she realized that she was providing cover for his nakedness.

"How did they escape the dungeon?" the sultan asked suddenly, his gaze fierce as he directed it at his son.

Ertuğrul winced. "I will go there next to investigate," he replied. "With your permission?" He bowed.

Ziyaeddin waved a dismissive hand, and his son, dragging the dead pirate by one arm, left by way of the door. After he closed it, Ziyaeddin lifted Charlotte into his arms and moved her to the bed. He kissed her forehead when his breathing had returned to normal.

"Well, that was rather exciting," Charlotte murmured, her hand going to the side of his face. Her breath hitched at seeing his continued look of worry. Of consternation. "Are *you* all right?"

Stunned by her question—and by how calm she sounded—he stared at her. "I would not have let him take you," he whispered, his brow furrowing. "I feared he would hurt you, though. Cut you with the blade."

"I know," she replied.

"I will do what is necessary to keep you safe," he vowed.

The sultan's claim that he would not have allowed the pirate to take her replayed in her head. The way he had rushed to her as she slid down the wall and taken her into his arms had the oddest sensations gripping her heart.

Desire to reward him had her burying one cheek into the small of his shoulder and kissing the warm skin of his chest. His heartbeat was strong against her ear, as if he still hadn't recovered from the excitement.

His manhood certainly hadn't. It was engorged, its length pressed into her thigh so she could practically feel its pulse. The combination of danger and fright and the sultan's regard for her made for a heady mix, her own arousal apparent by how her breasts swelled.

"Make love to me," she whispered, her words coming out in more of a command than a request.

Ziyaeddin's eyes darkened as his brows furrowed in confusion. "As you wish, Your Grace." His hand moved to the top of her thighs, and he hesitated when she spread her legs for him. When she arched her back as his palm pressed against her quim, he allowed a growl of surprise upon feeling her damp curls.

He felt satisfaction in hearing her mewls of pleasure as he rubbed her womanhood with his thumb. And then he sobered when she reached down to wrap his turgid manhood in her fist. He inhaled sharply when one of her thumbs brushed over the end of it, spreading the bead of moisture over its tip.

"You're wet for me," she teased.

He growled and was atop her, his manhood buried inside her in a single thrust. Her thighs cradled his, which had him seated more deeply within her. He groaned and gasped for air. When one of her hands gripped a buttock whilst the other cupped his sac, he was at her mercy.

Or perhaps she was at his.

In only moments, Charlotte cried out his name as ecstasy swept over her and through her. As the waves of pleasure washed away any thoughts of what had happened at dawn.

This time, Ziyaeddin did not delay his release to watch hers. Instead, he gripped her tightly in his arms and simply rode the waves with her.

Only the day before, he had thought one night with the duchess might be enough to satiate his need of her. Reignite his desire to share his bed after weeks of sleeping alone. Surely he would be satisfied to summon one of his favorite kadins to his bed for subsequent evenings.

Had that been the case, then he might have allowed the pirate to take her. He would be rid of her and her stubbornness.

But his thoughts went back to when she had been

brought into his throne room. To the dagger-filled stare she had directed at him. To the reminder of what he had felt for Afet. To how long it had taken for Afet to fall in love with him. To what he had felt for Charlotte.

What he still felt for her.

Three nights, he decided then. He would require she stay three more nights, and then he would allow her to leave.

Those were his last thoughts before sleep took him.

*M*eanwhile, Charlotte relaxed beneath his prone body, one hand cupping the back of his head as it rested in the small of her shoulder. Blissfully unaware of his thoughts for their immediate future, she began to think about what it might be like if she did stay with him. Perhaps she could afford to stay a month or more. After a month, surely he would be tired of her. Bored. By then, she would wish to resume her holiday. Eventually make her way back to England. Maybe even take a lover.

Those were her last thoughts before she dozed off.

CHAPTER 18
AN OFFER IS MADE

*L*ater *that morning*

Ziyaeddin awoke with a start, knowing it was later than his usual time to begin his day.

He knew the reason, of course. She was lying atop him, her eyes wide open. How she had ended up there when he remembered falling asleep atop her, he couldn't fathom. Then he wondered if he had made love to her whilst he slept. Surely he couldn't sleep through such an event, though. Not the way her soft body turned from temptress to tigress the moment he impaled her. Not the way her hands played over his skin and gripped him in such a possessive manner. Not the way her lips suckled his most sensitive areas.

His eyes focused to discover she was staring at him with the most beatific grin on her face.

"What is it, My Duchess?" he asked, not bothering to hide a matching grin. His chest constricted at seeing the joy in her expression, the delight in her eyes. He lifted himself onto his elbows, and she rolled off of his chest.

Charlotte's hands went to either side of his head, her fingers smoothing out his tousled hair. "I've made a horrible mess of your hair," she replied. "Which has me wondering how bad mine must look."

He chuckled. "The veil still covers most of it," he said, pinching the edge of the silk between two fingers. The fine fabric covered the pillow beneath her head. "Your maid must have stuck your hair with lots of pins to keep it on your head like that."

"I don't have that many," she argued. "Most were lost when the..." She stopped speaking, the events of the early morning coming back to haunt her. "On the ship," she finished lamely.

Ziyaeddin rolled off of her. "I have been thinking."

"Oh, dear," Charlotte replied. When she noted his furrowed brows—he had obviously taken offense at hearing her attempt at a joke—she quickly added, "As have I. You go first."

"Three nights, Charlotte," he stated. "Spend three more nights with me, and if you still wish to leave the palace, I shall allow it." Surely she would declare her love for him before that.

Charlotte blinked. She was about to say, "Only three?" but thought better of it. She had been prepared to accept his offer of a month if that's what it took. Instead, he was giving her an option that would allow her to resume her holiday and go back to England much sooner.

A generous offer.

Surely she could abide three more nights with the sultan.

If they were anything like this past night, she thought she could live the rest of her life not ever warming another man's bed. Unless... "In a row?" she asked.

He frowned, as if he were parsing her words.

"Consecutive nights?" she clarified. Perhaps he meant to only bed her once a week or once a month or...

"Yes," he answered, although he did so as if he thought she might be trying to trick him.

"Then I accept your offer," she stated. When he didn't react, she lifted herself onto an elbow, leaned toward him, and said, "We shall seal our with deal with a kiss." Then she kissed him on the lips.

He returned the kiss, finally pulling away when he realized his need for her would be too great in another moment. "It is late for me to be waking," he said. "I cannot stay abed any longer."

"I understand." She glanced around the room in search of her clothes, realizing she would have to put on her red gown from the night before. "Will you help me with my buttons?"

Ziyaeddin stepped off the bed and turned to help her out of it. "You're wearing my robe," he accused.

Despite the sunlight that streamed into the chamber, she slipped out of it and helped him into it. Although she wouldn't have done such a thing the day before—her chemise was practically invisible in the beam of light— she thought him seeing her in daylight might remind him she was a matron. That his body, two years older than hers, would appear so glorious in the morning light had her sighing in dismay.

"What is it?" he asked as he looked down.

"How is it you can be eight-and-forty years old and have the body of a god? And I, two years younger—"

"Look like Aphrodite?" His arms wrapped around her shoulders, and he kissed her on the forehead.

Charlotte inhaled softly before she swallowed. "I might have to give you four nights for that," she murmured as she stepped out of his hold and into the middle of her discarded garments. She bent and pulled up the petticoats and gown in one economical move and then tied the petticoats to her waist. Threading her arms through the sleeves of the bodice, she turned so her back was to him.

He chuckled as he smoothed the gown across her back. "What were *you* thinking? Before you told me to go first?"

Lifting the veil so he could do up the two buttons, Charlotte considered how to respond. Now that she agreed to stay only a few more days, she didn't need to offer him a month or more. "During my tour with Sevinc, I couldn't help but notice you have a garden. Perhaps we could go for a walk there before dinner tonight? Or after?"

He turned her around, arranging the veil so it covered her back. Then he picked up her shawl and wrapped it around her back. "Perhaps," he hedged. "It will depend on what is on the schedule for the day. I am already late, although I expect I am excused for what happened at dawn."

Charlotte nodded her understanding. "I'll wear the purple gown."

He paused as he pulled on a silk tunic. "I look forward to seeing you in it."

Thinking she had been dismissed, Charlotte curtsied and was about to take her leave, when he said, "You will join me for dinner again?"

She hesitated. "Yes, of course."

He paused as he arranged his kaftan, his gaze intense.

"What is it?" she asked, glancing down at her gown when she thought he had seen something was wrong with it.

When she lifted her eyes back to his, she gave a start. Ziyaeddin was striding toward her, his expression unreadable.

"I wish to kiss you," he said, as if she should have known. He placed his hands on either side of her face and pressed his lips to her forehead.

Charlotte held her breath, half-expecting he would take her lips with his. But he didn't. He simply stared at her.

Not sure what to do, Charlotte murmured, "Have a good day, Ziyaeddin." She curtsied once more and took her leave, her corset gathered into one of her hands.

CHAPTER 19
TEA TIME

*C*harlotte wasn't surprised to find Elena waiting outside the sultan's chamber. She was surprised when the Greek hurried up to her displaying a look of worry.

"You are well?" Elena asked. 'You are not hurt?"

Charlotte blinked. "I am fine." When she realized the Greek servant must have heard about the pirate, she added, "I was not hurt by the intruder."

"And the sultan?"

"He is fine." They walked in silence for a moment before Charlotte asked, "Tell me, have you heard how it was the pirates were able to escape the dungeon?"

Elena glanced around before she lowered her voice to say, "The dungeons are old, Your Grace. Over five-hundred years. The iron bars had rotted, so it was possible for the pirates to break them."

Charlotte nodded her understanding and then immediately realized who Ziyaeddin would blame for their condition.

Ertuğrul.

"The sultan will not be pleased when he learns of it," Elena whispered when they arrived at Charlotte's chamber door.

"That's what I'm afraid of," Charlotte murmured before the guard opened her door. "Could you see to hot water for a bath?"

"Yes, Your Grace," Elena replied before she bowed and backed away.

Charlotte furrowed a brow when she realized the servant had never shown her any deference in the past, and yet now she seemed determined to help.

Her thoughts still on Elena's change in behavior, Charlotte turned around to discover Parma staring at her with a grin. "What is it?"

"You look as if you have been thoroughly tumbled, Your Grace," her lady's maid teased.

Not about to chastise Parma for the comment—she hadn't seen her lady's maid look so happy in a very long time—Charlotte moved to the dressing table and stared at her reflection in the mirror. "I suppose I do," she murmured.

Parma stepped up and began removing the pins from the veil. "You have more color in your cheeks than you have had in over a year," she commented.

"And I will for a few more days," Charlotte remarked. "The sultan has agreed to let us go, but he has asked that we enjoy his hospitality for three more days," she explained.

Parma continued her work to take down Charlotte's coiffure in silence, which had her mistress frowning.

"You're terribly quiet. Do you think...? Am I... prostituting myself for having agreed to do this?" Charlotte asked in a whisper. Aukmed's words about her being a whore replayed in her head.

"He is a sultan, Your Grace. From what I have learned from the other servants, we were expected to be living in the harem with the rest of the women by now. They all wonder what you have done to gain a private chamber," Parma replied, hinting that she had been privy to gossip among the palace servants.

"I take it they don't see me as a guest of the sultan?" Charlotte asked.

Parma winced. "Too many learned how we were brought to the palace by the pirates. If the pirates hadn't been sent to the dungeon, they would have assumed the sultan paid for us or that we were gifts."

Inhaling sharply, Charlotte realized that tongues had been wagging in the palace much as they would in a Mayfair parlor. "Guests would have come willingly," she agreed, sighing in disappointment.

"Is it really so bad to be here?" Parma asked suddenly, her manner timid.

Charlotte blinked. "As I recall, you were the one who didn't wish to be here," she accused, remembering how frightened the lady's maid had been when she realized they were in the throne room of a sultan.

Parma appeared suitably chastised. "That was before I met the other servants. Before I learned more about palace life," she replied. "It's much like working in a large household. Everyone does their part to see to the cleaning and laundry," she added as she brushed out Charlotte's hair. "It's all very equitable."

"So... you *like* it here?"

Parma shrugged. "I don't dislike it," she admitted. "Although I was looking forward to seeing the Kingdom of the Two Sicilies—"

"We will," Charlotte insisted, staring at her reflection in the dressing table mirror. She gave a start at seeing how much younger she looked with her hair down. Or perhaps her time with the sultan had simply youthened her. One thing was certain—her nether regions felt tender, a sort of delicious soreness she hadn't felt in over twenty-five years. She looked forward to immersing herself in the warm water of a bath.

A knock sounded at the door. "That will be the bath water," she said happily.

Parma opened the door, and several female servants entered carrying jugs of steaming water. Behind them, Sevinc appeared.

"May I come in?" she asked meekly.

"Sevinc! Of course," Charlotte said as she stood and took the young woman's hands in hers. "What brings you on this fine day?" She dared a glance beyond the door, expecting to see a eunuch hovering nearby.

Sevinc dipped a curtsy. "I brought tea," she said as she waved another servant into the chamber. Behind that one came another bearing a small table. The two servants set up the table and the tea service before they filed out.

"How wonderful," Charlotte said as she hurried to take a seat on a cushion next to the low table. "I can pour," she offered, thrilled to see cakes and unusual biscuits included on the ornate silver salver. She waved for Sevinc to join her as Parma busied herself with preparations for the bath.

"I have interrupted," Sevinc stated, her gaze on the tub.

"You haven't. I can take my bath after we finish our tea," Charlotte said. "I cannot tell you how much I have missed having tea since I left England. And I am starving."

"You can have it here every day, if you'd like," Parma said as she watched Charlotte prepare the cups and pour the tea. "You only need to let Elena know."

"Oh?" Charlotte hadn't thought to ask for it. "Do you take sugar. Or milk?" she asked, glancing into the sugar-pot to discover the lumps were all the same size and shape.

"Milk, please," Sevinc replied. She helped herself to a biscuit. "My father says you are staying for a few more days," she commented. "I had hoped you might stay longer."

Charlotte blinked. "You must have spoken to him in the past hour?" she guessed.

Sevinc nodded. "We shared a quick breakfast. I heard about what happened with the pirate. Ertuğrul Efendi is sick with worry that you wish to leave because of it—"

"That's not why I wish to leave," Charlotte interrupted. "Besides, Ertuğrul saved me from the pirate. I owe him my life."

Blinking, Sevinc stared into her teacup. "Then are you disappointed with Baba? Did he do something...?" Her face flushed, and she dipped her head. "Say something? Was he a beast?"

Charlotte angled her head to one side, stunned at hearing the young woman's concern. "Oh, I am not disappointed with your father. Far from it," she said quietly. "He is a very fine man, Sevinc." She hesitated to add her other thoughts about his abilities in bed. His daughter didn't need to know about *them*. "If my circumstances were different..." She cleared her throat, surprised at the sudden sorrow she felt. "I have a family, you see. Two sons. My daughter-in-law is expecting a baby by Christmas," she added with a grin.

"You miss them," Sevinc stated, her gaze once again going to her tea.

Charlotte chuckled. "I never thought I would feel homesick, but there is that," she admitted. "And my youngest son isn't even in England. He is on his Grand Tour, somewhere in Greece. Probably on one of the islands," she explained. "He won't be returning to England for over a year," she added.

At the mention of a son, Sevinc straightened on her cushion. "How old is he?"

Charlotte grinned. "He's a couple of years older than you. More handsome than he has any right to be. Loves anything to do with Ancient Greece and..." She paused and inhaled softly.

"And?" Sevinc prompted.

"I really wish you two could meet. I think he would find your curiosity about the world rather refreshing. He's not overly fond of English girls, you see."

Sevinc grinned. "Perhaps I will meet him if Baba ever allows me to travel," she said.

"Well, if you ever come to England—"

"I have been there, but only once."

Charlotte blinked. "You have?"

Sevinc nodded. "I went along when Father took two of my brothers there. To enroll them in university. He had to... make special arrangements," she added.

"Because they are Muslim?" Charlotte guessed.

Sevinc shook her head. "Oh, no. There have been other Muslims at the university. My older brothers. And some from Persia," she explained. "He wished for them to be settled in housing specially built for students. I went along because I was hoping to enroll, too, but they would not take me."

Charlotte shook her head. "They don't enroll any girls at Cambridge or at Oxford," she said on a sigh, helping herself to a slice of cake. She murmured her appreciation of the flavor, sure the confection included dates.

"If your circumstances were different, would you stay?" Sevinc asked.

Blinking, Charlotte dared a glance in Parma's direction before she shrugged. "I... I might," she finally replied. "If I could say something..." She paused and dipped her head. "Entirely inappropriate for a young, unmarried woman to hear..."

"Oh, please, do," Sevinc said with some excitement.

Tittering, Charlotte grinned and then quickly sobered. "Men sometimes become easily bored with their wives. They seek out other women to warm their beds—"

"You are speaking of mistresses?" Sevinc asked.

"Yes. And... and of concubines," Charlotte said carefully. "You see, as much as I like your father, and I do, I think he would grow bored with me rather quickly. Besides, I never had to share my husband with another, nor do I think I could share a lover." She felt her cheeks grow hot at hearing the words aloud, knowing she was practically admitting her *affaire* with the sultan to his daughter.

"He loves you," Sevinc blurted.

Charlotte blinked, nearly spilling her tea. "Oh, I rather doubt he can be in love with me. We've only known one another a few days," she reasoned.

"You do not believe in love at first sight?" Sevinc asked, her disappointment apparent.

Giving a start, Charlotte remembered the first time she had met Joshua. Remembered how she had felt about him. But that had been at her come-out. Surely love at first sight was reserved for the young at heart. "Your father might *lust* for me now, but after a few nights, I expect he'll be happy to have one of his concubines in his bed. And I will simply continue my holiday," she said with a shrug. Even as she said the words, the Green Monster had her doubting them. The thought of him in bed with another woman had her chest constricting in a most unexpected manner.

"So... you don't love him?" Sevinc asked in a quiet voice.

Charlotte swallowed. "Uh. I... really... I really can't say," she stammered.

"But you could?" Sevinc countered. "After a few more days perhaps?"

"Maybe," Charlotte replied, hearing a slight whine in her voice. "I've accepted his offer to stay for only three more days, though." It was then she remembered Sevinc and the sultan had shared a breakfast that morning. Had Ziyaeddin sent his daughter to learn more about Charlotte's intentions? To discover if she had feelings for him?

"You will not stay longer?" Sevinc asked. The girl looked as if she was about to cry.

"Maybe a day or two more," Charlotte hedged, thinking the young woman might report back to the sultan. She felt tears prick the corners of her eyes. "I suppose it all depends on your father. And if there is a ship that can take me to Syros. Or to Athens."

Sevinc's eyes widened. "Please do give Baba a chance," she said. "And besides, you must stay. What if you carry his child?"

Charlotte gasped, and this time her tea did spill. The incorrigible sultan had obviously shared too much with his daughter. "I rather doubt that's possible," she said, using a napkin to wipe the tea from the satin gown. "I think I am too old," she added. A memory of her last monthly courses having occurred during the voyage had her adding, "Or not," in a whisper. She gave a start at seeing the delight in Sevinc's eyes. "Another sister," the young woman whispered.

Blinking, Charlotte inhaled softly. Oh, if only she had a daughter like Sevinc. The trouble the two of them could get into would surely vex the sultan. But then he would truly regret keeping her around.

That last thought had a frown turning down her lips as a frisson skittered in her abdomen.

"I will go now so that your water will still be warm enough for your bath, Your Grace," Sevinc said. She easily stood from the cushion and executed a perfect curtsy.

"Thank you. For thinking of tea," Charlotte said.

Although it would have been easier to keep her thoughts on Sevinc and her return to England, Charlotte spent her entire bath thinking of the sultan.

She almost wished he would make an appearance so she could scold him for using Sevinc as a spy.

Scold him and then thank him with a kiss.

CHAPTER 20
A GARDEN OF DELIGHT

L *ater that afternoon*

After donning the purple dinner gown, Charlotte took a quick look in the dressing table mirror. Parma had done her hair much as she had the day before, but without the veil.

"I don't think he expects me to wear it since I told him the red would clash with purple," she explained when Parma offered to pin it into her hair. When a knock sounded at the door, Charlotte said, "That's probably Elena."

Parma answered the door and then returned to stand behind Charlotte.

"It's almost as if someone was listening. A purple veil has just been delivered, Your Grace," the lady's maid said as she brought the folded fabric to the dressing table.

Charlotte gasped at the sight of the fine silk, the color rich and dark. The edges were trimmed in tiny beads, and the same beads were woven into the fabric every few inches. "This is stunning," she murmured as she unfolded the silk. "Was there a note?"

Parma shook her head. "Sevinc Sultana delivered it," she said as she took it from Charlotte and used the few remaining pins to secure it onto her coiffure. "It's perfect with your gown."

"It is indeed." Anxious to learn what Ziyaeddin thought, she moved to the door. "I'm off. I doubt I'll be back before the morning." When she opened the door, she nearly collided with Ziyaeddin.

"Your Highness," she said as she dipped a deep curtsy, immediately noticing his manner of dress—a long, dark blue top coat worn with light pantaloons and a white shirt. His two-toned turban appeared gold in the late afternoon light.

"Your Grace," he countered, his gaze going down and then back up as she straightened. "Purple becomes you," he added.

"Thank you. And thank you for the veil. It's gorgeous," she replied as she held out one edge of the silk.

His expression faltered for a moment, but he quickly straightened.

"You look positively European in that suit," she added with a grin. When his brows furrowed, she said, "Very handsome."

"I should be wearing a fez," he stated as he led them down the corridor.

"Oh?"

"All the men in the empire are required to wear fez," he explained. "So that their religion and economic circumstances cannot be discerned from what is atop their heads."

Charlotte furrowed a brow. "Those are the hats made of scarlet felt?" she asked, remembering the others she had seen on the few men she had spotted in the palace. Her eyes widened when she realized they were descending stairs. "That's the only color I've seen them in."

"Indeed," he replied. "They are named for the town where the scarlet dye is made," he explained.

"Well, it's just as well you don't have one here at this palace. It would clash with your suit," she said, wondering at his pensive mood.

Ziyaeddin chuckled as they emerged from the stairway and into the large atrium she remembered from her first night in the palace. His steps were quick as he exited the building and took a turn towards an iron gate. He held it open for her before he shut it behind them. "Your Grace wished to take a walk in the gardens, so..." He lifted a hand and waved it at the expanse of greenery and flowers before them.

"Oh, Ziyaeddin," she breathed. "It's beautiful."

The sultan inhaled deeply. "I admit I have been remiss in not coming here on occasion," he murmured. "I take the time to come to this palace in the spring to be closer to the Mediterranean, but I am rarely able to enjoy it." When Charlotte glanced up with a look of concern, he added, "I am determined to change the circumstances. Require more of my sons to do their part to see to the empire."

"Your gardener is to be commended," Charlotte said

as she waited for him to catch up to where she stood before a colorful flowerbed.

"My gardener is actually three concubines," he replied. "They have what I think you call 'green thumbs'," he added. "This is what they do for their part in maintaining the palace."

Charlotte angled her head at hearing the comment, her notions about the harem once again changing. The garden was finer than those at most English country houses. "They are quite skilled then," Charlotte remarked, her ears perking at hearing running water. "Is that a fountain I hear?"

Ziyaeddin grinned at her enthusiasm. "Indeed. Ertuğrul had it modeled after one in Rome, although I think this marble is far better, and he had the Egyptian obelisk replaced with a dolphin."

Charlotte gasped at seeing the replica of the Fountain of the Four Rivers. With four shade trees towering around it, the fountain wasn't visible from the palace windows. Although she had never seen the original in person, she had seen a color plate of an illustration in a book. "How is it you can remain in your palace all day when you have such a gorgeous garden so close?" she asked. "You could work out here."

He chuckled again. "It's rather hot out here in the middle of the day," he commented. When he noticed her pensive expression, he arched a brow. "What is it?"

Charlotte hesitated before responding, deciding this was as good a time as any to ask for clemency for his son. "Please do not hold Ertuğrul responsible for what happened this morning," she blurted.

Angling his head to one side, Ziyaeddin eyed her with suspicion. "Why do you think I do?"

She inhaled to respond and then thought better of telling him how she had learned about the bars in the dungeon. "If Ertuğrul is responsible for all the government buildings, it stands to reason he is responsible for this palace. For the dungeon. For the iron bars that apparently failed to keep the pirates in gaol. But he is only *one man*, Ziyaeddin. And a young one at that."

"A pirate invaded my private chamber," he stated, his sudden anger apparent.

"And Ertuğrul saw to it he is no longer a threat," she countered quietly.

Ziyaeddin straightened, his fierce gaze going to the fountain. He stared at the water beneath the marble statues for several moments before he sighed. "For you, I shall not punish him," he finally said.

Charlotte gasped and stepped up to him, lifting herself on tiptoes to kiss him on the corner of his mouth. "Thank you," she whispered.

"You're going to owe me another night," he stated, although a smirk slowly appeared to wipe away his expression of anger.

"It would be worth it," she said. "I would not mind."

He gave a start and then wrapped his arms around her shoulders. "Do not toy with me, Duchess."

"I would not. And I'm not," she countered. "I liked spending the night with you."

"But?"

She shrugged. "But nothing," she replied. "Other than I have a family I don't wish to be away from longer than is necessary." She sighed. "I didn't expect I would be homesick whilst on holiday."

He dipped his head. "If you did not have this family...?"

Charlotte blinked and then understood his query. "I... I would stay, I suppose. At least, until you grew bored with me..." She paused to wince. "Which I expect will be in three or four days."

His arms tightened their hold on her. "Charlotte," he whispered before his lips took hers in a crushing kiss.

Charlotte returned the kiss in equal measure, determined not to cower from him. His arousal was immediate, his hardening manhood apparent through his top coat and her gown. For a moment, she thought he might have his way with her right there on the garden lawn, and she knew she would do nothing to stop him. The fountain was immediately behind him, though, the rim of it deep enough to use as a bench.

When he finally pulled his lips away but left his forehead pressed to hers, she unhooked the buttons of his top coat and the fastening at the top of his pantaloons.

"What are you doing?"

"Sit down," she ordered as she helped to free his turgid manhood from the pantaloons. "I wish to make love to you."

His silver eyes rounding, Ziyaeddin did her bidding. He used both hands to grip the hem of her gown and lift it to her thighs before she climbed atop him, placing her knees on either side of him. His hands moved to the globes of her bottom as she impaled herself, lifting and lowering her hips until he was completely sheathed inside her.

Although the surrounding trees provided a canopy of leaves above them, a thought that someone might be paying witness to their carnal activity had Ziyaeddin ensuring that the veil that hung from the top of her hair hid any evidence of what they were doing.

He would have to discover who had arranged its delivery.

Thoughts of the veil left his mind when she lifted her hips again, her satin covered breasts sliding over his silk covered chest. The cold marble beneath them did nothing to cool their ardor, nor did the fine mist from the fountain spray.

Although she had begun the rhythm that would bring him his release in only a few minutes, it was his thumb pressed to where their two bodies met that sent Charlotte into oblivion immediately after.

Ziyaeddin watched in wonder as her head fell back and he heard his name spoken as if it were a prayer. He pulled her close and buried his face into the space between her neck and shoulder. Drunk on the scent of her perfume, his words of adoration were spoken in his native tongue.

*I*t might have been mere moments or even an entire hour before Charlotte realized her legs were falling asleep. Helping herself to the ruffled handkerchief poking out of one of his pockets, she held it against the top of her thighs and whimpered when she lifted her body off of his, his manhood not yet limp. "Apologies," she murmured, as she turned and wiped away the evidence of their joining.

"Why would you apologize for making love to me?" he growled, one of his arms keeping her steady until she found her footing.

Her lips trembled as she considered how to reply. "I did not ask."

"There was no need to ask," he replied. He put his garments to rights as Charlotte shook out her dinner gown. He glanced back at the fountain, chuckling when he realized they had been seated in front of the statue of the Danube River in Europe. "I will happily remember what we have done here every time I come to this fountain," he added. "I would not have thought to do such a thing here."

Charlotte managed a wan grin, glad the waning light hid her embarrassment. Noticing a sudden change in how the light illuminated the fountain, she faced west, her mouth dropping open in awe. The colors in the sunset matched her gown and her hair as a slight breeze had the purple veil billowing behind her.

Ziyaeddin stood and followed her line of sight. His gaze wasn't on the sunset nor even on Charlotte, but rather on the dock.

On the dock and on the ship pulling into it.

CHAPTER 21
A SON TO THE RESCUE

"*Gardiyan!*" Ziyaeddin called out at the top of his lungs as he raced to the garden gate. A guard appeared on the other side, and behind him, several others were already running towards the dock.

Ziyaeddin scrubbed his face with his hand as Charlotte joined him. "Is it the ship from The Netherlands?" she asked, remembering he had mentioned that one was due.

"It's Greek," he said with derision. "I cannot say for sure, but I think it is the same one that brought you here."

Charlotte gasped. "You think they've returned for the pirates they left behind?"

"They can have their bodies," Ziyaeddin growled, once they were beyond the gate. "You should return to your chamber," he added as his strides quickly carried him to the path that led down to the dock.

Not about to go back into the palace, Charlotte hurried after him. She couldn't help but notice his scowl when he realized she was nearly running to keep up with him. "I feel far safer with you than alone in the palace," she said between her labored breaths.

He slowed his pace, his brows furrowing at hearing her claim. Reaching for her hand, he placed it on his arm. When her confusion was evident, he said, "Then we shall watch from up here," he stated when he halted.

Charlotte stepped up next to him, her gaze finally turning to the deck of the Greek ship. She inhaled sharply. "It is the *Sun of Apollo,*" she said quietly. "But those aren't the pirates. Those men... they are the *crew,*" she added with excitement, her delight made more so when she recognized Captain Popodopolos. "They took back their ship."

"You are sure?" Ziyaeddin asked, his attention never leaving the deck. His guards had lined up at the end of the dock, their weapons at the ready.

"Captain Popodopolos is at the wheel," she replied. "I am so relieved he is not dead."

Ziyaeddin grumbled something unintelligible, and Charlotte glanced up at him. "He promised to see me delivered to Syros," she reminded him. "Apparently he intends to keep that promise."

The sultan finally tore his gaze from the ship to regard her with an expression that conveyed anger and betrayal. "He cannot take you," he hissed.

Reeling at hearing the anger in his voice, Charlotte understood almost immediately what he was thinking.

That she would break her bargain with him.

She placed a hand on the side of his face. "Ziyaeddin.

I owe you three nights, and you shall have them," she said quietly.

The sultan swallowed, his anger slowly ebbing away. He placed a hand over the one that she held to his face and then lifted it away and to his lips. He kissed her palm.

Charlotte inhaled softly at the sensation of his lips touching her there. Tremors darted beneath her skin, reminders of what they had been doing only a few moments before.

Shouts from below had the two of them turning to see young men racing down the ramp. "Mother!" one of them called out, one arm waving frantically.

"Mother?" she repeated in a whisper. Her eyes rounded. "That's James," she said in disbelief. "That's my son!" She gasped again. "And David. That's his friend. My best friend's son."

Ziyaeddin glanced between her and the dock, his impassive expression not giving away the turmoil he felt just then. "*Gardiyan*," he yelled.

One of the guards turned and ran up the steep path and then bowed before the sultan. Ziyaeddin gave him orders in Turkish.

His momentary surprise evident, the guard quickly recovered and said, "*Evet Sultanım.*" He once again bowed and then moved to rejoin his troops.

"What did you tell him?" Charlotte asked.

"They are to be given quarters and treated as guests," he replied on a sigh. "All of them."

Charlotte inhaled softly. "Oh, thank you, Your Highness," she said before she stood on tiptoes and kissed him on the cheek.

The gesture seemed to calm him, although he was obviously still bothered about something.

"Mother!" James said as he hurried up the hill. David was close on his heels, although his attention wasn't on Charlotte but rather on the sultan.

Charlotte rushed into her son's arms, squealing when his hold on her had her feet leaving the ground as he spun her in a circle. "James!" she half-scolded. "Oh, dear. Whatever are you doing here?" She leaned back. "Have you been eating enough?"

He laughed and kissed her on the cheek. "Enough, Mother. Are you all right?"

"I am, thanks to Sultan Ziyaeddin," she said as she waved a hand in the direction of the sultan. "He saved me from the pirates."

Meanwhile, David stood in awe before the sultan. "Your Highness," he said. He knelt before the ruler and kissed the hem of his topcoat before bringing it to his forehead. He glanced back up and added, "I am David Bennett-Jones, heir to the Bostwick viscountcy. Please, forgive our intrusion." He directed a grin at Charlotte. "How do, Your Grace?"

Ziyaeddin angled his head as his brows furrowed. "You are forgiven," he replied before he glanced in Charlotte's direction.

James hurried forward to perform the same ritual David had done with the sultan's topcoat. When he stood and stepped back, he said, "I am James Wainwright. Thank you for rescuing my mother, Your Highness."

His dark gaze critically surveyed the two young men for a time before Ziyaeddin finally said, "Cambridge men?"

James chuckled as a huge grin lit David's face. "Indeed, Your Highness," James replied. "We have met your sons."

Ziyaeddin's stern expression faltered. "Damnation," he muttered.

It was David's turn to laugh. "They do you proud, Your Highness."

Straightening, Ziyaeddin once again looked like the sultan he was as his attention went to the Greek sailors who slowly climbed the path. In the lead was their captain, whose own fierce gaze remained fixed on the sultan.

David moved to stand before Charlotte. He lifted her hand to his lips while James displayed a look of worry. He remembered the captain's tale about what had happened during the war and wondered how the sultan would react to being reunited with the man who had sunk his ship.

The young men stepped aside when Captain Popodopolos joined them.

"You look well, Sultan," Popodopolos said after he bowed. He didn't kneel nor show any other deference to the sultan.

"As do you, Poppy," Ziyaeddin replied as he held out an arm. The captain grasped it near the elbow, and the two hugged briefly before pounding one another on the tops of their shoulders.

Charlotte's eyes rounded at seeing their exchange. "You *know* one another?" she asked in a murmur.

"He sank my ship," Ziyaeddin stated, his expression stern.

"I rescued his crew," the captain countered with a shrug.

"I still hate him for it," said Ziyaeddin, although a smirk gave away his amusement.

"Your Grace, I cannot tell you how relieved I am to see that you are alive and well," Popodopolos said, his attention on Charlotte. He bowed and took her hand to his lips.

"I share in your relief, Captain. I was so worried about you and your crew. Am I to assume you dispatched the pirates?" she asked after she dipped a curtsy.

"We did," he replied. "Lost one of my crew in the sword fight," he added with a wince.

"How ever did you overcome them?" she asked in wonder.

He shrugged. "They put us in our own brig for the trip to Rhodes," he replied. "But... the brig was never completed before I took command last year. So... it was easy to escape."

Charlotte inhaled softly before she displayed a wan grin.

"Are you hungry?" Ziyaeddin asked of all those who stood before him.

"We're starving," Popodopolos replied. "Been going since sunset last night when we left Rhodes. I was about to order the cook to make us a meal."

"No need. Let us enjoy a feast in my dining room," Ziyaeddin said before he gave instructions in Turkish to one of the guards. The man bowed and hurried off.

Ziyaeddin set off with the captain at his side while Charlotte was flanked by the two young men. Behind them, the rest of the crew followed, word making its way through the group that they were guests rather than prisoners of the sultan.

"Do you suppose Sevinc and Ertuğrul—or any of your other children—could join us for dinner?" Charlotte asked as they made their way into the palace.

From Ziyaeddin's expression, it was evident he hadn't given a thought to inviting anyone else to the dinner. He waved a hand at a servant who hurried up to him and bowed. Instructions were given in Turkish, and the servant hurried off.

By the time they were seated on cushions in a large dining hall—Ziyaeddin at one end, Charlotte to his right, Captain Popodopolos, James, and David to his left, and the sailors taking up most of the remaining spaces—the long low table in front of them held a variety of dishes, and a number of female servants had appeared with bowls of water and linens so that each guest could wash their hands.

"How did this happen so quickly?" Charlotte asked in a whisper.

Ziyaeddin shrugged. "I ordered that it be done, and so it was," he replied. When he saw her look of awe, he quickly added, "There are nearly a two hundred people in the palace for every meal. Ten more at one dinner hardly matters." His attention went to David, whose gaze was caught by the mosaics on the ceiling. "Very few look up when they are in the palace. I see that you do."

David blinked. "Always, Your Highness. I have an

appreciation for architecture and the decorative arts. This palace is an amazing example of Seljuk architecture. That it still stands after over five hundred years is a testament to its designer," he remarked. "And the builders, of course."

Ziyaeddin gave him a nod. "I shall see to it you meet my son Ertuğrul. He oversees our buildings and is working on the designs for the next palace."

David's eyes rounded. "That would be magnificent, Your Highness."

Ziyaeddin lifted a disc of *pide* and tore it in half. He handed one piece to Charlotte and the other to James. When James saw how Charlotte tore her piece in half and passed it to the next person, he did the same. In the meantime, Ziyaeddin tore more pieces, and they were passed down the table until everyone had bread. Then the sultan indicated they should begin eating.

Aware that the empty cushion next to her was about to be occupied, Charlotte looked up to discover Sevinc had joined them. Dressed in coral *şalvar* and a deeper coral *entari*, she also wore an ornate headdress and drop earrings set with red gems.

Except for the sultan, all the men around the table stood upon realizing a young woman was in their presence.

"Your clothes are exquisite," Charlotte whispered as Sevinc knelt down.

"As are yours, Your Grace," Sevinc replied. "I had hoped the veil would be delivered in time."

Charlotte inhaled, her gaze darting between

Ziyaeddin and Sevinc. She had thought the sultan had sent it.

Sevinc turned her attention to her father. "Apologies, Baba," she murmured. "I came as soon as I received your invitation," she added. Her gaze swept the table as the men retook their seats, but it lingered on the two young men who sat across from her, one of them staring at her in wonder. "I see we have visitors. Welcome all," she added in a voice loud enough to be heard by the Greek sailors. Even though most of them didn't understand English, they seemed to understand the gist of her greeting.

"My daughter, Sevinc Sultana," Ziyaeddin said as he waved in her direction.

Sevinc nodded as the men around the table murmured their acknowledgments.

"Sevinc Sultana, may I introduce my son, James, and David Bennett-Jones, heir to the Bostwick viscountcy?" Charlotte said as she held out her hand in the direction of the two young men, well aware of how her son was staring at Sevinc. "Captain Popodopolos brought them here to... uh... rescue me," she added, indicating the ship's captain.

Sevinc bowed her head. "It's an honor to meet Englishmen and you, Captain Popodopolos," she said as her cheeks took on the same color as her outfit. Her expression suddenly changed. "Do you intend to take Duchess Charlotte away from us?"

"Not if you don't want me to," James replied in a faraway voice. He suddenly blinked and appeared flustered. "I... uh... you speak English," he managed to get out.

Sevinc grinned, darting a quick glance in Charlotte's direction. "I do. I learned because I had hoped to attend Cambridge University with my brothers," she replied.

"They don't take young ladies," David stated. "Which is unfortunate. We had occasion to meet your brothers, though. They play cricket quite well."

Her dark brows furrowing, Sevinc sighed. "Only because I taught them how."

Ziyaeddin chuckled. "My second daughter has been to England only once but seems determined to return there," he explained.

"Compared to here, it's very damp," David warned.

"I adore rain," Sevinc commented. "But I should also like to see the rest of the world. I can imagine only so much from the books I have read."

Charlotte had begun eating her soup but paused when she noticed how James continued to stare at Sevinc. "James," she scolded in a whisper.

He blinked and murmured an apology before turning his attention to the food before him. From the way he filled his plate and held his spoon, Charlotte realized he was already familiar with many of the dishes and the proper way to eat them.

Ziyaeddin, whose attention went briefly to James, furrowed a brow but addressed the Greek captain, and soon their conversation had the sailors settling in to enjoy their dinners.

Happy to have her son so close, Charlotte ate while he and David told her of their travels. Sevinc occasionally asked questions, her curiosity evident. When everyone claimed to have had their fill, cups of sherbet were brought by the servants and drunk with appreciation.

Another servant appeared to lead the sailors to their guest quarters for the night while yet another waited for James and David to finish their conversations with Charlotte and Sevinc.

"I suppose we can stay a few days longer," the captain said, obviously in response to something the sultan had said as the sailors looked to him for direction. "I sent my cargo on to Syros with another captain from Rhodes."

"So you and your crew shall stay as my guests," Ziyaeddin stated, as if he wouldn't consider another answer. "Join me on a hunt in the morning. The grouse have about taken over my lands. My servants will see to your crew."

"You expect me to miss the opportunity to bathe in your Turkish bath?" the captain countered as he displayed a teasing grin.

"We will bathe after we hunt," Ziyaeddin countered, sharing in Popodopolos' humor. He turned his gaze on James. "Lord James, will you join us as well? While Mr. Bennett-Jones meets with my architect?"

James opened his mouth to respond but directed his attention to his mother.

Charlotte nodded. "Of course you should go," she urged. "Perhaps when you return, His Highness will allow Sultana Sevinc to give you a tour of the palace."

Ziyaeddin's friendly expression faltered for a moment, but he said, "If she is in agreement—"

"I am, Baba," Sevinc said with a nod.

The sultan managed an impassive expression. "Then she will do so after our luncheon."

"Thank you, Your Highness. I am honored by your invitation," James replied.

Popodopolos finally nodded. "As am I. And I will stay. But then I really must depart for Syros," he said. "I've a schedule to maintain."

"I will send a servant when our hunt is ready to begin," Ziyaeddin said, rising to his feet. He held out a hand to Charlotte, and she allowed him to help her to stand.

"Thank you, Your Highness."

A servant approached James and David to lead them away. "Mother?" James asked as he slowly got to his feet, a look of worry aging his features. "What about you?"

"Parma and I have our own quarters," she said as she moved around the table to embrace him. "Sleep well, you two," she said, giving David a kiss on the cheek. "I'll see you at luncheon."

"We're to stay for three days?" James asked in a whisper.

She nodded. "Surely you can abide three days in a palace," she teased.

"How long have *you* been here?"

Inhaling softly, Charlotte managed a shrug. "A few days. It has not been a hardship, I assure you," she said, loud enough for Ziyaeddin to hear.

"I know I could stay here for far longer than three days," David said, his enthusiasm apparent. "Why, just documenting these tile patterns could take weeks."

Charlotte grinned, glad the young man would have

something to keep him occupied for a few days. She hoped James might discover something equally engaging. "Off to bed, you two."

Reluctantly, James turned to follow the servant, but he paused to speak to Sevinc. "I look forward to the tour, Your Highness."

Sevinc grinned. "You may call me Sevinc. May you have luck on the hunt." She covered her mouth with one hand as James took her other to his lips and kissed the back of it.

David followed suit as he bowed. "Your Highness."

"Good night," she said, giving the two a deep curtsy. She watched the young men take their leave before turning to discover her father staring at her. "Good night, Baba, Your Grace," she said, giving them a curtsy.

"Good night, daughter," he replied, suppressing a grimace.

"Sleep well," Charlotte said, glancing around to discover that with Sevinc's exit, she and the sultan were the only two left in the dining room. Stepping closer to him, she placed her head in the small of his shoulder and embraced him. "Thank you," she whispered.

Ziyaeddin didn't immediately return the hug, but finally wrapped one arm around her shoulder and kissed the top of her head. He took a deep breath, glad when the scent of her perfume enveloped him. "Will you join me in my bed?"

She glanced up in surprise. "Of course."

The assurance seemed to settle him somewhat. Without another word, he led them out of the dining room and to his private chamber.

They spoke not another word as they undressed one another. They were quiet as they moved to the bed. Before Charlotte could lie down, though, Ziyaeddin captured the side of her head with one hand and pulled her to him. He kissed her, open mouthed.

Charlotte did her best to return the kiss, her shock at his sudden move a surprise that had her mouth open to meet his. When he finally pulled away, he left his forehead pressed to hers. "What you did to me... at the fountain," he whispered.

Inhaling softly, Charlotte attempted to see him through the curtain of her lashes. "I've never done anything like that before," she claimed. "Outside. In the open like that." She sighed. "You're a terrible influence, you must know."

Ziyaeddin straightened, and whatever tension he had been exuding during their dinner seemed to leave him all at once. "I should like for us to do it again."

"Now?" Charlotte asked in alarm.

He chuckled. "Not now." His attention went to the balcony. "However..." Grabbing his dressing gown from the bed, he hurried to the balcony and spread the garment over the ledge of the stone railing.

"What are you...?"

Charlotte's query was cut off when he directed her to stand before him as he sat on the ledge. Even in the dark, Charlotte could see his manhood, already hard with his arousal, jutting from the dark nest of curls at the apex of his thighs.

"Are you quite sure about this?" she asked in a whisper, glancing over the edge. With only a waxing moon in the eastern sky, she couldn't make out the details of the ground below. "Someone could see us."

"It's dark. Don't look down," he warned, placing his hands on either side of her hips to lift her. "Open for me, Charlotte."

Her hands immediately went to his shoulders, gripping them until she could place her knees on either side of his thighs. Excitement at what they were about to do combined with her fear of falling made for a heady combination.

Already wet with anticipation, she impaled herself on his turgid cock, inhaling when his mouth covered one of her breasts. "Oh!" she gasped.

Despite her position, Charlotte allowed him to do most of the work of lifting and lowering her as he thrust into her. She was glad for the cooling night breeze that lifted the veil from her back and caressed her naked skin.

Afraid they would fall over the edge, she leaned back, her spine arching as her arms straightened. Ziyaeddin's low growl filled the quiet night as one of his hands gave up its hold on her bottom so he could press his thumb where their two bodies met.

Determined to remain quiet—she feared someone might hear them and appear on an adjacent balcony—Charlotte mewled through her ecstasy as a wash of warmth filled her lower body.

She continued to mewl as his arms wrapped around her and held her, his mouth covering one of her breasts.

His body jerked again and again when she repeatedly clenched his manhood, as if she intended to incite every possible bit of pleasure in their joining.

When his labored breaths evened out, Ziyaeddin moved his mouth to cover her other breast before he pulled away slightly and instead nibbled on her nipple.

Charlotte clung to him, her breaths uneven. Her mewls quieted to slight inhalations of breath and finally to a long sigh.

Sure he would fall asleep at any moment, Charlotte was about to straighten one of her legs when he stilled her movement with a hand. "Wrap your legs around me," he ordered.

Hesitating for a moment—she wasn't sure she could —Charlotte was about to put voice to a protest when he leaned to one side. "Ziyaeddin," she scolded, fearing he might fall backwards. But the move gave her the space she needed to straighten her leg and then wrap it around his back. When he leaned in the other direction, she did the same with the other leg and then hooked one foot around the other. In the dark, she could make out his huge grin. "What are you going to do?"

"Hang onto me," he said as he leaned forward and straightened from the balcony's ledge. With his cock firmly inside her and his arms wrapped beneath her bottom, he was able to make it to the bed.

"You've done this before," she accused.

His brows furrowed. "I have not," he responded. "Nor would I have thought to if you hadn't taken me at the fountain."

"Taken you?" she repeated as she displayed a brilliant smile. "Is that what you think happened?"

He chuckled. "No one has ever ordered me to sit down before."

She sobered slightly, stunned at how he stared at her. "There is a first time for everything, I suppose." She glanced down at the bed. "Now what?" He had made no move to let her down.

"Lie atop me. I wish to remain inside you," he murmured.

"All right," she agreed.

He backed onto the bed, and as her legs lowered to his thighs, he straightened. She felt the muscles in his arms bunch as he moved them farther onto the bed, and then she felt his entire body relax as he fell asleep.

Arranging the purple veil so it covered her backside, Charlotte settled onto his body, her head resting in the small of his shoulder. Given the excitement they had shared on the edge of the balcony, it was a long time before she closed her eyes and even longer before she finally succumbed to sleep.

CHAPTER 22

THE DECISION FOR A DAUGHTER IS MADE

The following morning
"I cannot stay abed this morning," Ziyaeddin whispered as he allowed the edges of the purple veil to slip between his fingers.

"You're going on a hunt," Charlotte murmured, remembering the arrangements that had been made over dinner. She stretched and rolled off his body, the veil wrapping itself around her torso.

He lifted himself onto one elbow and fingered the edge of the silk again. Charlotte noticed, wondering at his odd expression. "Sevinc had it delivered yesterday. It arrived only moments before you came for me."

Ziyaeddin gave a start, and he sat up. "Oh," he said before he grunted.

Charlotte's eyes narrowed. "From where did you think I got it?"

He stared at her a moment before he glanced away. "I did not know, and I admit it had me most vexed."

Sitting up on the bed, Charlotte stared at him. "Why didn't you simply ask me?"

He stood from the bed and made his way to the balcony to retrieve his dressing robe, the sight of his morning tumescence causing Charlotte's nipples to tighten. They stood out in silhouette behind the translucent silk of the veil, and Ziyaeddin noticed when he returned to stand next to the bed.

"I may have feared the answer," he grumbled.

She scoffed. "Who else would have given it to me?"

Ziyaeddin sat on the edge of the bed. "Word has reached my concubines that I have favored you these past few nights."

Charlotte inhaled softly. "Are they... jealous?" she asked in a whisper, watching as he turned his body and crawled toward her.

"Or they are relieved. I can never be sure with some of them," he murmured as he pulled one of her hands to his face and kissed the palm. He pressed his nose to her wrist and inhaled deeply, humming softly as the floral scent of her perfume filled his nostrils. A smirk lifted the corners of his lips, and he suddenly appeared years younger. "I have not visited the harem in a very long time, so I do not know their thoughts," he admitted. "However, they know better than to complain." He nudged her knees apart with one of his, and she lifted her knees to press them against his thighs.

"What happens if they do?" she asked, her voice breathy.

"I marry them off to someone in my..." He struggled for the English word.

"Cabinet?" she offered before he slid his cock along her wet folds until his sac pressed onto her womanhood. She gasped as he reversed direction until his tip was at her entrance.

"Cabinet," he affirmed. He thrust into her, and Charlotte arched her back in response, crying out his name as she clenched him.

He kept his arms straight as he thrust into her again and again, his moves quickening until his release had him stilling his body. His head thrown back, he growled as the cords in his neck became visible.

Charlotte watched in fascination, the morning light from the balcony casting him as a golden god. She could only hope it was doing her the same favor.

She guided his body down onto hers, grinning when he kissed the side of her neck. "When you said you were going hunting, I didn't think you meant for me."

He chuckled, but the reminder of the hunt had him rising. She hissed when he pulled his still engorged manhood from her body. Wrapped in the purple veil, Charlotte felt as if her entire body was quaking from the quick bout of lovemaking.

"I do hope you do not think of yourself as prey, my duchess," he remarked as he moved to dress. "But I shall be on the hunt for you again tonight."

Charlotte turned onto her side, holding her head up on a hand as her elbow pressed into the bed. She watched him pull on a pair of trousers and a shirt. "So you have not tired of me?" she asked, secretly glad when he gave her a quelling glance.

"There is still much for us to learn about one another," he replied as he pulled on a waistcoat and quickly buttoned it.

Hearing the rebuke in his voice, Charlotte decided to change the subject. "Thank you for allowing Sevinc to join us for dinner last night," she commented.

"It was good practice for her. She will need it in her role as a wife for one of my... cabinets."

Charlotte sat up in alarm. "Ministers... *viziers*," she corrected. "Does that mean you have decided on someone?" she asked in worry.

About to pull on a coat, Ziyaeddin paused. "I have."

"Does he know?"

"Not yet."

"Does *she* know?"

Ziyaeddin shrugged. "I have not told her who I have chosen, but she knows she is to marry." He narrowed his eyes. "Why do you look like that?"

Swallowing, Charlotte blinked a few times. "She is so inquisitive. So anxious to see the world. I do hope whoever you have chosen for her will appreciate her desire for knowledge."

Ziyaeddin sighed as he finished buttoning up his coat. He placed a simple turban on his head and straightened it before turning his attention back to Charlotte. "He will have to," he said, although his words did not sound convincing. Plucking a large silver ring from a nearby table, he thrust it onto one of his thumbs.

"What is that?" Charlotte asked.

He glanced down at his hand before lifting it in her direction. "My bow ring."

She blinked. "You're hunting with bow and arrows?" she asked in surprise.

It was Ziyaeddin's turn to blink. "I cannot use a sword."

Charlotte swallowed, hoping James had been practicing his archery.

"I must go." He leaned down and kissed her forehead before giving her a grin.

"Where is your cravat?" she asked. At his look of confusion, she said, "Neckcloth."

He scowled. "I am going hunting," he replied, as if that was answer enough. His silver eyes suddenly darkened. "I like you wrapped in a veil," he murmured. "I shall have another sent to you for tonight."

Charlotte felt the heat of a blush color her face. "Will I see you when you return for luncheon?"

"I will send for you," he said, leaning over to kiss her again on her forehead.

"I'll be ready," she replied. She watched him depart, the oddest sensation gripping her chest.

It was a long time before she dressed and left the sultan's bedchamber, her thoughts on their bargain.

Two more nights.

Surely he would grow bored of her after two more nights. Wouldn't he?

But what about her?

CHAPTER 23
A GARDEN LUNCHEON BRINGS NEWS

*L*ater that day
        Parma had just finished dressing her mistress in a pale yellow sprigged muslin gown when there was a knock at the door. "Oh, Your Grace. I haven't finished pinning up your hair," she said. While most of Charlotte's hair was captured in a loose bun atop her head, a large lock hung down over Charlotte's shoulder. Given there were only oil lamps by which to heat the curling iron, it took longer than usual to complete a coiffure.

"I quite like it like this," the duchess said, angling her head in both directions as she regarded her reflection in the mirror. "Reminds me of styles from the last century."

Parma answered the door to discover Sevinc on the other side.

"I am to escort Duchess Charlotte to luncheon," Sevinc said happily. "And to deliver this." She held out a bundle of blue silk.

"Another veil?" Charlotte asked as she joined the

sultana. Her day gown was a stark contrast to Sevinc's hunter green ensemble. She responded to the young woman's curtsy with one of her own. "The color of this is gorgeous," she remarked as she fingered the blue fabric. "I must thank your father for thinking of me." Handing the veil to Parma, she turned and was about to leave the room when she noticed Sevinc hesitating to join her. "What is it, My Sultana?"

"Your head," Sevinc whispered. "It must be covered, Your Grace," she said carefully. "Luncheon is being served outdoors. In the gardens."

"Oh, that sounds delightful," Charlotte replied, wondering if the choice of venue had been up to the sultan. "I'm quite sure I have something appropriate," she added. She returned to the dressing table as Parma retrieved a silk flowered hat from one of the trunks.

Sevinc watched in wonder as Parma pinned the hat into place on one side of Charlotte's coiffure. "There are times I wish I could wear such a hat," she murmured when Charlotte caught her reflection in the mirror.

"Why can't you?"

Dipping her head, Sevinc said, "They do not match with our clothes," she said as she held out her *entari* in one hand and her *şalvar* in the other.

"I have one that would be perfect for your ensemble," Charlotte argued, instructing Parma to retrieve the hat from her riding habit.

Sevinc grinned as Parma removed her headdress and set the hunter green hat in its place. "It's perfect," she announced, grinning at her reflection in the mirror.

The two left the chamber, Sevinc's arm hooked into

Charlotte's elbow. "Have you heard if the hunt was successful?" the duchess asked as they made their way down the steps to the atrium.

"I was watching from a balcony when the men returned," Sevinc admitted. "They appeared to have a goodly number of birds." She dipped her head and added, "Lord James rides well."

Charlotte grinned. "He should. He's been riding horses since he was three years old," she said. "But I don't think he's hunted with a bow and arrow."

They emerged from the palace into sunshine and a pleasantly warm day. "It's like a summer day in England," Charlotte commented as they passed through the iron gate of the gardens. A low table and cushions had been arranged on the largest open area of the garden, and several gentlemen stood about conversing. Although the sound of the fountain was evident, it wasn't in sight.

Upon seeing Charlotte, the sultan was quick to step away from two younger men to take her hand to his lips.

Charlotte's eyes rounded at seeing him perform the courtesy. "Your Highness," she murmured as she curtsied. "I trust you have had a good hunt?"

"There shall be grouse for everyone in the palace for this evening's dinner," he replied in a loud voice. He turned his attention on his daughter, who smiled broadly as she took his hand to her lips and then to her forehead.

The happy expression on Ziyaeddin's face faltered when he noticed his daughter's manner of headdress. "I suppose this was your idea?" he asked as he fingered the brim of the green felt.

Sevinc shook her head, her eyes darting in Charlotte's direction. "I admit to saying I wished I could wear a hat."

"I think it's perfect with her clothes, Your Highness," Charlotte stated. "Don't you?"

He lowered his voice. "You might have warned me about your son's ability with a bow. He took more birds than I," he complained.

Blinking, Charlotte's attention went to her son, who was making his way in her direction. "I knew he was proficient in archery, but I had no idea he could hunt with a bow," she replied in awe. Joshua had taken her sons hunting many times, but always with guns.

"Mother," James said with a grin. He kissed her cheek. "You look as if you could be one of the flowers in this glorious garden." He turned his gaze onto Sevinc. "And you the loveliest, Sultana Sevinc."

Tittering, Charlotte felt heat color her cheeks as her gaze caught the sultan staring at her. "Careful, James, or we will assume you are after a favor," she said.

James moved to stand before the sultana. "I look forward to your tour this afternoon, Your Highness," he said as he took her hand to his lips and brushed them over her knuckles..

"As do I," Sevinc replied, dipping a curtsy.

"May I have the honor of escorting you to a seat?" he asked as a line of servants appeared bearing trays and bowls of food. They distributed them along the length of the table and then just as quickly disappeared.

Sevinc nodded and the two stepped away as Ertuğrul and David approached.

"Your Grace," David said as he bowed and took her hand. "Your Highness."

"Good afternoon, David, Ertuğrul," she replied. "Have you had your fill of architecture this morning?" she asked, remembering David was to spend time with the sultan's son.

"Hardly, Aunt Charlotte," he replied with a chuckle. "Ertuğrul has several projects in the works in all manner of architecture. Hard to believe for someone who is only twenty years old."

"There are others besides the new palace?" she asked.

"My son is designing what will be our first bank and has already designed our first university," Ziyaeddin remarked.

Ertuğrul jerked upon hearing the pride in the sultan's voice. "It is my honor to do so, My Sultan," he said.

Charlotte wondered about the nearly inaudible huffing sound Ziyaeddin made before he said, "Come. Let's be seated."

Having taken a walk about the gardens, Captain Popodopolos joined them as his sailors were led into the gardens by a servant. From their fresh clothes and scents, it was apparent they had retrieved clothes from their ship and had taken advantage of the Turkish baths.

"Captain, did you enjoy the hunt?" Charlotte asked when he bowed before her. He was dressed much like he had been during their dinners on the ship.

"It was a unique diversion for me," he replied as he moved to his seat to the right of the sultan. "Can't say I was especially effective."

"He shot as many birds as I did," Ziyaeddin claimed as he knelt on the cushion at the end of the table.

"Like I said...," the captain teased, the huge grin on his face making it apparent the two had enjoyed their outing. He turned his attention to Charlotte. "Your Grace, I need a moment to speak with you about our... our schedule."

"Oh?" she responded as James assisted her to kneel.

"There is a storm approaching from the west. Given the direction of the winds, the tide, and the fair weather, I have decided we must depart for Syros tonight," he murmured.

A moment of uncertainty had Charlotte darting a glance in the sultan's direction. She was sure he knew of the change in the plans, but his impassive expression didn't give away his thoughts on the matter. "But... I cannot be ready to leave that soon," she argued. "Besides..." She turned first to David and then to James, wondering if they knew of the captain's plans. Both had their attentions on their food and on Ertuğrul and Sevinc, with whom they seemed to have shared a private joke. "I have accepted His Highness' invitation to stay for at least two more days," she added. She stared at Ziyaeddin until he locked gazes with her. His silver eyes seemed to blaze under the midday sun, but she couldn't discern if they did so in anger or lust or something else. "Unless of course, he has... changed his mind." She almost said, "Grown bored with me."

Ziyaeddin's almost imperceptible shake of his head had Charlotte dipping hers. She had an opportunity right then and there to accept the offer of an early departure from the palace. A chance to continue on her holiday or return to England once they reached Syros.

Or stay two more nights.

She owed Ziyaeddin at least that much. She didn't wish to risk angering him, nor have him thinking ill of her. The oddest sensation flitted in her chest at the thought of leaving him now.

"Captain, I shall find other means of traveling to Syros," she said. "Of course, Lord James and Mr. Bennett-Jones—"

"Are welcome to stay here as long as they'd like," Ziyaeddin stated.

At her mention of their names, the two young men looked up in confusion. "What's this?" James asked in a whisper.

His gray brows furrowing slightly, Captain Popodopolos glanced between Charlotte and the sultan. "If you're sure," he said.

Feeling lighter than she had in days, Charlotte gave him a grin. "I am, Captain. Being here at the palace has been a rather auspicious start to my holiday, and I shouldn't want it to end too early." She said this last in a louder voice, intending for everyone at the table to hear it.

"Do I understand you correctly, Your Highness? You're inviting us to stay?" David asked, hope in his voice.

"I am," Ziyaeddin replied with a nod.

David exchanged a quick glance with Ertuğrul before he said, "I am honored, Your Highness, and I should like very much if I might continue my study of your palace.

Of the plans for your new buildings," he said with excitement.

"What about you, James?" Charlotte asked, well aware his gaze had settled on Sevinc.

"I... I would be happy to stay," he replied. "Whilst on our hunt earlier today, I have discovered a number of Ancient Greek sites near here," he said. "I should like to study them. After my tour of the palace, of course," he added, his attention darting to Sevinc. "Or perhaps we could go this afternoon."

Ziyaeddin spread out his arms, his manner entirely different from when they had taken their seats around the table. "Ah, it is settled then. Please, eat," he said.

Charlotte's gaze stayed on the sultan until he once again glanced in her direction. One of his brows furrowed in question.

She gave him a grin. "Thank you. And thank you for the gift."

He straightened on his cushion as he acknowledged her with a nod, and then he resumed eating.

Buoyed by the fair weather and the good food, conversations resumed around the table in three languages until a servant appeared. He stood off to one side until Ziyaeddin finally waved him over.

They exchanged words in Turkish, but Charlotte could tell the sultan was annoyed by the news.

"I must return to the palace," Ziyaeddin announced, the words said in a growl. "But please, continue eating, and do not stand up on my account."

Charlotte angled her head to catch his attention as he

was about to walk past her. "Is everything all right?" she asked in a whisper.

He leaned down, his lips close to her ear when he said, "I've an appointment with my... my minister of agriculture," he whispered, briefly stumbling on the word for one of his cabinet members. "I will come for you for dinner."

A frisson skittered down Charlotte's spine. "I look forward to it, Your Highness."

She watched him go, and when she was turning her attention back to her plate, she found Sevinc grinning in delight.

Although she blushed when she realized others had noticed the sultan's attention on her, Charlotte returned Sevinc's grin and resumed eating.

CHAPTER 24
YOUNG LOVE

*L*ater *that afternoon*

As David and Ertuğrul set off for the work-room the latter had adopted as his office, Captain Popodopolos and the Greek sailors headed for the *Son of Apollo*. Only Charlotte, James, and Sevinc remained in the gardens.

During the luncheon, it had become evident to Charlotte that the two young people enjoyed one another's company. They conversed easily about Ancient Greek artifacts, Roman ruins, and Egyptian pyramids.

"Perhaps Sevinc could take you on that tour of the palace now," Charlotte suggested, deciding she would like the gardens to herself for a time. "Or mayhap to the Ancient Greek ruins near here."

James regarded Sevinc for only a moment. "Could you?" he asked. "I understand there must be a chaper-one," he added, as if he expected Sevinc would beg off for that reason.

"It would be my honor, my lord," she said happily.

Easily rising from his place at the table, James hurried to the other side to assist Sevinc to her feet. "Should I speak with your father? Or... or someone else?" he asked nervously.

She grinned at seeing his anxious manner. "One of the eunuchs will accompany us."

James' happy expression faltered for a moment. "Do you mean that barrel-chested man over there whose arms appear to be the size of a ham shank?"

Sevinc followed his line of sight and giggled. "Him, yes," she said before turning her attention on Charlotte. "May we have your permission to leave the table, Your Grace?"

"You have it," Charlotte replied. "However, my son must help me up first," she added.

James held out a hand and easily lifted his mother from her cushion. "Do you wish me to escort you anywhere before we take our leave?" he asked.

She shook her head. "I'm going to remain in the gardens for a time," she replied. "You go on."

Sevinc curtsied and James bowed before he offered his arm to the young lady.

Glancing at it at first with confusion, Sevinc's face suddenly brightened. "I have seen this done in England," she murmured. She placed her arm on his, her shoulders lifting as her head dipped with her excitement.

The two walked though the gate and were met by the eunuch, whose dark expression had James halting.

"The sultan's guest, Lord James, wishes to visit the site of the Greek ruins, and I have been instructed to guide him there," Sevinc claimed in Turkish.

His brows furrowing, the eunuch regarded the two with suspicion for a moment before he loudly sighed in resignation and waved one beefy arm. "I will follow," he replied, his voice higher than James would have expected of a man his size.

Sevinc provided directions for a few turns, but once they were off the palace grounds and on the path to the ruins, James knew the way from his time on the hunt earlier that morning.

"Is it true you shot more grouse than my father?" Sevinc asked.

James winced. "I did, but I tried not to," he claimed. "I do not think the sultan's mind was on the hunt, though," he added. "He was..."

"Distracted?" Sevinc offered, when he seemed at a loss for words.

"Yes. I thought perhaps there was a matter of state that had him worried."

Sevinc sighed. "He has been not himself of late," she said, struggling with finding the English words to describe her father.

"Is something wrong?" James asked, worry evident in his voice.

"I think he feels his mortality," she replied. "And he misses... constancy." She shook her head. "I don't think that's the right word."

"Has something happened that has interrupted the constancy of the empire?" James asked, deciding he could reassure her by using the same verbiage.

"Other than the loss of more lands, no," she replied.

"He does not seem anxious to go to war to keep them," James murmured.

"He is not. And although owning more lands means more taxes can be collected, the costs of keeping those lands are sometimes higher than the taxes which are collected."

"You cannot run a country at a deficit," James agreed. "Just as my brother cannot run the Chichester dukedom at a loss. But I suppose others may not see it that way."

"Exactly!" Sevinc said with excitement.

James blinked, rather glad he had said something she seemed to find profound. "I suppose running an empire is not much different than running a dukedom," he hedged. "Although the scale is obviously much larger."

Sevinc stared up at him in awe. "How is education handled on a dukedom?"

Chuckling, James said, "Well, tutors at first, then public school, then university," he replied. "But the public school and the university are not run by the dukedom but rather by the state..., uh, by the *country*," he explained. "Does the Ottoman Empire have a university?"

She shook her head. "Not yet, but my brother Ertuğrul has designed one based on the one in Paris."

"Your brother...Ertuğrul. You seem to get along rather well with him, but am I understand you were not raised together?"

Sevinc dipped her head. "He is my twin—"

"Twin?" James interrupted. His eyes narrowed. "There is a resemblance."

"We have the same eyes. I have been told they are the

same as my mother's were," Sevinc said with a wan grin. She lowered her voice. "Since our real mother died, Ertuğrul and I were raised by different women in the harem. When we learned we had the same birthdays, it was easy to sort that we were twins, since my Father loved only our mother and no one else for over a year."

"Why not just tell you?" James asked in confusion.

She shrugged. "I don't know, and I've never asked. Ertuğrul said there must be a reason, but he is never in good stead with our father, so has never broached the subject."

James furrowed a brow. "Ertuğrul is so knowledgable. So good at what he does... I cannot imagine why he wouldn't be in good stead with the sultan."

Sevinc once again dipped her head. "Our mother died the day after giving birth to us. I was the first, and then I think something must have gone wrong. Ertuğrul survived, but just barely," she explained. "I cannot help but think Baba blames him for her death."

Wincing, James shook his head. "Hardly fair to blame a babe," he replied quietly. "Especially when he's... what? Twenty years old?"

She nodded. "Twenty and the architect of several buildings," she said proudly. "Baba has already decided that two universities shall be built here in the empire. One in Konya and one in Constantinople."

"Will you be able to attend one of them?" James asked.

Inhaling to answer, Sevinc suddenly furrowed her dark brows. "Baba has not said," she replied in a faraway voice.

"You would put all the male students to shame, Sultana Sevinc. You are the most clever woman I have ever met," he claimed.

Sevinc stared up at him, her steps slowing. "Clever?" she repeated. "Is that...?"

"It's a compliment, My Sultana," he replied, hoping to set her mind at ease. His gaze swept the grounds before them. "We're here," he said, noticing a line of short columns that had at one time been the bases for much taller versions. "This must have been a temple," he reasoned, as he led them along the phalanx of short marble cylinders.

"But for which god?" Sevinc asked, one of her brows arching.

James counted the column bases and began pacing out the length of the temple's foundation. He turned to the right and frowned, seeing only one more column base in the distance. He led them to it, counting his exaggerated paces as he did so. Glancing to his right again, he spotted several that were in line with the first set of columns. Sevinc giggled as she struggled to keep up. "Do you count thirteen on the long sides?"

"Indeed," James agreed, repeating his pacing for the last side. "I believe there were six on the short sides." He finally came to a halt and said, "Which means this was likely a temple to Zeus." He regarded her for a moment. "Did I get it right?"

Sevinc blinked and shrugged. "I do not know," she replied with a grin. "That's why I asked you."

James laughed and pulled her into an embrace. "Oh, you minx," he said before he realized the eunuch had nearly reached them, his expression suggesting James was about to suffer some sort of punishment for having touched the sultana.

He let her go and quickly stepped back, his hands in the air. "Apologies!" he called out.

"*Durmak!*" Sevinc shouted, holding up one hand in the direction of the eunuch.

The eunuch slowed his pace, his labored breaths loud. He said something in Turkish, but Sevinc shook her head. She said more to the servant, her manner suggesting annoyance. Reluctantly, the eunuch stepped back, but his murderous gaze remained squarely on James.

"Was that because I... because I hugged you?"

Sevinc nodded. "I did not mind... but touching a woman in Baba's harem is not allowed," she explained.

"Harem?" he repeated. "How are you—?"

"All of my sisters, our mothers, his sisters before they married, some of their mothers, the female servants, his other concubines... we are all members of his harem," she explained.

James pulled his head back, which briefly made him appear as if he had a double chin. "Oh," he finally said. Remembering the sultan's behavior with his mother, he frowned. "Tell me, Sultana Sevinc. Is my mother part of his harem now?" he asked in a whisper.

Sevinc blinked. "He would like her to be," she replied. "She would be his favorite. Has been his favorite. Ever since her arrival," she admitted. "I think he has fallen in love with her."

James swallowed. "Is she in love with him?"

Her head angling to one side, Sevinc winced. "She

misses her family. She says she cannot stay away from England any longer, even though her holiday was supposed to last two years." She straightened. "Tell me, my lord—"

"James. You can call me James," he offered.

"James," she repeated before a wan grin lifted her lips. "Are all women in England as vexing to their husbands as your mother is to my baba? With their... contradictions?"

Blinking, James couldn't help the burble of laughter that suddenly erupted. "I suppose some are," he hedged. "But my mother..." He paused and furrowed his brows. "I have never known her to contradict herself. She's usually very steadfast. Knows exactly what she wants, and sees to it she gets it," he explained. "Knows exactly what to do, as well. I suppose she's had to be like that as a duchess. Decisive."

The two meandered to another set of ruins. "She has told my father she must leave so she can resume her holiday. Then she told him she must return to England because she is needed there," Sevinc explained. "She told me she had not expected to feel homesick when she left on her holiday, and that is why she wishes to return to England. She..."

Blinking, Sevinc hesitated in saying anything else, although she had been about to tell him what Charlotte had told her over tea. That the duchess was of the opinion the sultan would grow bored with her and turn his attentions to another concubine.

Rather than wait for that day to come, she supposed the duchess was merely guarding her heart. She was sure the woman was in love with her father. She had seen tears in her eyes when they spoke of him.

James scoffed. "She is a *mother*," he stated, as if that's what Sevinc had been about to say. "Of course she is of a mind to think my older brother and his wife need her, but..." He swallowed. "They really don't. John's wife Arabella is the daughter of a marquess, and well versed in the responsibilities of a duchess," he explained. "And, yes, Arabella is due to have a babe by Christmastide, but my mother's presence won't be required. I'm quite sure Arabella's mother will be there."

"Then you would not mind if your mother stayed here?" Sevinc asked in a quiet voice. "When you resume your holiday?"

His gaze on a marble block, James thought about her query for a moment before he shook his head. "I would not," he replied, but his expression appeared troubled.

"What is it, James?" she asked, her attention going to the marble block, thinking that perhaps he was bothered by something about it. "It's Parian marble," she said, a fingertip tracing one of the visible veins in the stone.

"I wonder how long your father intends to host David and me? I shouldn't want to overstay our welcome—"

"We do not return to Constantinople for another month or more," Sevinc interrupted. "Not until it's too warm to stay here. I am quite sure you would be welcome until then, and maybe even at one of the palaces in Constantinople after that," she claimed.

"*One* of the palaces?" he repeated. "How many are there?"

"Three," she said with a grin. "It will be four after the next one is built."

James stared at her for several seconds. "I would only wish to go to the one where you are in residence," he murmured, his gaze going from the marble to her. "You're terribly lovely."

Sevinc blinked. "Terribly?" she repeated, her happy expression faltering.

"Forgive me," he said, giving his head a shake. "You are *very* lovely," he corrected. Then he dipped his head, realizing what he had said aloud. He moved one of his hands to the back of his neck as if to scratch it.

"Thank you," she murmured, a blush suffusing her face. "When I told your mother I wished to live in England, she said that all the young men at a ball would wish to dance with me."

"That's because they would," James replied. "Me included. I would only be allowed two dances with you, though, but you can be assured they would be both be waltzes."

Sevinc's eyes widened. She was about to say something when the eunuch moved closer.

James noticed and immediately offered his arm. "There may be the remains of a theatre over here," he remarked in a loud voice, pointing toward the edge of the ruins.

Giggling, Sevinc allowed him to lead her to the edge of a large depression. "You are right about it being a theatre," she said, indicating a curved line of marble blocks that marked the top row of seats. She pointed off in the distance, where the shoreline came into view. "And the foundations for some houses are along that ridge. There are even some broken statues," she added. "I think one of them might be Artemis, but I could not be sure."

Following her line of sight, James inhaled sharply. "I might have to stay for an entire month just to study all of this," he breathed. "Perhaps you would be able to... assist?"

Sevinc dipped her head. "You will have to ask my father. I will ask permission for myself, but he will wish to know your intentions," she said.

"And if my intentions are...?" He swallowed.

"Honorable?" she offered.

He blinked. "Well, they would be honorable, of course," he hedged. "But also... selfish."

Her brows rising in confusion, Sevinc stared at him. "Selfish?"

"Tell me, Sevinc. How old are you?"

"Twenty years," she replied.

"Are you betrothed to anyone?"

It was her turn to swallow. "Not that I know of," she replied. "But my father does plan to marry me off to one of his viziers." When she saw him struggling to understand, she said, "Ministers of his cabinet."

"Oh, God, no," James whispered.

"What is it?"

"You are the most clever girl I have ever met. And the loveliest. I would never grow tired of seeing you when I awaken every morning," he blurted. "Something tells me you would even enjoy joining me on these treks," he added, waving to the ruins surrounding them.

Sevinc inhaled softly, her gaze darting between his

eyes and his lips. "Oh, I would. Very much," she whispered.

"I really wish I could kiss you right now," he said, his eyes darting to where the eunuch was leaning against a marble block, obviously bored.

Her gaze followed his and she shook her head. "He will hurt you," she warned. "And then my father will—"

"Then I shall have to be satisfied with only imagining it," he interrupted.

"And so shall I," she replied sadly.

James nodded and began walking down the center of what had been the theatre seats. He led them to a line of columns that would have been the front of the theatre. When they were behind one of them, he stopped and placed his hands on either side of her face. He kissed her forehead, much like what he'd seen the sultan do to his mother.

Grinning, Sevinc crossed over to the next column. When James was hidden from the eunuch, she did the same to him, standing on tiptoe in order to kiss James' forehead.

"Is there any chance at all I could be your husband?" he asked as they wandered to the base of what had been the theatre's propylaea.

Sevinc's eyes rounded. "You wish me to be your wife?" she asked in surprise.

He nodded. "You are the daughter of a sultan, so I believe you would have to be the one to propose marriage to me, would you not?"

Giggling even as tears pricked her eyes, Sevinc shook her head. "If only that were true," she replied. "I would have proposed marriage the moment you took me into your arms," she claimed.

James blinked. "I accept," he said as a huge grin lightened his face. He glanced around, in search of the eunuch, and when he was sure they were out of sight from him, he pulled her into an embrace and kissed her.

The first touch of their lips was tentative, the two testing what to do until their heads were angled just so. All at once, their lips locked and James moaned his appreciation as Sevinc lifted a hand to the side of his face. She purred and pulled away to stare up at him.

The sound of heavy footsteps crunching through the stone-littered sight had James stepping back and turning to stare at the marble. "I should like our house to be made from Parian marble," he remarked casually as he lifted one of his hands to a seam, pretending to study how the blocks had been joined.

Understanding his scheme to make it appear as if nothing had happened between them, Sevinc moved to an adjacent block of marble and did the same. "It would appear white in the midday sun," she replied with a grin. "But keep us cool in the summers."

A nearby grunt had James turning to discover the eunuch regarding him with annoyance, his huge arms crossed over his chest. "Excuse me, sir, but do you speak English?" he asked.

Sevinc giggled. "He does not," she said. "Very few in the palace do," she added. "What did you wish to tell him?"

"I didn't wish to tell *him* anything, My Sweet Sultana,"

James replied. "I want to verify he doesn't understand me when I tell you that I'm in love with you."

Dipping her head, Sevinc gave him a brilliant smile. "Is this when I'm supposed to say you are a... a bounder?" she asked as her brow crinkled.

James laughed and said, "But I am *your* bounder and no one else's."

They might have continued their words of affection, but the sun had begun its descent into the Aegean Sea.

"We have to go back," Sevinc said, sobering. "It will be dark soon."

Disappointed but aware she spoke the truth, James once again offered his arm, and they hurried off toward the palace. The eunuch followed, but he stayed much closer than he had on their way to the ruins.

"I will request an audience with your father," James said as they made their way. "To ask his permission to marry you."

"I will do what I can. To encourage him to consider it," Sevinc promised. "But..." She gave a shrug. "If he has already promised me to someone else..." She didn't complete the sentence, but it was apparent she feared it might be too late for them.

"I will beg if I must," James claimed as they rounded the path that led to the palace entrance.

A brilliant sunset colored the western sky, and as they paused to watch, James wondered why there had been talk of an impending storm.

CHAPTER 25

CONVERSATIONS IN THE GARDENS

*E*arlier, in the gardens

Charlotte watched her son and Sevinc depart through the iron gate, a wan grin the only sign of her conflicted thoughts as she wandered the garden paths. From the moment Sevinc had appeared for dinner the night before, it was apparent James had a crush on the sultana's daughter.

Given she was seated next to Sevinc both for dinner and that day's luncheon, Charlotte wasn't sure how Sevinc felt about James. There had been some shyness between the two, even though it wasn't usually how James behaved among young ladies.

He tended to be outgoing. He made friends easily. He was certainly less serious than his older brother, but she supposed as the spare heir, James knew he wouldn't have the same responsibilities as John.

How much they might share with one another—other than thoughts about Greek ruins—had her wondering if

Sevinc would tell him what she knew of the sultan and Charlotte sharing a bed.

She was about to take a seat on the edge of the fountain when Captain Popodopolos appeared.

"Captain," she said in surprise.

He approached and bowed before her. "Your Grace." He held out a small box he had clutched in one hand. "I believe this belongs to you."

Charlotte's eyes rounded at seeing her jewel box. "Oh! I thought the pirates would have taken it," she said as she took the box.

"Your son found it under a table but left it in your cabin."

"I may have helped it to fall to the floor and then kicked it under the table during the scuffle with the pirates," she admitted as she undid the latch and opened it. Although the jewels inside were tossed about, there weren't any missing. "They're all paste, so it wouldn't have been a terrible loss had they been taken," she remarked. "Thank you for bringing it to me."

Popodopolos nodded. "I've also come to discover if you might have changed your mind about staying. It's not too late if you have. I can have your trunks brought on board—"

"I am staying," Charlotte replied, motioning for him to join her on the fountain's bench. "Sultan Ziyaeddin has invited the boys to remain as his guests, and they are both happy to stay for entirely different reasons."

"And you?" he asked gently.

Charlotte sighed. "At first, I wished to leave as soon as I could. After what happened with the pirates, I wanted to return to England, but at the same time, I wanted to resume my holiday," she said on another sigh. "I wanted to see all the sights. I was so torn. I have never been like this," she claimed.

"Like this?" he repeated.

"Indecisive," she replied. "Wishy-washy," she added on a sigh.

"And now?"

She turned to regard him with confusion. "Truth be told, I'm still not sure what to do. Ziyaeddin has invited me to stay here at the palace. Make it part of my holiday. I agreed to remain here for a few days, and then you arrived to rescue me."

The captain chuckled. "Don't take this the wrong way, but when I learned the pirates planned to sell you to him, I knew you would be in good hands, if indeed he was in residence."

Staring at him in wonder, Charlotte furrowed a brow. "Then... why did you come back for me?"

Humor once again lightened the captain's face. "Three reasons," he replied. "I made a promise to Mr. McElliott that I would see to your safe arrival on Syros."

"I'm absolving you of that promise," Charlotte stated.

"Your son and his friend were quite adamant that you be rescued, and another captain agreed with them. He took my cargo to Syros on my behalf."

"And?" she prompted.

He grimaced. "If the sultan hadn't been in residence at this particular palace, the pirates would have sold you to a slave trader or to someone else," he stated. "I could not live with myself if I discovered that had happened."

"Even if slavery isn't allowed in this empire?" she asked in dismay.

Giving her a quelling glance, the captain didn't respond.

"That was rather naïve of me to say, I suppose," she murmured. They sat in silence for a moment before she asked, "How is it you two can be friends after what happened? Did you really sink his ship during the war?"

He grinned as he nodded. "One of the best days of my life," he claimed as he chuckled. "One of the worst, too," he added as he sobered. "Lost a lot of crew. Both of us did. But we respected one another. Learned to trust one another. I brought him here—to this palace—when we knew for sure the war was over," he explained. "Times were tough, and when I couldn't find a husband for my daughter, he agreed to hire her as a servant," he added on a sigh.

Charlotte inhaled sharply. "Elena?" she guessed.

He nodded. "The fourth reason why I agreed to come back. I'm welcome to see her whenever Ziyaeddin is in residence here," he explained.

"You hardly had any time to spend with her," Charlotte lamented.

"Oh, I had enough. Last night after dinner. Then again this morning during breakfast. Before the hunt."

Charlotte blinked. "Then I suppose she told you about me and..." She blinked again, this time in an attempt to stave off tears.

"He's not a bad man, Your Grace," Popodopolos remarked. "And according to my daughter, he's quite fond of you."

"His daughter Sevinc Sultana says that as well," she murmured.

"Well, you might consider putting him out of his misery," Popodopolos remarked. "Until this morning, I'd never been on a hunt with him when he bagged the fewest birds of all of us," he claimed. "His mind definitely wasn't on hunting."

Charlotte blinked. "How do you know his mind was on me?" she asked.

The captain chuckled and stood. "Because he told me," he said as he turned to face her. Giving her a bow, he took her hand to his lips and kissed the back of it. Without another word, he took his leave of the gardens.

Staring after the captain in wonder, Charlotte was about to resume her tour of the gardens when she realized she wasn't alone.

"Please pardon my interruption, Duchess Charlotte," Ertuğrul said as he bowed.

Charlotte dipped a curtsy. "Why, you're not interrupting at all. I was just saying my farewells to Captain Popodopolos," she added. "Please, join me," she said as she waved to the fountain. Her eyes suddenly rounded. "Oh, dear. Has David driven you out of your office? I know he can be—"

"He has not, Your Grace. He is tracing tile patterns in the baths," he said as he held up a hand. "And I appreciate his presence. He is quite knowledgable, and he has very good ideas."

They settled onto the marble ledge of the fountain. "He comes by it naturally," she said with a grin. "His grandmother is Italian. He has been to the Kingdom of the Two Sicilies twice in his life and is about to return again as part of his Grand Tour," she added. She frowned when she noticed Ertuğrul's expression. "But that's not why you've come out here," she guessed.

"I wished to thank you for speaking to the sultan. On my behalf," he said. "I am responsible—"

"It was not your fault," Charlotte stated. "I only wished to be sure your father didn't blame you, and besides, you saw to it the pirates were... dispatched," she added, attempting to hide the wince she knew appeared whenever the pirates were mentioned. The young man had killed them, and she briefly wondered if it had been the first time in his life that he had taken another's.

"He told me as much," Ertuğrul said. He dipped his head, as if he was hesitating with his next words.

"What is it?" she prompted.

"I could not help but overhear what the captain told you. About the sultan and his regard for you."

Charlotte blinked. "Oh," she replied. Unsure of his position on the matter, she asked, "Does it bother you? That a complete stranger has shown up out of nowhere and apparently driven your father to complete distraction?"

He gave a start. "Not at all, Your Grace. I merely wondered why it has taken so long for you to come into the sultan's life," he said as one of his brows arched.

It was Charlotte's turn to give a start. "You say that as if you think it was my destiny," she accused.

"Do *you* not think that?" he countered. "He has been waiting a very long time for you. And now that you're here, you seemed determined to leave—"

"'I've agreed to stay for a time," she countered.

"But not for the rest of your life."

Charlotte inhaled sharply. "I have not been asked to do so," she said, attempting to keep annoyance from sounding in her voice. "Probably because your father knows that wanting something is sometimes more satisfying than the having. That he will grow bored with me—"

"He will not, Your Grace. He loves you," Ertuğrul said in a hoarse whisper. "I believe he loves you as much as he did my mother."

Dumbstruck, Charlotte stared at the emir. How was it that three people could make the same claim in two days? That they all seemed so sure of Ziyaeddin's regard for her? How?

"Did he ask that you speak with me?"

Ertuğrul's eyes widened. "Never, Your Grace. He would be angry with me if he learned I was here."

"He does have an odd temper," Charlotte remarked.

"But he's not a bad man."

Charlotte inhaled softly. "I didn't say that he was."

"Yet, you seem hesitant to stay." He lifted his arms and turned in the direction of the palace. "You could have the run of this place," he claimed. "A duchess like you? You could run the next one. Be the *Valide Sultan.*"

Furrowing her brows in confusion, Charlotte stared at Ertuğrul, realizing almost at once he was attempting a different tactic with her. "What are you saying?" she asked, suspicious.

"Since his mother died last year, there is no one to oversee his harem. No one to oversee the running of the... the household," he struggled to get out. "The eunuchs do what they must, but a powerful woman really should be in charge."

"Did he tell you this?"

"He didn't have to," Ertuğrul replied. He sighed with disappointment. "We have all been living on seashells wondering what he will do."

Charlotte furrowed her brows. "Do you mean... 'walking on eggshells,' perhaps?"

He nodded before a grin of embarrassment broke out to lighten his face. All at once, he went from looking like a middle-aged, worried man to someone closer to her son's age.

"I cannot share him with anyone else," she said softly. "He is married, and I hate myself that I..." She shook her head. Ertuğrul obviously knew she and the sultan had shared a bed, but she didn't have to say it out loud.

"He will divorce her. He has already made the decision to do so."

"And how many years will that take?" she asked, hardly believing what she was asking.

Ertuğrul paused before answering, apparently parsing her words. "None. He need only tell her so."

Charlotte's eyes rounded. "And his concubines? I admit I am a jealous woman. I never had to share my husband, nor would I share your father," she claimed, sure her condition would be a deal breaker.

"I cannot say for certain, Your Grace, but I believe he would do anything for you," Ertuğrul said quietly.

Angling her head to one side, Charlotte considered how to respond. "I owe him two more nights," she murmured, annoyed that the mere thought of sharing his bed had her body responding as it did at that moment. "You have given me much to think on," she added, not about to admit that she was already contemplating almost everything he had already mentioned. "Now, will you tell me why it is your father is so hard on you?"

Ertuğrul stared at her a moment, and from the way his lips moved, she could tell he was repeating the question to himself. He dipped his head. "Because I was the reason his favorite wife died," he finally said. "He holds me responsible."

Charlotte furrowed a brow. "Afet was your mother," she remembered Sevinc telling her. "Did she die in the childbed?"

He nodded and allowed a long sigh. "She did. I have been told bearing twins is always difficult for a woman, and I was the second to be born," he explained. "She died the day after." Expecting the duchess to respond with words of sympathy or a sorrowful expression, Ertuğrul was surprised when she did neither.

"That incorrigible *beast*," she fumed. "Holding *you* responsible for your mother's death in the childbed?" She rolled her eyes. "The insufferable tyrant." After another moment, her features softened and she angled her head to one side. "Apologies for my outburst, Ertuğrul. Please accept my condolences on the loss of your mother. I realize it's been far too many years since it happened, but apparently my arrival was expected long ago."

He stared at her before he sighed. "Thank you, Your

Grace." His gaze darted to the sky. "I must go. I didn't realize how late it has grown."

He stood and gave her a deep bow before he backed away and then hurried off to the iron gate.

Left by herself in the gardens, Charlotte kicked off her slippers, hitched up her skirts, and turned around on the marble. She heaved a heavy sigh as she placed her feet in the cool water and planted her elbows on her knees.

With her chin resting in one hand, she stared at the statue representing the Nile River and was pondering what she would do when she remembered Ertuğrul's mention of being a twin.

Afet bore me a son and a daughter twenty years ago, Ziyaeddin had said the very first day he had spoken to her.

There is only one daughter who is twenty, Charlotte remembered as her eyes rounded.

Sevinc.

Sevinc and Ertuğrul were twins, and yet their father's regard for each of them was entirely different.

Charlotte felt a flash of annoyance. While Sevinc was Ziyaeddin's favorite, he held Ertuğrul in contempt—held him responsible for Afet's death.

Not sure there was anything she could do about it, Charlotte stared at the falling water and wept.

CHAPTER 26
ONE ENLIGHTENING NIGHT

*L*ater that evening
Having eaten his fill of dinner, Ziyaeddin relaxed on the sofa in his bedchamber, his dressing robe opening at the top to reveal the dark hair on his chest. He regarded Charlotte with an appreciative gaze. "The blue veil is perfect with your eyes," he murmured. "And it highlights your other features in a most erotic way," he teased.

Charlotte glanced down at her manner of dress. "I feel like a harlot," she complained. Given the translucency of the veil that was wrapped twice around her body, she had worn a mantle whilst making her way to the sultan's private chamber. There had been enough fabric in the veil to cover her torso, but her arms and legs were completely bare.

He leaned over and kissed her forehead. "And yet you are not," he replied. "If it makes you feel... uncomfortable, you have my permission to remove it."

Charlotte gave him a quelling glance. She had nothing else to wear but her mantle. "You are incorrigible," she accused.

He grinned and returned to his lounging position on the sofa again. "I am too full to go to bed," he said. "So let us speak of matters other than..." He struggled for a moment.

"Sexual congress?" she guessed, thinking that by now, they would usually be on his bed.

This night's dinner had been delayed, though. A combination of the Greeks departing for Syros—she had experienced a moment of panic at the thought it might be a long time before another ship appeared—and the sultan's late meeting with his viziers meant it was dark outside by the time he came for her. Given her late afternoon in the gardens, it was just as well. It had taken her a good deal of time to consider what both Captain Popodopolos and Ertuğrul had said to her.

When Parma asked what she wished to wear to dinner, Charlotte's gaze had settled on the length of blue silk.

She had already been wearing her mantle when Ziyaeddin had arrived to escort her. His look of disappointment had been apparent until they reached his chamber and she doffed the garment once the door was shut.

His face had lit up in delight in seeing how one corner of the silk had been secured over a shoulder and pinned at the back whilst the rest wrapped at an angle around her body. The opposite corner reached the top of a thigh and was secured with a pin. "Some presents are too beautiful to unwrap," he had whispered before he kissed her on the forehead.

"Bounder," she had accused.

*R*ecoiling at hearing the words "sexual congress," Ziyaeddin shook his head. "That is the term in English for making love?" he asked in dismay.

She tittered. "It isn't a very good one, is it?"

He seemed to think on it a moment. "I suppose when it is merely a physical joining, it cannot be lovemaking," he murmured. Charlotte was about to ask what he thought they had been doing for the past few nights when he added, "We have been making love, have we not?" He held out an arm in invitation for her to join him.

Charlotte moved to sit next to him. When the arm behind her captured her shoulders, he pulled her closer. "At first, I was not sure," she murmured.

One of his fingers trailed down her bare arm. "But now?" he prodded.

She gave him a curious glance. "You have not tired of me," she replied.

He winced. "Do you want me to be?"

Not expecting such a query, Charlotte shook her head. "Of course not." She sighed. "But I am concerned. For my future."

"I have been thinking—"

"Oh, dear," Charlotte whispered, but she made sure he saw her teasing grin.

"I would like you to stay. For... for another month. At least until it is time for me to return to Constantinople," he said. "Consider this part of your holiday," he added. "We'll take time to go out on the boat. Visit the ruins. Go shopping at the bazaar."

Charlotte experienced a moment of mixed feelings. From her time in the gardens that afternoon, she had surmised the longer she spent with the sultan and away from England, the less certain she was about continuing her holiday. At least with James in the palace, she knew he was safe. "What about James and David?"

"They are welcome to stay," he quickly replied. "They have avocations that will occupy their time." He pulled her closer and rested his cheek atop her head. "When another ship comes, they can either leave or stay."

The words brought her discussion with Captain Popodopolos to mind. "Before today's luncheon, did you and the captain discuss his early departure?" she asked, suddenly suspicious.

"We did. During our hunt this morning," he acknowledged.

Charlotte narrowed her eyes. "Is there really a storm brewing?"

He scoffed. "Can't you smell it?" he asked.

Blinking, Charlotte removed herself from his hold and stared at him. "What?" For a moment, she was sure he had mangled his English.

"The rain," he clarified. "I expect we'll have a downpour by morning. The winds will increase by tomorrow afternoon..." He didn't bother finishing the sentence when Charlotte hurried out to the balcony. He reluctantly rose from the sofa and followed her, then stood behind her as she gazed westward. She inhaled, the familiar scents of ozone, the sea, and rain reminding her of brief visits to Brighton.

"I understand," she said, as Ziyaeddin wrapped his arms around her and pulled her so her back was pressed to his front. "But doesn't that mean that they're sailing right into the storm?" she asked suddenly.

"They will make it to Syros before the worst of it arrives," he replied. "Probably midday tomorrow," he reasoned.

"You sent them into a storm," she accused.

Ziyaeddin recoiled at hearing her rebuke. "He did not wish to stay, Charlotte. Can you blame him? His sailors are Greek. They were growing nervous," he explained. "I gave Poppy an honorable means by which to leave early. That is all."

Charlotte relaxed in his hold, her conversation with the captain coming back to her in bits and pieces. "Why didn't you tell me Elena was his daughter?" She felt him shrug, and she angled her head to look up at him.

"I did not think it important," he replied. "And I am surprised he told you. Or did she?"

"He did," Charlotte replied. "Before he left. Why are you surprised?"

Ziyaeddin winced. "Remember when we spoke of daughters? That we are to treat them better than we do anyone else?"

She nodded.

"I think he has always been embarrassed that he could not find a suitable husband for her. Or perhaps he realizes now that he was too..." He struggled for a word.

"Picky?" Charlotte offered.

"Prideful," he countered. "Every man wants a rich husband for their daughter," he clarified. "But that time... right after the war... rich men were not to be found, and she was too old for the young men who returned to Syros."

"So he brought her to you," Charlotte murmured. She suddenly inhaled. "Did you think to make her one of your concu—?"

"No," he stated firmly. "I had an agreement with Poppy, and I have honored it," he added. "She was to be a paid servant, and that is what she is. One of the best, in fact."

Charlotte tried to calm her thoughts, but her conversation with Ertuğrul came to mind. His revelations had been enlightening as well as troubling.

Behind her, Ziyaeddin chuckled. "What has you vexed?"

She inhaled softly. "How did you know that I am?"

Turning her around in his arms, he dropped a kiss onto her forehead. "I feel it in your bones," he replied.

Charlotte attempted to suppress a chuckle as she settled her head onto his chest. His pulse was evident against her cheek, and she took comfort in the steady rhythm. "Do you love any of them? The women in your harem?"

Ziyaeddin pulled away from her, his brows furrowing. "Of course. My daughters, my aunts—"

"Your concubines. Your *kadins* and *ikbals*," she clarified.

Running a hand down one of her arms, Ziyaeddin hesitated to respond. "I do because they are my responsibility. Part of my family, I suppose. The mothers of my children especially," he replied. "I admit, when I was younger, I had a strong appetite for sexual congress." He said the last with an arched brow, as if emphasizing he did not consider it lovemaking. "I liked bedding my women. I liked being waited on hand and foot. I liked when they were round with child, and I loved holding the babes in my arms after they were born. They smelled heavenly," he murmured. "I wept for the ones who died and gave thanks to my god for all of them. But unlike the sultans of two-hundred years ago, I did not allow my harem to interfere with my responsibility to the empire."

Charlotte gave a start. "Are you saying those sultans ignored running the government in favor of... of sexual congress?"

He winced. "I am. For years, there were sultans who were too young or too incompetent to run the government, and their mothers schemed to give themselves more power. More money. The empire suffered greatly for it," he explained. "Remember how I told you that my concubines are paid? Imagine if there were a hundred of them. A thousand of them," he amended. "Girls belonging to the sultan as well as all the princes, all merged in one palace. The costs to the sultanate were enormous. Those all had to be paid from the taxes collected from the various lands under the empire's control."

Realizing he was trying to educate her on some of the sultanate's history, Charlotte listened in fascination. "So the empire was... bankrupted?" she asked in alarm, not sure if she used the right term.

"Nearly," he replied. "Change had to happen, of course, and it did. All those princes... they used to be kept sequestered in a palace so that they could not undermine a sultan's rule."

Inhaling softly, Charlotte's eyes widened. "Keep your friends close. Your enemies closer?" she guessed.

Ziyaeddin chuckled. "Indeed. They were sometimes killed to prevent a coup, and sometimes they were put in charge of running the provinces on the fringes of the empire. Out where they couldn't do much harm."

"And now?" Charlotte prompted. "What did you do differently?"

Inhaling deeply, Ziyaeddin paused a moment before he said, "I did not take on more concubines than I could afford to support. My brothers' harems are not merged with mine but are kept in the provinces over which they are responsible. They must see to paying them from their own funds. We were planning to split up our sisters among the harems, but they were all married off before my brothers came of age. The few who are housed in my harem are widows. And because I am generous with my brothers, I am on good terms with them. I do not fear an attempted coup."

Charlotte stared up at him. "How many brothers do you have?"

"I had five. Only three survive. Two of them died in

the past few years," he murmured, his Adam's apple bobbing as he swallowed.

Sensing his sorrow, Charlotte said, "I am sorry for your loss."

He glanced down at her. "A century ago, I would have been taught to hate them," he said. "To suspect them of undermining my rule. Five brothers from five different *kadins*?" he added on a sigh. "But our father insisted we be friends. That we learn to trust one another, and value the empire above all else. And so I have taught my sons the same," he explained.

"And it's worked?" she asked gently.

Ziyaeddin chuckled. "Well, I am not dead, and I am still the sultan," he replied as he tightened his hold on her.

"And the empire? Is it solvent now?"

"It is," he acknowledged. "This new palace and the two universities will cost the treasury a good deal, but they will then exist. There will be something to show for the expenditures," he explained. "And next I will see to sorting a new banking scheme for the empire."

Angling her head to one side, Charlotte regarded him by the dim light from the bedchamber and sighed. "And your... *appetite* for sexual congress? Judging from the past few nights, I am of the opinion you are still a rather hungry man."

Ziyaeddin stared at her as if he wished she had come to a different conclusion. "I am older. I am not in need of a different woman in my bed every night. And every spring solstice, I am reminded that I once loved a woman from the first moment I first met her."

Charlotte inhaled softly, her gaze going to his lips. A moment later, and he was kissing her with an intensity she had never felt in him before, as if he was pouring every ounce of his passion into it. Charlotte moaned as his hands splayed over her back and smoothed down over her scar and finally cupped the globes of her bottom so he could lift her onto the ledge of the balcony.

After she had wrapped her legs around his back and her arms around his shoulders, he entered her slowly. As the first drops of rain fell, she felt his lips on her ear and neck and inhaled softly when he pushed into her again. His moves slow and deliberate, he had her begging for him to move faster. Begging for him to hurry. When he finally increased his thrusts, she was practically weeping with need.

Her ecstasy led to a blessed oblivion, her insides tumbling about in waves of pleasure and a wash of warmth as Ziyaeddin experienced his own release, his head thrown back to accept the cooling shower of rain that fell from the inky blackness above.

They were both soaked when he finally straightened and carried her inside. She welcomed the feel of the silk dressing robe he used to dry her skin. Sighed when she felt him unhook the pin that secured the veil over her shoulder. Reveled in how he unwrapped the soaked silk from around her body. And finally she purred when he placed her on the bed and settled in next to her, the warmth of his body enveloping her in comfort.

She knew he had fallen asleep from the moment his head hit the pillow. About to follow him in slumber, his last words reminded her of Ertuğrul. Of the young emir's comment about his mother, Afet.

The love of Ziyaeddin's life had died after giving birth to him, and the sultan held him responsible.

CHAPTER 27
ONE BAD AWAKENING

Dawn, the following morning

The sensation of being watched followed by the rumbling of thunder in the distance had Ziyaeddin on alert as the rest of his body followed in wakefulness. The scents of rain and warm skin had him wishing he could simply remain where he was, but when he felt a touch on the tip of his morning tumescence, his eyes shot open.

Charlotte gasped and quickly pulled her hand away. For a moment, she looked so startled he nearly chuckled. His gaze darted down the rest of her body. She was completely naked, the first time she had been so in his company. No headscarf, no veil, no chemise to hide her puckered nipples or soft skin from his view.

Day Three, he thought with a mix of excitement and dread. Surely she would tell him she loved him. Agree to stay with him for the rest of her life. Afet had done so, her stubbornness not withstanding.

So he was entirely unprepared for her query.

"Do you hold Ertuğrul responsible for Afet's death?" she asked in a whisper.

Ziyaeddin blinked several times and lifted himself onto an elbow. Then he lowered his head to kiss and then suckle one of her nipples. Even as her hand speared his hair so her fingernails scraped his scalp and sent shivers down his spine, he sensed she would not give in to his attempts at lovemaking until he answered her.

Sighing, he covered her other breast with a hand, as if he had to hide it from view in order to speak coherently. "She died after she gave birth to him," he stated. "I know it is illogical, but I am reminded of it every time he is in my company." He winced. "He took her from me."

Despite his hold on her, Charlotte was able to wriggle out from under him and sit up, a lock of her sleep tousled hair falling in front of one of her eyes—eyes that blazed as they had the night she had been dumped on his throne room floor by the pirates. "So you *do* hold him responsible," she said in disbelief. "Even though she gave birth to Sevinc as well?"

"Who told you?" he asked, an expression of worry aging him a decade.

"You did, when you said Afet gave birth to a son and a daughter," she replied.

"She doesn't know," he whispered.

Charlotte scoffed. "Why ever not?"

Ziyaeddin winced. "The concubine who nursed her—who raised her from birth—she asked that Sevinc be considered her daughter. I agreed."

"Don't you think she should know her real mother

was a woman you loved?" She took two labored breaths and then made a move to get off the bed.

Ziyaeddin was faster, though, one of his arms wrapping around her middle to pull her back to the center of the bed. He wasn't prepared when she struggled, her legs kicking and her arms flailing in an attempt to free herself. "Let go, you *beast*," she cried out.

From the way his entire body stilled, his arm relaxing his hold on her, Charlotte knew she had hurt him. Either that or she had angered him. She couldn't be sure when her gaze locked onto his.

"Beast?" he repeated in a hoarse whisper. "Is that what you think of me?"

Charlotte's chin lifted even as she was about to counter his words. "You would hold a baby responsible for the death of his mother?" she whispered. "Is that true for the other two who died in the childbed?"

One of Ziyaeddin's brows furrowed, realizing almost at once that she would have learned of them from Sevinc. "I did not love them. Not as I did my Afet," he murmured.

"So you *do* blame him?"

"It's not like that, Charlotte," he stated, wincing once again.

"He tries so hard to please you, but he'll never be able to, will he?" she asked, as if she hadn't heard his last words. "For the rest of your life, he'll know that there was nothing he could have done to earn your regard," she accused.

"You do not know of what you speak," Ziyaeddin countered, his silver eyes blazing. As if to punctuate his claim, a flash of lightning lit up the opening to the balcony. A crack of thunder quickly followed, and Charlotte jerked in his hold.

"Then... then explain it to me," she challenged.

Frustration had him pulling her down to the bed, covering her with his body so that she couldn't escape. His manhood throbbed with need of her even as he cursed himself for his reaction to her. He knew nothing he said to her would make her understand. "I expect more of him," he whispered in dismay.

"And Sevinc? Will you force her to marry a man who will not appreciate her knowledge? Her curiosity? Her wish to learn? She is your favorite."

Ziyaeddin winced. "She will do so because it is our way, Charlotte," he replied tersely. "It will be up to her husband to decide if she's allowed to pursue more education."

Charlotte lay beneath him, staring up at him with an expression of defiance and defeat. Perhaps she understood his need of her, for her legs parted and she opened for him. With his tip at her entrance, he knew she was wet for him and wondered how she could be so angry with him and yet so in need of him.

Much like he was for her.

Burying his manhood to its hilt in a single thrust, he took heart when she didn't curse him or cry out. Instead, her legs lifted higher on his thighs and her chest rose from the bed.

She met every one of his thrusts in equal measure, even as he increased the rhythm. He restrained his force, though. He wasn't angry with her. Not now. Not when she was letting him have what he needed.

One last time.

Even with her head thrown back on the pillows and her insides clenching his manhood to incite every ounce of pleasure she could into their coupling, Ziyaeddin's release came with the realization this would be their last time together.

He watched her fight her own ecstasy, felt relief when she finally allowed it. He smoothed a hand over her belly with the hope he might provide even more pleasure before he pulled himself from her. Landing on his back, he growled in a combination of satisfaction and frustration.

Ziyaeddin knew she had left the bed when he reached out for her. Opened his eyes to discover she had already pulled on her mantle and was at the door.

"You will not leave," he said, his words coming out far harsher than he intended. He had meant for them to be a plea that she stay.

She whirled around, her blue eyes glinting despite the gray beyond the balcony. "I dare you to stop me, you stubborn, incorrigible, insufferable *tyrant*," she stated in a low voice that grew in intensity with her every word. With that, she took her leave.

Ziyaeddin fell back to the bed, his gaze going to the mosaic tiles that decorated the ceiling above the bed. Obviously the artist had a sense of humor, for an image of a naked Aphrodite stared down at him.

He had always thought the goddess taunted him from

above, but when he angled his head in the pillows and narrowed his eyes, her expression changed completely.

Sucking in a breath. Ziyaeddin sat up and stared at the closed door. "I think she loves me," he whispered in awe.

CHAPTER 28
A MOTHER LISTENS TO HER SON

a few hours later
Wracked with a multitude of emotions, not the least of which was heartache, Charlotte followed Elena to her son's chamber. "Can you see to it tea is brought?" she asked. She struggled to hold back tears. Had done so for the past two hours. Managed to keep her head up as Parma saw to her coiffure and the choice of a bright blue day gown. Feared that once she was behind the protection of her son's chamber, the dam would break and she would burst into tears.

Despite her lady's maid's good cheer, the early gloom of the morning dampened Charlotte's spirits even more.

"I can have it delivered to the dining room, Your Grace," Elena offered. She appeared about to say something else, but took a step back and waited.

"That would be lovely," Charlotte replied as she knocked on the door. No guards stood on either side of the entry, which had Charlotte realizing the boys could come and go as they pleased. A hint of annoyance merely added to the mix of emotions she was trying very hard to keep from showing on her face.

The parting words she had said replayed in her mind, and she winced. She rather doubted they had made the situation between her and Ziyaeddin any worse than it already was, though.

When there wasn't an immediate answer to her initial knock, Charlotte was about to knock again when she noticed Elena's gaze on her. "What is it?"

Elena dipped her head. "My father feels awful about what's happened to you."

Charlotte allowed a shrug. "It was not his fault," she replied. "I was so worried for him and his crew." She angled her head. "His departure yesterday... it was rather quick given the sultan had invited him and his crew to stay longer."

Her eyes downcast, Elena said, "Some of his crew fought in the war. They did not wish to partake of the sultan's hospitality. The rest... they wished to return to Syros. To see their families."

Charlotte nodded her understanding, "Which meant you could not spend as much time with your father."

Elena allowed a wan grin. "A little is enough, and if I am homesick, the sultan allows me to travel to Syros for a fortnight."

Blinking, Charlotte stared at the servant a moment before she said, "He sounds very generous."

Her eyes darting to the side, Elena said, "He is. I thought you would know that by now."

Charlotte gave the servant a watery grin. "I suppose I do." She sucked air through her teeth at the reminder of how she had left things with him. "I fear I have angered him past the point where he'll ever be generous with me again." She was about to knock one more time when the door suddenly opened to reveal James, his hair wet and his cravat still untied.

"I will see to the tea right away," Elena said as she curtsied and hurried off.

"Mother," James said before he leaned over and kissed one of her cheeks. "You're just in time to help me with my cravat."

Charlotte followed him into his bedchamber, her mouth dropping open at seeing the array of furnishings and the overall opulence of the room. "How is it you have real beds and a sofa?"

James shrugged. "David arranged it with someone. I think he's met just about every man of influence in this palace."

Moving to stand in front of her son, Charlotte took the ends of the cravat and began wrapping the silk around his neck, alternating them until the ends were short enough to make a mail coach knot.

"Still rather conservative with your knot choice, I see," he remarked when he checked his reflection in a mirror.

"It's the only one I know," she countered. "Your father's favorite." The reminder of Joshua had her blinking, although it didn't have tears forming as it would have back in England.

"We missed you at dinner last night," James said as he combed his damp hair into the current style.

"I ate with the sultan," Charlotte replied, now

wishing she had declined the invitation. Feeling as heart-sick as she had that morning, she hadn't tried to eat any of the breakfast Parma had offered. She knew tea would help, though. "I've arranged for tea to be delivered to the dining room. I thought you and David might like to join me."

"I'd love a cup of tea," James replied. "Could we invite Sevinc Sultana?"

Charlotte nodded. "Of course. When Elena returns, I can mention it to her." She strolled to one of the chamber's windows, her eyes rounding at seeing the view. "What a wonderful vantage," she commented.

"Isn't it?" James murmured as he pulled on a pair of boots. "Sevinc and I watched the sunset last night. The colors were brilliant."

"I didn't get a chance to ask how your tour with her went," Charlotte hinted, wincing when she remembered Ziyaeddin's claim that arrangements had been made. Sevinc would be marrying one of the *viziers*. From the way the sultan had said the words, she had the impression he was glad to be rid of his favorite daughter. Glad she would be someone else's problem to sort. "Did you see all of the ruins?"

"Not by half," he replied as he indicated she should take a seat on the sofa. "I could spend a fortnight just studying the amphitheater. I'll bet I could find names carved into the blocks of the bottom row if I could just dig down a few inches."

"You and Sevinc seemed happy together."

A huge grin appeared on James' face. "Oh, indeed," he claimed. "She is smart and clever and knows so much of the world, Mother, and yet... all of her knowledge is gleaned from books," he said, his gaze on his mind's eye.

Charlotte stared at her son, seeing once again the evidence of his having fallen hard for the sultan's daughter. "Ziyaeddin has said she will marry a member of his ministry," she warned, wincing once again at the thought of the bright girl forced into a loveless marriage.

James gave a start. "She cannot," he said as his head shook. "She has accepted my offer of marriage."

"*What?*" Charlotte's eyes rounded in both surprise and worry. "Have you spoken with His Highness?" She knew he hadn't. Unless their paths had crossed that morning, she knew her son hadn't been in the sultan's presence since their luncheon the day before.

"I have sent word with the Greek servant that I wish for an audience. I am told it could be several days or more before he will see me," James replied with a grimace. "Mother, I have never felt this way about a girl in all my life. It's as if..." He allowed the sentence to trail off as his face reddened.

"You were struck by lightning," Charlotte finished for him.

He nodded, his pained expression betraying his thoughts.

"I felt it, too," she said as she sat down next to him. "The air between the two of you fairly sizzled," she whispered. "You would make a perfect husband for her, if you can abide the fact that she is probably better educated than you are."

Despite his melancholy, James grinned. "I don't mind. Truly. I'm never going to find an English miss who shares my fascination with Ancient Greece or dead civilizations," he added on a sigh. "She will make an excellent traveling companion. She is curious and—" He paused when he saw how his mother stared at him. "What?"

Charlotte swallowed. "What would you think of me if I told you...?" She stopped as her face flamed red.

"That you and the sultan are having an *affaire?*" James guessed, his brows lifting in a tease. "Or had one?"

Her mouth dropped open in shock. "James William Joshua Alexander Wainwright," she scolded.

"*Now* I'm in trouble," James said as he rolled his eyes. "I thought you'd forgotten all my names." Although the words were said in a serious tone, a smirk lifted the corners of his lips.

She gave him a quelling glance even as tears pricked the corners of her eyes. "Do you think me a harlot?" she asked in a whisper.

James scoffed. "Hardly," he replied. He dipped his head. "Truth be told, I'm glad you... you decided to be adventurous for once in your life. You took a risk leaving England on a holiday with only your lady's maid," he went on.

The mention of risk had Charlotte chuckling softly. "It was not the first time, you must know."

James inhaled. "What are you saying?"

She gripped one of his hands in hers. "When I learned your father had been burned so badly when he attempted to rescue his sister from the fire... I arranged for his care. Had him brought to London. Stayed with him in hospital. He didn't even know I was there until... well, several months later when my father arranged for me to marry the Earl of Gisborn—"

"*What?*" James nearly bolted from the sofa. "Henry Foster? Hannah's Henry? He's... he's practically my uncle."

Charlotte nodded and then shook her head. "Father thought he was doing right by giving Ellsworth Park to Henry as a dowry. Before Henry had even secured a promise of marriage from me," she explained. "Father didn't have any money. He had gambled it all away, you see," she whispered.

"You never told me this before," James said in a quiet voice. "Does John know?" he asked, referring to his older brother.

Charlotte nodded. "I told him before he married Arabella. He had always thought your father and I had an arranged marriage, so I had to explain matters to set him straight."

"So... how did you put off Henry?"

Sighing, Charlotte decided to tell him the entire story. "I had always loved your father, even when I was betrothed to his brother, the *bastard*," she replied.

"Mother!"

"Oh, I did not mourn John the Second when he died in that fire," she stated, remembering how she had despised the original heir to the Chichester duchy. He had been a rake of the worst kind. If Joshua hadn't intervened on her behalf several times, she would have lost her virtue before she'd had her come-out.

Charlotte inhaled deeply as the memories surfaced.

"When Joshua had recovered enough, he took on the ducal duties and returned to Wisborough Oaks. Mr. McElliott was overseeing the repairs on the estate. He was already acting as a foreman, you see," she explained. "I had no intention of marrying Henry—we were like a brother and a sister growing up—so I ran away to Wisborough Oaks."

James stared at her for a long time before he asked, "How?"

Charlotte angled her head to one side as tears once again threatened. "My godfather. The one we call Grandby, but who is really the Earl of Torrington," she said as a watery grin appeared. "He lent me his traveling coach and told me to do what I must to claim my duke. So I did. Took Parma with me, of course," she said as an afterthought. "Henry followed a week later, and I told him he should marry Hannah. I had already moved into Wisborough Oaks. Had already taken on the decorating choices—your father wanted nothing to do with it—and..." She shrugged. "Your brother was born nine months later. After we were married, of course."

His expression conveying a moment of confusion, James scoffed. "So you're the one responsible for choosing that awful wallpaper in the parlor?"

Inhaling sharply, Charlotte stared at her son, her mouth opening and closing much like a fish. "You think it hideous?"

"It's a bit much," he said with a scowl.

Charlotte tittered. "I was thinking about that wallpaper when I decided to go on holiday."

James barked a laugh that had her grinning even as

tears fell down her cheeks. "It would have been far easier to have it replaced, don't you think?"

She sniffled and said, "I suppose." Sobering after a moment, Charlotte thought of what had happened since that fateful day at Wisborough Oaks. Remembered the voyage on the *Sun of Apollo* and all the sights she had witnessed from the rail of the ship. The excitement when the pirates had overtaken the vessel. The combination of fear and awe she had felt upon meeting the sultan. The disbelief she had felt at being wanted by a man who had so many other women he could be with.

"I think I've made a horrible mistake," she murmured as she struggled to catch her breath.

"The wallpaper isn't *that* bad, Mother," James said, his brows furrowing at seeing her so distraught.

She raised her gaze to meet his. "It's not about the wallpaper," she whispered. She swallowed. "Arabella is going to have a baby. Probably by Christmas."

James blinked at the sudden change of topic. "Well, this is good news," he said with a grin, surprised she didn't remember having told him the first night of his arrival. "I'm going to be an uncle. And you're going to be a... a grandmother," he added in a murmur. "So... what is this horrible mistake you think you've made?"

Her gaze meeting his, she said, "I think I'm in love."

James lifted a shoulder in a shrug. "So now you know how I feel," he replied. "Miserable, isn't it?" he teased.

Charlotte grabbed a pillow and hit him in the chest with it. "I've spent the last week thinking I should be in a hurry to return to England—"

"Why?" he asked as he straightened. "You've only just

started your holiday. Not on the best foot, but... ending up in a palace on the Aegean Sea? With a handsome sultan? If the matrons in Mayfair had any idea where you've been and what you've been doing, they would be green with jealousy," he claimed.

Although she didn't care one whit about the opinions of the matrons in Mayfair, Charlotte knew her son had a point.

Why was she so anxious to go back?

Family.

John and Arabella. James. They needed her.

Didn't they?

"What do you suppose your brother would think if he learned I had no plans to return to Wisborough Oaks? At least, not anytime soon?"

James blinked several times. "If I tell you the truth, do you promise not to cry?"

"What?" It was Charlotte's turn to straighten on the low sofa. She would have to stand soon or her legs would fall asleep.

"Before I left England, John was worried about you," James said. "That you would become a hermit, and live out your days in the old wing of Wisborough Oaks, staring out the windows," he added.

Charlotte swallowed hard. "That's why I decided to take a holiday. Well, that, and because Elizabeth and Hannah encouraged me to go," she explained. "What if I don't go back? What about you?"

James shrugged. "You needn't worry about me. John has assured me he'll continue my allowance. He knows how much I want to travel. How much I want to be an archaeologist." He chuckled softly. "I don't think he expected me to want to marry so soon, but... why shouldn't you have another chance at loving someone?"

Charlotte turned to regard her son with tear-filled eyes. "Oh, who are you, and what have you done with my son?" she asked as she sniffled.

He paused a moment, his brows furrowing. "I must admit, Mother, I wouldn't have expected you to fall for a sultan. Doesn't he have a... a harem?" His eyes suddenly rounded. "Are *you* part of his harem now?"

"Aaaand... he's back," Charlotte said as she directed another quelling glance at her youngest son. She huffed. "I am *not* part of his harem," she stated, her thoughts returning to that morning. To the moment before she had left his chamber. Ziyaeddin's anger had been palpable. "In fact, given how much I angered him, I don't expect I'll ever see him again."

James furrowed his brows, apparently deciding it was best he didn't ask what she had done. "A harem is a sign of a sultan's power," he stated. "An indication of the size of his state. The influence he has over his country," he explained. "One sultan is said to have had over a thousand concubines in his harem."

Charlotte grimaced. "He could take a different woman to his bed every night for over three years without a repeat," she murmured. Ziyaeddin's harem wasn't nearly as large, but he could still enjoy variety in his bed for several weeks.

So why did he want her?

They had spoken of sexual congress. Of lovemaking. The difference between them.

The oddest sensation gripped her chest just then, a small ache in her heart at what she could have if she wasn't so determined to return to England.

"Tell me, Mother. Is Ziyaeddin's anger because you... you turned down some sort of offer?"

Charlotte buried an eyetooth in her lower lip as she took a deep breath. "I did not mean to offend him," she replied. "I made a bargain with him so he would let me go, and I've kept it, but..."

"He reneged."

She shook her head. "I think he will let me go, but he must get past his anger. His hurt." Or perhaps she should consider his son's thoughts on the matter.

Destiny.

Fate.

"Well, I want to marry his daughter," James stated. "I want to spend the rest of my life with her."

Charlotte nodded her understanding even as determination had her straightening on the sofa. "Then I shall see what I can do about that." She furrowed a brow as she glanced around the room. "What's become of David?"

James chuckled. "He's made friends here in the palace. One of the sultan's sons—the one called Ertu..." He struggled with the name for a moment.

"Ertuğrul," Charlotte offered, realizing she had said the name correctly for the first time.

"Yes, that's it. They've been discussing architecture. Apparently Ziyaeddin is having another palace built in Constantinople."

Charlotte inhaled softly and nodded. "Indeed, he is,"

she replied, remembering her discussion with the sultan. "A very expensive built-in garden," she added, remembering what they intended to name it.

Perhaps one day she would see it, but for that to happen, she would have to make amends with Ziyaeddin.

The sooner, the better.

CHAPTER 29
A FATHER COMES TO TERMS

Meanwhile, in Ertuğrul's workroom
Dipping his quill into the ink pot Ertuğrul had offered earlier that morning, David wrote a few lines in his journal and blew on the wet ink. "I hope you do not mind, but I am fascinated by this particular part of the design," he said as he pointed to the architectural drawings spread out on a high table in the middle of Ertuğrul's workroom.

Ertuğrul joined him to survey the portion of the palace that had David so impressed. "There will be plants in there. Like in a..." He shook his head as he struggled for the English word.

"Courtyard," David offered. "I've seen many of these in Italy. The design makes it possible to have windows where there wouldn't usually be any, and the interiors tend to be cooler during the hottest parts of the day."

Studying the design for the courtyard, Ertuğrul noted there were no windows indicated for the courtyard walls.

"Ah, I shall add windows here and here," he said, using his own quill as a pointer.

"Why not on this wall?" David asked as he pointed to one of the adjacent walls. "For morning light."

The sultan's son shook his head. "That is the royal bedchamber," he replied. "My father would not always wish to be awakened by the sun."

"Ah," David replied. "I understand." He returned his attention to his journal, jotting down more notes.

Ertuğrul straightened. "I do not mean offense, but I wish to ask why it is you are so interested in this project."

David inhaled and gave a shrug. "I have always been interested in architecture. In buildings. Especially in such unique designs," he replied. "Did you do this?"

"I did," Ertuğrul acknowledged. "Most of it. I had to work with a stone mason to be sure it could be constructed on the land where it will go. To be sure it won't... sink. It's to be near the water. On the Bosphorus Straight."

Nodding his understanding, David pointed to another area of the drawing. "Despite our love of gardens, we don't have anything like this in England," he said. "I do hope you have painters—an artist—who can document it. Mayhap when it is complete, I might be allowed a tour of it?"

Ertuğrul nodded. "If I am still employed in this position, then I shall see to it," he said.

David gave a start. "Why wouldn't you be? Your work is... amazing. This is obviously not your first design."

Dipping his head, Ertuğrul said, "It is not. I have seen to many in the four years I have been in this position."

Gasping, David asked, "How old are you?"

Ertuğrul dipped his head. "Twenty years. I apprenticed under an old architect when I was but twelve, and when he died..." He gave a shrug. "I have had the position ever since. I fear the sultan is not pleased with me, though."

Furrowing his brows, David shook his head in disbelief. "How can that be? And aren't you related to him somehow?" Despite the few days he had been in the palace, David was still struggling to understand all the relationships among those he had met. Nothing seemed to track given all the possible mothers. Even inheritance among the sultan's heirs was nothing like it was in England.

"I am his fifth son," Ertuğrul stated. "Of the eleven who still live."

David boggled at the thought of that many sons. In England, only the eldest would inherit. The rest would be beholden to the eldest for their livelihoods if they did not take employment.

"My mother was his favorite, but she died giving birth to me," Ertuğrul said quietly.

From the emir's expression, David understood why he seemed concerned for his future. "He holds you responsible for her death?" he asked in a whisper. "But that's... that's ridiculous," he added. "It's not a babe's fault if a woman dies in the childbed."

Ertuğrul shrugged. "Out of nineteen babes born to

the sultan who are still alive, my mother and two of his *kadins* are the only ones who died."

David inhaled softly. "Nineteen children," he said in awe. "I was thinking I would be happy to sire maybe three or four."

"As would I. Apparently the sultan is searching for a wife for me," Ertuğrul said, his lack of enthusiasm suggesting he didn't expect his match to be a good one.

"I have a sister who is not yet wed. Adeline. But she's only seventeen this year. She'll make her come-out..." He paused a moment. "She's *made* her come-out," he quickly amended, realizing the first ball of the Season had already happened. He chuckled softly. "She's probably the only aristocrat's daughter to have already been to the Kingdom of the Two Sicilies," he murmured. "Twice."

"I doubt your father would want his daughter wed to a Turkish man," Ertuğrul replied.

"My father is not like most Englishmen," David claimed. "My grandmother was born in Italy, so my mother is half-Italian," he explained, his brows waggling. "He fell in love with her at first sight."

Ertuğrul grinned. "No matter whom I'm to marry, I shall honor my wife," he said. "It is our way here."

"I am glad to hear it," a deep voice said from the arched doorway.

Both Ertuğrul and David turned to discover the sultan standing with his arms crossed and leaning against the wall next to the door. The long sleeves of his gold and red brocade kaftan weren't moving, which suggested he had been standing there for some time.

Both young men bowed deeply.

"Your Highness," David murmured.

"My Sultan," Ertuğrul said in Turkish.

Ziyaeddin regarded the two for a moment before his gaze rested on David. "Duchess Charlotte and Lord James are in search of you. For tea," he stated. "They are in the dining chamber."

"Thank you, Your Highness. I... I lost track of time," David replied. Realizing he was being dismissed, he bowed again and slowly left the room, bowing once more before he disappeared beyond the door, closing it behind him after he gave Ertuğrul a look of worry.

Ziyaeddin lowered his arms to his sides and strode farther into the room. His gaze briefly darted to the architectural drawings, but his attention quickly returned to Ertuğrul. "How long have you known your mother was my favorite?" he asked quietly.

Ertuğrul blinked. "As long as I can remember."

"How long have you thought I held you responsible for her death?"

There was a pause before Ertuğrul said, "As long as I can remember."

Dipping his head, Ziyaeddin said, "It is true what you think... to a point," he said. "But it is only because you are Afet's only son that I seem to wince whenever I see you. Not because I blame you, but because you are a reminder of how much I miss her," he explained.

"Then perhaps it would be best if you sent me away. Denied my birth," Ertuğrul suggested.

Ziyaeddin gave a start, his dark brows furrowing before he once against crossed his arms. "Is that why you don't call me *baba* when we are in private?"

Ertuğrul considered the query before he said, "You have never said I could."

Sighing, the sultan moved toward the clear-glass window and looked out. From this vantage, the Aegean was visible, its turquoise waters nearly still despite the wind left from the early morning storm.

He took a steadying breath. "Today is a very auspicious day," he stated.

Ertuğrul's eyes rounded. "Sir?"

"You are my fifth son," he stated. "And given my disgust for your older brothers and their desire for war, you have become my favorite."

Gasping, Ertuğrul stared in disbelief at his father. "So, we are going to war?" he asked, his gaze quickly darting to the drawings of the palace. "The construction is to be put on hold?" Even though he was in awe of his father's words, the sound of disappointment in his voice was evident.

Ziyaeddin shook his head. "There will be no more wars, at least, not for the time being. I am to meet with your older brothers in a few minutes on the matter." He moved toward the table and indicated the drawings. "You will see to it the palace is built—with the windows looking out to the courtyard—and I appreciate your thoughts on not having any windows on the east wall of my bedchamber."

Ertuğrul's face flushed red when he realized his father had been present for most of his discussion with David. "Yes, My Sultan." When Ziyaeddin gave him a quelling glance, he quickly added, "Yes, Baba." Emboldened, he asked, "When you said today was a very auspicious day, to what were you referring?"

His father chuckled. "You will choose your own wife."

Ertuğrul's eyes rounded. "I will?" His eyes darted sideways before he chuckled. "Does that mean I can return to England? For a Season?"

Ziyaeddin's laugh could probably be heard through half the palace. "If you wish to do so," he replied. "Then do so."

Shocked at his father's response, Ertuğrul rushed to embrace him. "Thank you, Baba. I will. Next spring. Or the one after, when the new palace is finished."

Hugging his son—hard—Ziyaeddin finally stepped away and said, "Now it seems you are late for tea. Do join our guests in the dining room, won't you?"

Ertuğrul blinked. "Yes, Baba," he replied. "Won't you be there, too?"

Wincing, Ziyaeddin dipped his head. "I have a meeting with your older brothers," he replied. "But I will walk with you."

The two took their leave of the office, Ertuğrul striding abreast of his father as they made their way.

CHAPTER 30

AN AUDIENCE WITH A FATHER

en minutes later
James glanced over at his mother as he escorted her in the direction of the throne room. "Are you sure about this?" he asked.

Charlotte nodded. "I have never been more sure about... anything," she responded. "Now off with you. Elena will have seen to the tea being delivered to the dining room. I'll meet you there shortly."

Giving Charlotte a worried glance, James bent down and kissed her cheek before he turned around and headed for the dining room.

Girding her loins, Charlotte approached the door to the sultan's throne room and caught the surprised look of the two guards. "I wish an audience with the sultan," she stated.

The guards obviously didn't understand English, for they merely blinked and looked about the corridor for someone to provide a translation.

When neither moved to open the doors, Charlotte

stepped forward and gripped the handle of one of the doors, intending to let herself in.

When a guard placed the palm of a hand above hers to keep the door closed, his head shaking side to side, she angled her head and gave him her most haughty expression. "I wish to speak with the sultan."

He visibly swallowed before he lifted his head in the direction of the other guard. That guard opened the door closest to him and disappeared inside.

A moment later, not one, not two, but three of the sultan's viziers exited the throne room. Their gazes darted away when she glanced in their direction, and Charlotte was left wondering what sort of meeting her presence had interrupted.

Were the viziers upset at her arrival? Or was that relief she had paid witness to when they departed?

And why did they look so familiar?

The guard reappeared from within and held the door open for her.

Taking a steadying breath, Charlotte entered the chamber to find Ziyaeddin standing in front of his throne. He wasn't facing her, though. His attention was on one of the colored glass windows, the red and yellow beams casting him in a golden light.

Charlotte inhaled at the sight, her insides tumbling about in a combination of tremors and nervousness and desire and despair.

How could he have that effect on her by simply standing there?

She waited until he turned to acknowledge her before

she dipped a deep curtsy. "Your Highness," she said before rising.

In the meantime, Ziyaeddin had stepped down from the raised dais and stood before her. "Your Grace," he replied, his expression far more friendly than she was expecting.

"Were those rather handsome men your sons?" she asked.

He rolled his eyes. "They are," he replied. "You have come at an auspicious time."

"Oh?"

"My ministers of defense have come to an agreement. Probably for the first time ever."

Charlotte's eyes widened. "On a war?" she whispered, her lips quivering at the thought of Ziyaeddin leading forces against another country.

"Peace," he stated. "We cannot afford a war at this time. Even if it means losing lands, I will not sacrifice my men."

Staring at him in awe, Charlotte waited a moment before she said, "I am very glad to hear it, Your Highness." She took a steadying breath. "With your thoughts on peace, perhaps we can come to one of our own?"

His dark brows furrowed, and for a moment, it seemed anger would overcome the sultan's attempt to remain calm. "You have a proposition for me?"

Charlotte thought the word an odd choice, but a reminder that English was not his first language had her reconsidering. "First, I wish to apologize. For what I said this morning."

His brows arching in anticipation, Ziyaeddin said, "For calling me a tyrant?"

Charlotte winced. "For calling you a beast," she countered, ignoring his look of confusion. "I have given it a good deal of thought and discovered only today that I am not as needed as I once was. Therefore, I am not of a mind to return to England," she stated. "At least, not for some time."

Ziyaeddin's expression softened for only a moment before he once again appeared as fierce as the day they had met. "Are you requesting... continued hospitality?"

Giving a start, Charlotte realized her discussion with him would be more difficult than she thought. "I suppose that all depends," she replied. "I have come to realize that I love you, but that is not the issue I have come about on this day."

His brows shot up. "It is not?"

"My son wishes an audience with you."

His head lifted as his eyes seemed to scan the elaborate tiled ceiling. A cherub armed with a bow and arrow seemed to take aim in his direction, and he wondered why he had never noticed it before. "I am aware. Elena informed me earlier today" he replied. His eyes continued to dart about as if he were still trying to sort her earlier words, a different goddess capturing his attention. One of Zeus' daughters, Persephone.

"It's about Sevinc."

Now his eyes narrowed as they turned on her. "Did you tell her?"

"Of course not," Charlotte replied.

"Has something happened to her?"

Charlotte huffed. "I suppose you could say that."

"She is to marry my minister of agriculture," he stated, briefly thinking the middle-aged man bore a passing resemblance to the mosaic image of Hades positioned near that of Persephone.

"Yes, you told me that, but if you learned there was a young man who wished to spend the rest of his life with her, the brother of a duke, would you consider him instead? One who values her mind and would show her the world?"

Ziyaeddin's expression of confusion turned suspicious. "Are you speaking of your son?"

"I am. Lord James loves her. And I adore her. To have her as my daughter..." She stopped as tears threatened. "Well, I would be honored."

For a moment, Ziyaeddin stared at her, as if he was replaying every moment they had spent together in his mind's eyes. "Are you asking on his behalf?" he asked finally.

Charlotte swallowed. "He has asked for an audience with you so that he might plead his case. To ask your permission to wed Sevinc," she explained.

"So... why are you pleading his case for him?"

Inhaling softly, Charlotte allowed a wan grin. "I am here to plead *my* case, Your Highness. I wish for Sevinc to be my daughter-in-law." She swallowed again. "I will do whatever you wish."

His eyes widened slightly. "Whatever I wish?" he repeated, his attention once again turning to the colored glass window.

"I know I have hurt you," Charlotte whispered. "I did

not intend to, My Sultan. I've been attempting to fulfill my end of the bargain not realizing there would be... other repercussions."

"Repercussions?" he repeated, as if he was struggling to remember its meaning.

"Consequences. Effects," Charlotte offered. "I thought you would tire of me after three nights."

He grimaced, remembering his thoughts from the their first night together. "There was that possibility, I suppose," he admitted, his gaze still on the window.

She inhaled softly at hearing his confession. What she had thought was merely lust apparently was more. Far more. "I have also learned that apparently I am not needed. At least, not in England," she murmured.

Ziyaeddin's eyes narrowed. "Did your son tell you that?"

Dipping her head, Charlotte moved closer to him. "He reminded me that my eldest has a wife to take care of him, and that he is old enough to see to his own life." Tears pricked the corners of her eyes. "If after everything that has happened, you still want me with you, I would be happy to stay," she offered. "But I cannot share you."

"Happy to stay?" he repeated.

She nodded. "Oh, Ziyaeddin, I didn't think I was capable of falling in love again."

"Nor did I," he whispered as one of his hands rubbed his face and smoothed his short beard.

Charlotte took the three steps to where he stood, her face raised so the golden light washed over her. "Do you love me?" she asked.

He moved his hands to either side of her face and

placed a kiss at the top her forehead. "From the moment I met you," he murmured, inhaling to capture the floral scent that surrounded her. He closed his eyes and once again kissed her forehead. "I shall not be shared."

Wrapping her arms around his chest, Charlotte settled her head into the small of his shoulder and hugged him hard. "Given my age and the shape of my body, I suppose I should have known it couldn't be lust that had you wanting me in your bed," she murmured.

Furrowing his brows, Ziyaeddin pulled away enough to look down at her. "Are you questioning my desire for your wisdom and soft body?"

Charlotte tittered before she stood on tiptoes and kissed the corner of his mouth. "That all depends. Will you invite me to your bed tonight?"

Gazing down on her, he asked, "Would you come if I did?"

She grinned. "Oh, in more ways than one."

It took him a moment to understand her response, but when he did, he chuckled softly. When he suddenly sobered, Charlotte stiffened. "What is it?"

"If I give Sevinc to Lord James, then I must offer a different daughter to Ahmet."

"You say that as if you are lacking in daughters," she teased. Remembering the names he had mentioned on their first walk together, she asked, "Is Ekin of an age to marry?"

He gave her a suspicious glance. "She is nineteen," he replied. Then his eyes lit up in delight. "Ah, I see what you are thinking," he murmured. "Ekin means harvest. Vizier of Agriculture. Why did I not think of her first?"

Charlotte smiled, relieved she had saved Sevinc from a loveless match and would gain a daughter in the process. "Perhaps your mind was on other matters, Your Highness."

"No doubt," he murmured, once again kissing her on the forehead. When he noticed she still seemed bothered by something, he stiffened. "What else has you vexed?"

She inhaled softly. "Ertuğrul."

He gave a start and then chuckled. "Ah. Before my meeting with sons two, three, and four, I paid a call on number five," he said, delight in his eyes. "I explained that I do not hold him responsible for his mother's death. That he is merely a reminder of a woman I loved very much."

Charlotte angled her head to one side. "Then why do you seem so annoyed when he asks for an audience?"

Ziyaeddin winced. "I know I should not be," he admitted. "He merely tries too hard in his quest to please me. He offered to leave the palace—so that he would no longer be a reminder of Afet—but I could not abide his absence since he is to be my heir."

Charlotte's eyes rounded. "Your *heir*?" she repeated in surprise. A brilliant smile appeared as she nearly bounced on the balls of her feet. "Ziyaeddin!"

"I have had to expect more from him as my father did with me," he warned, suppressing a grin when he noted her excitement at hearing the news. "If he is to be a successful sultan, I must do so." When he thought she was about to scold him, he added, "I dared not tell him sooner, or he might have quit trying to please me. Now I know he is dedicated to seeing this empire thrive. A smaller empire, yes, but a stronger and more modern empire."

Charlotte inhaled softly as tears threatened. "Oh, Ziyaeddin," she whispered. "If I wasn't so hungry..." She sighed.

Ziyaeddin furrowed a brow and then chuckled when he sorted what she was about to say. "Tea has been served in the dining room," he reminded her.

"Will you join me?" she asked.

He glanced around the throne room. "My schedule appears to be open," he replied. Offering his arm, Charlotte placed a hand on it and they left for the dining room.

CHAPTER 31
A FATHER GIVES PERMISSION

few minutes later, in the dining room
The animated discussion involving a sister, a brother, and two best friends continued for several moments after Ziyaeddin and Charlotte quietly entered the dining room, the topic having something to do with mosaics and the nearby Greek ruins.

Ertuğrul was the first to notice the sultan and duchess, immediately coming to his feet. James was next, offering a hand to Sevinc so that she and David rose in unison.

"I do not wish to interrupt such an interesting conversation among young people," the sultan said as he escorted Charlotte to a cushion near the head of the table.

The four dipped their heads, and James was the first to kneel to bring the hem of Ziyaeddin's robe to his lips and then to his forehead. David and Ertuğrul followed. Sevinc merely took his hand to her lips and then pressed it to her forehead. "Good morning, Baba," she said.

He leaned over and kissed her forehead. "It is an auspicious day, despite the rain," he replied as he settled onto the cushion at the end of the table. Charlotte was already seeing to a cup of tea for him, the red liquid still steaming hot from the ceramic pot in the middle of the table. "What is it you were saying about mosaics?" he asked in an attempt to restart the conversation.

David exchanged a quick glance with Ertuğrul before he said, "I couldn't help but notice that so many of the mosaics in the palace include figures from Greek mythology. I suppose I thought it... unexpected," he said with a shrug.

"I explained that the palace was built at a time when such motifs were common in mosaics done by the artisans of north Africa," Ertuğrul offered.

"Although the mosaics in the churches on Sicily were supposedly done by the same Muslim artisans, and they feature scenes from the Old Testament," James continued with some consternation.

Ziyaeddin turned his attention to his daughter. "And what have you to say on the matter, Sevinc?"

Sevinc grinned at her father. "Unlike the mosaics found in the palaces of Constantinople, their originals built by the Roman emperors of the Byzantium era, those found in this western palace pay homage to the influence of Greek mythology on the Aegean shore of the empire. Before it was part of what is now the Ottoman Empire," she recited. "There used to be several Greek city-states located on these shores. Their ruins are located to the east and south of here," she added.

Ziyaeddin beamed with pride at hearing his daughter's response, his attention going to James. The young man was staring at Sevinc much as he had done when Afet was first introduced to him.

Much as Ziyaeddin had done when he was first introduced to the young man's mother.

"Why is the story of Persephone and Hades on the ceiling of the throne room?" Charlotte asked as she placed a biscuit on a plate and set it before the sultan.

Five sets of eyes turned to stare at her.

She scoffed. "I do know my Greek mythology," she said in her own defense. Her gaze darted to Ziyaeddin, who was staring at her in wonder.

"I haven't yet documented the mosaics in the throne room," David replied with some excitement. "Perhaps I might be allowed to when Your Highness is not using it?"

Ziyaeddin nodded his ascent. "I shall have word sent when it is vacant," he replied, his chin lifted proudly. When he realized Charlotte was still staring at him, he cleared his throat. "The story of Persephone is one of... compromise," he said, as if he struggled to sort the correct English word. "As Hades' queen and a daughter of Zeus, she had to live in the Underworld for half the year and in our world for the other half, so that crops might grow," he explained. He turned his attention to Sevinc. "Which is why I have decided your sister, Ekin, will wed my Vizier of Agriculture instead of you."

His daughter's eyes rounded. "She will be perfect for him," she murmured, even though she had only seen the emir from afar. She turned to James and said, "Her name means 'harvest' in our language."

James turned his gaze on the sultan and swallowed. "You said this was an auspicious day, Your Highness."

Ziyaeddin chuckled. "For you and for your mother, and for my favorite daughter and for me," he replied.

Swallowing, James said, "I have asked for an audience with you. With the intent of asking if I might have the honor of marrying your favorite daughter."

"You will have that honor," the sultan stated.

"Baba!" Sevinc said as she gasped. She was immediately up from her cushion, which had both James and David rising from theirs. She knelt before her father, kissing the hem of his robe as well as the back of his hand and then his cheek. "Baba," she whispered as tears filled her eyes. "*Teşekkürler.*"

Ziyaeddin glanced over at Charlotte, stunned to find her staring at him with tears in her eyes. He grasped one of her hands in his. "As you requested, she will be your daughter."

James' eyes widened as his mother displayed a brilliant grin and then launched herself into Ziyaeddin's arms.

Ertuğrul quickly averted his eyes as David grinned and James squeezed Sevinc's hand.

Ziyaeddin cleared his throat and straightened on his cushion. "Duchess Charlotte has decided to remain here as my... favorite," he said. "You..." He waved at both David and James. "May do so as well, although you..." He directed his pointed stare onto James.

"Will be marrying your favorite daughter and escorting her on the wedding trip of her dreams, Your Highness," he finished for the sultan.

Ziyaeddin angled his head left and right before he nodded. "You will be traveling for some time," he warned.

"I am counting on it, Your Highness."

Sevinc beamed in delight, although she resisted the urge to end up in James' arms.

"Will you marry my mother?" James asked. "You have my permission to do so, although you don't really need it."

Ziyaeddin gave a shrug. "That will be up to her," he replied carefully. "Apparently I am an incorrigible beast and an insufferable, stubborn tyrant," he murmured.

Charlotte directed her grin to the others at the table. "Oh, don't listen to him. He's merely a beast," she said with a brilliant grin. She turned her gaze up to him. "My beast," she whispered before she kissed him on the cheek.

Ziyaeddin's whispered response was spoken for only her to hear, and Charlotte blushed a bright pink. "I suppose I do owe you another night," she murmured.

EPILOGUE

Two years later, on the balcony of the sultan's private chambers

Streaks of coral, purple, and red painted the western sky as Charlotte stood on the sultan's balcony and watched the sun set into the Aegean Sea. She never tired of the sight and had made it a point to find a suitable vantage from which to watch it every evening.

In a few months, she and Ziyaeddin would be returning to Constantinople, the new palace's construction nearly complete enough for them to make it their home. Although he had promised the sunsets over the Bosphorus Straight would be as brilliant, she doubted she could watch them whilst wearing little in the way of clothing.

Behind her, Ziyaeddin stood with one arm wrapped around her middle while he held their slumbering year-old daughter Zehra against a shoulder. His attention wasn't on the disappearing red ball but rather on the ship that was pulling into the dock at the edge of the water below. When he tightened his hold on his wife, she turned her head to rest it on his shoulder.

"What is it?" she asked in a quiet voice, not wanting to break the spell of the moment. She was sure his nose had been buried in Zehra's curly hair, a practice he had continued despite the fact that she was no longer a tiny babe.

"Poppy is back," he whispered.

Charlotte gave a start. "You say that as if you were expecting him," she accused as her gaze went to the long dock. The ship was barely visible on the darkening water.

"I was," he acknowledged. "He brings important cargo. Come with me to greet him?"

"Of course," she said, her curiosity piqued. Glad she hadn't yet prepared for bed, she hurried alongside the sultan as his long strides took him out of their private chambers and down the long corridor to the stairs. "Is this why you seemed so restless all day?" she asked as they made their way down the steps to the palace's atrium.

"I wasn't aware I was," he said when he offered his arm.

Charlotte gave him a quelling glance. "You insisted the palace be cleaned from top to bottom even though I always ensure it is," she countered. Having taken on the running of the household, Charlotte Sultana, as she was now known, oversaw the servants and kitchen staff of the Aegean palace.

Given the size of the new palace in Constantinople, she was glad for the practice.

They were halfway down the path toward the dock

when a pair of figures descended the merchant ship's ramp, one of them wearing a long gown. Charlotte gasped. "Is that—?"

"Mother!" James shouted as he waved from the dock with one arm. On the other was Sevinc, a bundle held in her arms.

"James!" Charlotte called back, her gaze darting to Ziyaeddin. "However did you keep this a secret?" she asked in delight.

The sultan grinned as he lifted his chin. "I have known they would be arriving for at least a week," he claimed.

Inhaling softly, Charlotte had to turn her attention to her son, who was seeing to greeting Ziyaeddin and then Sevinc, who held back until her father beckoned her forward. With her free hand, she took his to her lips and then to her forehead. "Baba," she beamed as she straightened. "Charlotte Sultana," she added, the words barely out of her mouth before Charlotte's arms were around her shoulders.

"Oh, Sevinc, it's so good to see you. And, oh my, who might this be?" she asked with excitement, realizing the bundle had moved against her chest.

James cleared his throat. "May I have the honor of presenting Ziyaeddin Joshua Ahmet Wainwright?" he said proudly as Sevinc unwrapped the blanket to reveal a baby. "She was born at Wisborough Oaks, just in time to meet her newest cousin, James. Her oldest cousin, Jennifer, doted on them both."

Charlotte's eyes rounded as Ziyaeddin peered down at the three-month-old. "Oh, he's adorable," she whispered, her fingers spearing the scads of dark curly hair that surrounded his round face. Her thumb caressed his cheek, and the babe stirred but didn't awaken. "Arabella wrote she was expecting again, so I'm relieved to learn she gave John his heir."

"Oh, now who is this?" James asked with a grin.

"May I have the honor of presenting Zehra Elizabeth?" Ziyaeddin stated, turning so the sleeping baby's face was visible. James was quick to take her into his arms. "My first sister," he mused as he gazed on her dark hair and chubby cheeks. "She looks a lot like her nephew."

Ziyaeddin took the other babe from Sevinc and placed it against his shoulder, his face hidden by the blanket for a moment.

"Whatever are you doing to your newest grandson?" Charlotte asked in a hushed voice.

Sevinc tittered. "He does this to all the babies," she said as they made their way to the palace. "He likes to smell them."

"As do I," James remarked with a grin, his nose pressed onto Zehra's head. "They smell heavenly. Not at all what I expected. David had me believing Zi would smell of piss and vinegar—"

"James," Charlotte scolded.

Sevinc took her newest sister into her arms, the girl waking up to regard her in wide-eyed wonder before she displayed a huge grin. Giggling, Sevinc said, "Oh, I can hardly wait until you know how to read."

"Which reminds me," James added, smirking at hearing his wife's comment. "Where *is* David these days?

We last saw him in Constantinople. He and Ertuğrul were overseeing the installation of a ceiling mosaic in the new palace, but that was before Zi was born."

"David and Ertuğrul left for England only last week," Charlotte said as they made their way up the stairs. "Which has Elizabeth rather excited. They'll arrive in time for the Season. I think she is hoping David will take a wife soon, and I am of the opinion Ertuğrul will take one even sooner."

James chuckled. "If David isn't needed by his father, I expect he'll be back here in the summer. He wants to see Dolmabahçe in all its finished glory."

Charlotte tapped Ziyaeddin's arm. "It's my turn," she moued, taking the boy from him to hold it in the crook of her arm. "He's like a little cherub. Look at all that hair."

Ziyaeddin paused to watch her gaze at her second grandchild and then leaned closer in an attempt to catch a whiff of her perfume. He inhaled deeply, which had Charlotte glancing up at him. "What is it?" she asked in a whisper.

He chuckled. "If you like, I could see to it you have one of your own," he teased.

Scoffing, Charlotte angled her head to one side. "Oh, I'm quite sure I'll never be able to have another," she murmured.

Reminded of their conversation after their first night together, Ziyaeddin grinned. "Never say never, My Sultana."

AUTHOR'S NOTES

Charlotte and Joshua's story, *The Grace of a Duke* (The Daughters of the Aristocracy, Book 2), is available at all major book retailers in ebook, paperback and audio formats.

Did anything like this tale ever happen in real life?

There is no record of a British aristocrat ever having been sold to a sultan or otherwise becoming part of a sultan's harem. When aristocrats were kidnapped by pirates, they tended to be held for ransom.

There is a legend that Nakşîdil Sultan, wife of Ottoman sultan Abdülhamid (Abdul Hamid I) and mother of Mahmed II was really French heiress Aimée du Buc de Rivéry. Born in 1768 on Martinique, where her father had a plantation, Aimée was sent to France to attend a convent school. While returning home in 1788, she went missing at sea. Rumor has it she was captured by Barbary pirates and sold as a harem concubine, but this has not been proven.

The Sultan

Although some physical traits and accomplishments of Ziyaeddin are based on real Ottoman emirs and sultans, he is entirely fictitious. *The Lady of a Sultan* takes place during the reign of Abdülmecit I (1839-1861), a sultan whose time was notable for the rise of nationalist movements within the empire's territories. He promoted a number of reforms, most notably in the Army, which was reorganized. Non-Muslims were allowed to become soldiers for the first time. He also saw to abolishing the capitation tax, which had forced non-Muslims to pay higher tariffs. His other reforms brought about modern universities and academies, and an Ottoman School was founded in Paris. Under his rule, Ottoman paper currency was also introduced, and there were plans to abolish slave markets and to decriminalize homosexuality.

He would have made for a great character, but Abdülmecit I was only twenty-four years old at the time of our story.

His brother, Abdul Aziz, was the thirty-second Sultan of Turkey and was the first to develop good diplomatic ties with Britain.

How many wives could a sultan have?

Four wives and as many concubines as they wanted.

Ottoman sultans did not marry free women after the sixteenth century but instead took slaves as wives. Most were Greek, Caucasian, Georgian, and Abkhazians which meant their offspring, including the chosen heir, were always of mixed nationalities. Unlike wives, who had vested interests in their own family's affairs, slave concubines had no recognized heritage which could interfere with their loyalty to the sultan.

Headwear

The Turkish fez got its name from the Moroccan city of Fez, the source of the sanguine berry formerly used to paint the felt its distinctive scarlet color.

Wearing a fez as opposed to a turban or kufi was a giant step for the Ottomans. Since the 16th century, laws had governed clothing in the empire, distinguishing the sultan's non-Muslim subjects, mainly Christians and Jews, from their Muslim counterparts. When Sultan Mahmud II decided that all Ottoman officials would wear the fez in 1829, regardless of religion, this changed everything.

Mahmud II once declared, "From now on I do not wish to recognize Muslims outside the mosque, Christians outside the church, or Jews outside synagogue." At a time of distress and uncertainty, the fez became a symbol of secular citizenship and could be worn by every Ottoman man to bind all the sultan's subjects together.

The fez was subsequently outlawed in Turkey in 1925 as part of Atatürk's Reforms.

Ottoman Clothing

The upper-class or royal people in the Ottoman Empire wore fur-lined, embroidered *kaftans*. The middle class wore *cübbe*, a mid-length robe, and *hırka*, a short robe or tunic. The lower class also wore a collarless jacket called *cepken* or *yelek* (vest).

The *entari*, or robe, was the main element of women's

dress in the Ottoman Empire, worn together with a *gömlek* (chemise), *yelek* (vest), *cakşir* (underpants), and *şalvar* (baggy trousers). When out of doors, a *ferace* (a long loose robe) was worn.

Fountain of the Four Rivers

Located in Piazza Navona in Rome, this fountain was designed by Gian Lorenzo Bernini in 1651 for Pope Innocent X. The four statues at the base represent the four major rivers of the four continents through which the pope's authority had spread: the Nile, representing Africa, the Danube, representing Europe, the Ganges, representing Asia, and the Rio de la Plata, representing the Americas. Rising from the middle is a copy of an Egyptian obelisk topped with a dove carrying an olive branch.

ABOUT THE AUTHOR

A self-described nerd and student of history, Linda Rae spent many years as a published technical writer specializing in 3D graphics workstations, software and 3D animation (her movie credits include SHREK and SHREK 2). Getting lost in the rabbit holes of research has resulted in historical romances set in the Regency-era as well as Ancient Greece.

A fan of action-adventure movies, she can frequently be found at the local cinema. Although she no longer has any tropical fish, she follows the San Jose Sharks and makes her home in Cody, Wyoming.

For more information:
www.lindaraesande.com
Sign up for Linda Rae's newsletter:
Regency Romance with a Twist
Follow Linda Rae's blog:
Regency Romance with a Twist

Made in the USA
Monee, IL
21 February 2025

12446330R00194